THE
SAVAGE
AETHER

HENRY NEILSEN

Copyright ©2026 Hunting Sunrise Publications
Written by Henry Neilsen
All rights reserved.
ISBN (Paperback): 978-0-6489426-5-8
ISBN (eBook): 978-0-6489426-6-5

This is a work of fiction. Similarities to real people, places or events are entirely coincidental.

This work was created without the use of generative AI or other AI assistance programs.

Cover and title by Jon Stubbington
(www.jonstubbington.com)

Edited by Vicky Smith

Henry Neilsen is a member of Meridian Australis
(www.meridianaustralis.au)

A catalogue record for this book is available from the National Library of Australia

CONTENT WARNING

This is a horror story, and as such contains depictions of a dark, violent, and graphic nature. In the interest of saving the reader from spoilers, these are not detailed here. However, if you are concerned about particular triggers, please flip to the rear of this book for further details.

To Dave and to Crebes,
All the way to the finish

For thousands of years men have dreamed of pacts with demons. Only now are such things possible. And what would you be paid with? What would your price be, for aiding this thing to free itself and grow?

William Gibson, *Neuromancer*

PART ONE

CHAPTER 1

COLIN

Reality flickered in and out. Rain spattered and ran in rivulets down concrete walls. The buildings formed a chasm. Cold wind, colder water and mammalian hind-brain claustrophobia made Colin check behind himself as he trudged alone through the downpour. Lights from unreal advertisements shone in his eyes but failed to reflect in the crystal light thrown up from the pavement.

He had seen the broken wiring, cracked solar panels and general miasma of an Aug-hovel a few streets back, and it had set him on edge. The last thing he needed was some solar-junkie Aug jumping him. The rain kept the street in a nighttime dark, but Col could see the crisp gleam of near-dawn sun on the upper levels of the buildings around him. Nightmares had haunted him lately, and in those, too, he'd seen the shining edges of crystal towers, full of smoke and devouring flame.

His head hurt. A gust of wind drove a cold trickle of rain down the back of his shirt. He tried holding his arm up to protect his eyes, but the rain battered at his coat sleeve and seeped through. Trudging through the dark in the lurking space between safety and the unknown made him wonder how his sister did it. Cass was constantly risking her hide for work – clambering over rooftops to find evidence, confronting violent mobsters to their face, or crawling through abandoned sewer tunnels – and still gleamed like sunshine.

2   HENRY NEILSEN

And here he was, scared of walking down a street, brushing rain from his eyes, blood warmed by a press of adrenaline and growing unease.

The Library, his destination, loomed in the fading night, a black hulk between the false luminance projected by the Uplink onto the hab blocks surrounding it. Its windows were boarded up, and in daylight the remnants of scraped glue still faintly revealed the words *State Library* on the architrave. His eyes slid past it onto the in-retina displays that cajoled his consciousness. The Library was a hollow in the world.

A movement spat from an alley to his left.

There were two Augs, too far away to see clearly but close enough to hear, surrounded by the trash that always seemed to accompany them. Wiring, either stolen or abandoned. Printed circuit boards. Pistons, pumps and metal in various states of repair, and solar panels. Always solar panels.

One of them stood and faced him. The lights painted its eye sockets as black shadows and its emaciated frame was tense, coiled like a whip. Over the rain, he could hear the whirring of the servo motors in a prosthetic leg. The streetlight ringed its human form in a cold halo of light, and he could feel its eyes on him.

He turned from them and sprinted.

Still running, he jumped the ankle-deep stream of water in the gutter and mounted the sidewalk. He didn't trust himself to check if the Aug had followed him, instead shoving the large outer door open and stepping into the anteroom. The inner door checked his Ident through the link and hissed open. A small icon appeared in his vision, logging his time of entry.

ENTRY 0456H: COLIN P. MONTGOMERY

Col breathed a sigh of relief as the single sensor light turned on over his head, its dim luminance fleeing into the waiting night before being swallowed up and reflecting off the metal shelves of the Library stacks. Once a public space, the Library had been reappropriated by enterprise. The musty, bookish silence was now an electrical hum and blinking blue lights. Above the stacks, coiled cables were arrayed like so many feedlines in a slaughterhouse. They both fed into and siphoned off the vast multitudes of data spooling through the processors every second, throwing it into a rooftop transmitter. This was one node of the Uplink, and it pulled and pushed sensory data pseudotelepathically to everyone in radius.

Except the Augs, of course.

A thump from the doorway made Col jerk in fright. Had the Aug followed him? He listened. There was only the hum of the stacks and the blue flickering glow of the lights of the server.

Breathing out, he tried to concentrate on what he'd come here to do. He pulled a jeweller's screwdriver from his pocket and headed toward the bank of servers, calling up the Library's floor plan onto his Uplink as he did so. The world around him burst into a sea of blue-white lines arrayed across his retina. The names and operational status of the server pods in the stacks appeared as glowing numbers floating above the hardware. Lights flickered but didn't reflect off anything. He was still shaken, and the screwdriver quaked in his hand in concert with the muted cacophony of the rain outside.

In the stacks, he found the server box that had thrown the error, a deep red warning in the Link written over a darkness in reality where a blue light should have been. He had bent to his work and was gently unscrewing the box when another noise pierced the wash of the rain. A scraping from the back of the building, near an overflow room packed with old chips and parts. As he turned around, he thought he saw a small, dark figure sprinting across the aisle, heading into the stacks.

He swiped the overlay away and shook his head sharply to clear it, then stared at the stacks. The movement had disappeared, and the constant sound around him infiltrated his brain, his synapses hissing with data. His reason for coming to the Library long forgotten, he brandished the screwdriver in front of him like a shiv, dreading the thought of using it.

He crept along to the edge of the stacks, flinching every time his shadow played across one of the ancient shelves. At any moment he expected the Aug from the alley to leap out in a dark, violent blur. He flitted across the aisles, peering down each in turn, listening for sounds over the whitewash of rain and server hum. Afterward, he ducked back to the door to the storage room, and he held his breath as he edged it open.

Nothing.

Nothing but the blazed chipsets and distribution arrays from previous iterations of the Uplink's servers that had been abandoned in there, gathering dust and static.

Confused, he downloaded the security data and threw it into his on-retina display. No breaches from outside, and the only entrance in the previous twelve hours had been him, minutes before. He pulled a security recording and ran it. He could see himself, sodden and breathing heavily. The inner door opened automatically as he approached.

He sped the feed up to where he'd heard the first thud. The rain was beginning to slow, and he saw the faint edges of the morning light playing across the empty street.

Except it wasn't empty.

Col leaned forward, despite the image being projected on a display made from stimulation of his visual cortex, and replayed the moment.

It was barely perceptible, a small crescent of light, dancing off a moving object.

A *walking* object.

Here we go, then, Col thought.

CHAPTER 2

CASS

The Aug's mechanical eye whirred in its socket as a breeze drifted through the shattered window. Dawn sunlight, drab and silty, threatened to filter in despite the black fog of rain crouching over the city scant kilometres away. The floor was filthy, covered in rags mingled with electrical wires. The walls were stained with generations of sweat and piss and dried blood.

She could hear the whirr-thud of another Aug stomping down the corridor. The Aug Cass was facing had a grotesque mask where the left side of its face should have been. Burnished steel burst crudely through inflamed flesh to reveal an electrical orb that functioned as an eye. Angry scabs and sores pockmarked the rest of its face, where the Aug had tried to itch that which couldn't be scratched, for days and weeks and years.

Cass stepped closer to the window to get some fresh air. The Aug whirred. It wasn't taking its attention away from her, though it hadn't spoken since she'd walked in. A smattering of notifications chimed softly in her ears but not in the world outside, and her peripheral vision flickered with a roulette of icons. She dismissed them all and temporarily silenced her Link with a flick of the wrist, careful not to move too fast and spook the Aug.

The remnants of last night's downpour lay pooled on the windowsill and across the rapidly lightening sky. The last few days and nights had been inundated with the kind of rain that reminded her of her brother. When they were kids, rainwater would pour over the eaves of their hostel and Col had hated it. It seemed to drench his soul and drown him, turning him into a withdrawn and sombre caricature of himself.

She didn't know if it was something he had ever noticed.

She stepped closer to the Aug, electrical wires and dust creaking under her thick work boots, and spoke to it again. This time she tried a different tack.

'My name's Cassandra Montgomery. I'm a reporter on case for – ' She hesitated. It couldn't access the Uplink. Couldn't complain if she didn't perform the necessary disclosures. 'I'm a reporter. I'm trying to follow up on some rumours about Augs in this area finding a way into the Uplink. That something you know about?'

The Aug's fake eye focused. It was lidless; the Aug couldn't close it. What it must be like living with cold, digital data being press-ganged into your consciousness every day, Cass didn't want to think about. At least with the Uplink she could temporarily silence or stymie the endless feed of notifications, alerts and contacts. This Aug had no choice.

'Move,' the Aug said. Cass was blocking the morning sun from hitting a small solar panel that lay on the floor. The Aug's human eye stared hungrily at the black crystals. She knelt down slowly. The false eye buzzed, following her movement. She shot her hand out to the two alligator clips on a wire attached to the panel and wrenched them out of the Aug's reach. The Aug scrambled for them, snarling at her before collapsing supine into its own filth, cursing under its breath.

It was watching the window and the patch of light that was now beginning to play across Cass's jacket, the eye flicking frantically between that and the solar panel sitting in the dark. Cass could see its terminals; dark, ugly scars on the left arm that led up to the neck and disappeared at the back of the lower jaw. Set into the arm were two metal spikes, jutting out just above where the bones of the forearm met its wrist. Each of these were shiny from repeated use, in stark contrast to the dull surrounds. A spiderweb of blackened and cauterised skin splayed out where the electricity had burned the flesh.

'Whaddayawannaknow?' it said, rolling the words out as a single sound.

'We've had rumours that Augs are accessing the Uplink around this area. Do you know anything about it? Do you know why an Aug would want to get into the Uplink?'

The Aug laughed, catching her by surprise. There was no joy in it. It was harsh. Staccato. Bitter.

'I'm not who you're lookin' for.' It pointed to the ravaged robotic elements of the left side of its face. 'All this? Can't live without it now. Need it, like. 'Cause of that, I can't use your Link. Never could, even when it first started. I tried, at the start. I did, and me trying to find out left me nothin' but what's in this room. I ain't got much longer, and the last thing I want to do is spend my time tryna break into that place never wanted me. Was the world that didn't want me in it. Was the world that put everythin' in everyone's head but mine.'

For a while the Aug sat still and silent, trying to think its way to saying something that it didn't want to say directly. Its eye whirred, and it coughed, wet and sickly.

It probably wouldn't survive winter.

'On my better days, I go down the docks. Not when they're busy, mind. Dock workers don't like seeing ol' one-eye staggering about. Call me dangerous – pah!' It spat on the ground and coughed again. Cass saw blood in the spit, and looked away. In the corner she saw a small pile of belongings. Scrappy, worn clothes. A broken stool. A worn-looking filing cabinet. She hadn't seen one of those in a decade. She'd never used one. The Aug kept talking.

'Sometimes I hear things, in the dry dock. Sometimes. Hearin's not what it was, but you get to know your own sort. You listen for the noises they don't make, if ye take my meaning. Dock workers ain't spendin' time trying to not make noise, 'cause they're *supposed* to be there, right?'

Speaking so many words at once seemed to sap the energy from it. Its body was wracked by a more severe coughing fit.

'The docks, then?' Cass said. As she spoke, she stepped back and a sliver of grey light stabbed down onto the solar panel on the ground.

The Aug heard her move. With a flash of speed she didn't think it was capable of, it grabbed both alligator clips and pressed them onto the terminals above its wrist.

Cass jumped back in horror as sparks leapt across the terminals. It made a tinny crack, and the effect on the Aug was instantaneous. The spiderweb of burns lit at the edges with a searing yellow, tracing a diffuse lightning glow where its skin wasn't yet carbonised and calcified. The arm convulsed, and the wrist snapped up to the shoulder under the current of the electrical shock, quivering there as though ready to push further, threatening to break the arm at the elbow. The rest of the Aug's body went deathly limp. The face, what human part of it was left, relaxed into a glow of contentment and ecstasy. The frown was forgotten and both eyes dilated, the black pupil of the real and the light blue of the mechanical opening like wells into the mind.

Cass reckoned she could see the cable running from the terminal and into the jaw pulsing with the solar-generated hormones, electrifying the pleasure centres of the brain and pushing the Aug into a high beyond any pharmaceutical. The coughing stopped. Cass could see a fresh clot of mucous and blood on the mattress near the Aug's head, where his arm was now spasming and twitching with the electrical current.

She stood there a moment longer, taking in the blissful emptiness of the Aug's face. She had a sudden mental image of wires pricking the grey, wrinkled mass of its brain, shooting endorphins and imagery into the complex neural lace that made up the Aug's consciousness. It made her shudder and finally look away. She walked toward the door, then turned.

'What's your name?'

It looked at her blankly but didn't answer.

'Okay,' she said. 'Why don't you want to access the Uplink? Everything you need is there. Wouldn't you at least try?'

When it laughed, there was none of the harshness or bitterness that there had been before. A deep guffaw, starting down in the chest, climbed out of it and rumbled through the room. The laugh turned to a hacking cough, and flecks of blood and spit flew from its mouth and left bright specks of red on the ruined mattress. Arm still spasming, and with the levity of a barely suppressed giggle, the Aug spoke. Blood smeared its lips.

'I may have metal and wires and all sorts in me. But I know what's in my head is mine.'

With that, it burst into a fit of laughter, spasming and gyrating with pleasure on the mattress. The narcotic effect of the solar cell suppressed another cough instantly and the Aug fell back, staring at nothing, almost completely still, neither the real nor mechanical eye taking in the squalor of their surroundings. The Aug had gone into a trance, floating through an emptiness where it was, for a while, free.

Her boots crunched on the floor, her rapid footsteps creating a staccato polyrhythm with the heavy thuds of the Aug patrolling the hallway. She saw it this time. The entire left part of its hip had been ripped away and replaced with a clumsily installed four-axis robotic leg. The wiring, similar to the Aug in the room, ran under an ugly scar through its bare chest and into the lower jaw. From there, she guessed, into the motor control centres at the base of the brain. She nodded. It ignored her. The mechanical leg seemed to be moving on its own, and it was stepping awkwardly with its other. This Aug's face was drawn, haggard and grim, like it hadn't slept in days. She walked by, past the gaping maw of the ruined elevator shaft to the fire-exit stairs with the doors ripped off, and began her long walk back down to the outside world.

CHAPTER 3

COLIN

The whirring stepper motor of the stim dispensary thickened the sounds of the street from somewhere behind an acrylic panel. Inset into the wall, shelves of over-the-counter drugs and heavily preserved foods were arrayed in careful rows and accessed by a Link request to a product code. Col waited next to it, peering through the hash of scratch marks, trying to discern the robotic arm behind it. He rubbed the bridge of his nose to will away the tired throb behind his eyes. It didn't work. It just added a flash of stars to the notifications being projected into his consciousness, scrolling endlessly. He hadn't made it home after the incident in the Library, and his shift started soon.

There was a jagged hole in the wall next to the dispensary, loose electrical wiring and a hose dripping hydraulic fluid onto a few leftover packs of stimtab blisters. *Augs,* Col thought, checking behind himself again in the early morning light. They must have hit the place in the last week. How they'd ripped the second dispensary from the wall he didn't know, but in his mind he still saw the dash of a dark figure and a vidfeed showing the reflection of rain off an Aug's back. He collected his blister packs of stimtabs and painkillers and pushed them into the pocket of his rain jacket.

The rain had cleared as the morning had worn on, and now corded rays of sun crept their way into the chasm formed by the towers framing the Library. It made him think of childhood days on the docks with Cass, each of them holding sweets they'd managed to steal, small legs kicking in the sun as they stuffed sugar into their giggling mouths.

Those were the memories that appeared to him, more than anything, when the sun managed to break through the choking atmosphere and sulphur-yellow clouds and climb down to the street. To him, the sunlight was Cass, and he always thought of her when its rays warmed his face.

Two urgent reminders bled into his vision, flickering onto the inside of his eyes and jolting him from his daydreams. One was for an all-hands meeting that morning, the other a query about swapping chipsets in the Library databases, addressed to both him and Sal. He popped open the blister pack of painkillers and dry swallowed two of them.

Why did they want him to update the chipsets?

He pushed it to the back of his mind, flicking his task list away and pulling up a vidfeed of the Library from the night before as he started making his way back to his hab. He twitched and activated the feed, and images of the rain-soaked night bled into his consciousness, burning his neural pathways.

He saw himself, panicked and drenched, entering the gloom of the Library. He skipped forward, watching himself putter around, finding the offending portion of the server and replacing it. The walk through the stacks. He switched cameras several times to follow.

He turned onto his street and ducked under a makeshift awning that ran the length of an abandoned shopfront. He popped a stim from the other foil pack and put it into his mouth. The smooth, crisp chill of amphetamine rinsed his blood. As his acuity increased, he noticed someone walking behind the vidfeed; he almost didn't see them. A brief glimpse of red hair and pale features, caught in the moment before he stepped aside in the deluge.

There it was. In the camera view, he jumped, startled, then looked down and away from the stacks.

He'd have to get Sal to look into it. This morning he needed to understand why the urgency on the new chipsets. He'd look at the specification to see what the difference was between the new ones and the old, but *someone* needed to find out if the Library had been broken into. He'd been running the footage every way he could, but Sal had a knack for this kind of thing. Despite himself, Col twitched and changed the angle of the recording to an outside camera to watch it again. He muted the feed, found the timestamp of his entrance and scrolled backward by several minutes.

The Library stood in the dark. Crisp blue lights danced against the edges of the rain, and Col could see small rivers running through the street. It made the night seem like an old, low-resolution film. A grainy memory. He sped the feed up, trying to find the time when he'd been sent the alarm in the first place. Surely *it wasn't just that one sensor that had got him out of bed. The entrance wasn't breached, but it had to be –*

There. Col leaned forward and replayed the moment.

It was slight, a small crescent of light, dancing off a moving object. A walking object. It made its way to the door and –

He'd reached the front of his hab complex, a faux wooden entrance that drew him through a windowless hall. He headed to the end, shedding his coat at the door and sending a link request to Sal as he made his way in. The Library *was* being scoped, and he had seen something. He needed her to look into it while he dealt with whatever this chipset thing was.

He considered filtering the Link for Sal. His hab was untidy; a few empty stimfoils and food trays, and variously scattered and abandoned clothes. Sal had seen the place in worse condition – she was one of the few people he knew in close enough proximity to come and see the real thing. Cass was on the other side of town, and Col's job often turned into 13- and 14-hour days, so Sal was the one person he stayed in contact with regularly. More than one late night at work had turned to drinks in the stacks, and once had ended in a night of the kind of desperate intimacy that happens when two people have each other and nobody else. It was years ago now. They never talked about it.

Sal appeared in front of him, and he decided against filtering his background. She could deal with seeing his untidy hab. There was the usual hash of digital static that clipped through his auditory receptors as the vox and image initialised. Her image flickered at different sizes and positions until her heavy work boots looked as though they were standing on the floor. If Col had looked closer, the lack of reflection and shadow on the tiles of his hab would have given the Uplink away. If Col had decided to concentrate on it, his mind would have reeled, and he'd have ended up with nausea or confusion. The mind was good at letting things *seem* real; even better at glossing over what was entirely unreal. The model of the universe that was built by the human mind could easily fill the holes where reality made no sense, and the uncanny valley was not a place where people enjoyed spending time.

'Morning, Col. How's things?' Her voice quickly reconciled from digital static into her usual clipped but friendly tones.

She turned slightly to orient herself – or rather the apparition did, a slick correction. Her posture remained the same, but if he'd been watching, the boots would have slid around on the floor in a peculiar frictionless motion.

'Hi, Sal. I've got something I'd like you to look into for me.'

She listened carefully as he explained the phenomenon from the other night, the noises from outside, the shadow on the vidfeed... and whatever he'd seen inside. He gave the timestamp and passed on a temporary clearance for her Ident to the security system.

'I was going to look into it myself, but I've got – ' He paused. 'Actually, do you have any idea why they'd be doing this?'

He flicked his wrist, and the message about the chipsets flashed up between them. Sal read for a minute, then shrugged.

'I dunno. Those chips are pretty similar. They all are. They just interface with the feedlines, map it to some generic data struct and throw it back out to the server.'

Col frowned. Sal continued, 'I've got some backup system to install tomorrow as well, but I thought we already had a backup server? It's in that spare room up on level four, right?'

'Correct. Where's the new one going?'

Trying to hide his confusion, Col started rifling through the file network to find the two different chips he had to install.

'Uh, that main back room. Heap of wideband processors and training networks. Gotta do a transformer rollover as well. Doesn't make sense to me.'

Between them, she popped up a map of the Library with flashing indicators showing what was to be replaced. It looked like half the Library. They discussed it for a while, but they only became more confused. From what Sal told him, there wasn't anything pressing that would have necessitated the kind of heavy overhaul he was being shown. Sal, too, was trying to understand what it was that required such an increase in the power-handling side of the circuit, not to mention the training networks. After a few minutes, neither of them getting anywhere, they had to get back to work. Col bid Sal farewell, and she vanished from his vision.

Col's eyes adjusted to the light that had been there the entire time, but which his brain had told him a woman had been blocking for the last few minutes. The flash-and-fade effect of his pupillary response lent an air of drama to the mundane apparitions of the Uplink.

Col's headache was getting worse again; the painkillers weren't working as well as they should be anymore. He dry swallowed a couple more, then sank into the small couch crammed into the corner of the room next to the folded-up bed. He closed his eyes as he felt, rather than saw, the room disappear around him.

When he opened them again, he was in the Uplink-generated version of the stacks in the library. The space had a crisp uniformity of light that didn't exist in the gloomy, boarded-up twilight of the real space. In here, the windows were open with sunlight streaming in, a pale gold colour that rarely occurred but in uncannily good weather. Gone too were the umbilicals of cables to the ceiling; in their place was a series of visual switches indicating the data feedlines that were being employed by the too-smooth black boxes, floating in a caricature of the actual shelves.

In his apartment, Col's eyes were wide and unseeing. His index fingers twitched slightly as he navigated the ethereal quasi-reality of the Uplink-connected space. Before long, even these stilled as his consciousness calibrated with the Uplink more fully.

He pulled up the schema for both of the chipsets. The auburn glow of the false Library slipped away and a void enveloped him. Myriad neon lines spread, seemingly from his fingertips, and glistened like spider silk. These formed into three-dimensional glyphs with codes and numbers floating next to them. Col waved a hand and the lines turned a pale red. He pushed them over to one side. Next, a new set of lines, the wiring diagram of the *new* memory units, glimmered into being. These he coloured blue. With a series of small hand gestures in the dark, the two coloured webs overlapped one another. He pushed, pulled, zoomed in and out, and inspected the points of difference between the two diagrams. The shapes flew around and over and under and through him, shedding a false light on his too-smooth features from where the Uplink approximated his own location.

Before much longer, he was forced to drop back into the Library again. The flying schemas were making his head throb, and he hadn't found much of interest to differentiate the two memory types. Not enough, in his estimation, to cause one set to be ripped out and replaced. The only difference between the two was potential bandwidth. The older chip had an upper limit on the breadth of information it could receive, which in *theory* put an upper limit on the data transfer time and could cause a lag in communications between the terminals. In practice, though, there was more than enough for the Uplink. It sent visual and audio signals at a fidelity that was quasi-reality for almost anyone, and did it with processing to spare.

Col's mind felt like it was running hot, and he pulled himself out of the Uplink, leaning forward on the couch and rubbing his temples. The painkillers weren't working, and he didn't know why he was replacing these chips while Sal was being told to rip out half the infrastructure in the Library. Huge memory increases, bigger backups, more bandwidth. But why? The Uplink required upgrades regularly – ensuring a safe level of redundancy meant keeping the system size roughly consonant with population growth. But a delivery of this size would only make sense if the population was expected to triple or quadruple overnight.

An alert flashed into his vision. His meeting was starting.

He splashed filtered water on his face to try to ease the throb in his skull, and sat upright on the couch. Around him, the walls of his living room seemed to fold back – the floor shifted from ageing faux timber to gleaming white tiles. His oft-used couch morphed into a nondescript office chair, and the bookshelf vanished. Around him, one by one, men and women appeared in varying formality of dress. Each sat on an apparition of the same kind of office chair he did, except one. The woman in the centre of the room stood, ostensibly looking straight at Col. He knew, however, that no matter who in the room was looking at her, it would always seem as though the woman was looking straight at them. Thinking about it too much made his head burn even more than it already did – was it getting worse? It put him in mind of the picts of works by Picasso: every angle captured all at once.

'Good morning, all,' was all she said, before a meeting agenda dissolved into view.

Before Col could read it, a private message appeared on the screen. It was from Sal.

I've reviewed the feeds from the library. I found something.

CHAPTER 4

CASS

Behind the burnished haze of the city smog there was probably a beautiful sunset. The rich colours she saw in picts from long ago were no longer there – the pinks and oranges and iridescent reflections off clouds had long ago given way to the auburn of a slowly choking atmosphere.

The chilled bottle kissed her lips as she took a swig from a flavoured stim juice. Personalised advertisements bombarded her from the flat surfaces of the city, along with neon simulacra fighting for their space in the broken sky. She was at the age where the ads were shifting from fashion and recreational drugs to digital pets and fertility centres. She wondered if Col saw anything like the same sky she did.

His apparition reclined awkwardly in the second of the two beaten-up outdoor lounges that had been snuck onto the rooftop of her hab some time before she'd moved in. From where she lived in the older part of town, she could see the outline of the building where she'd spoken to the Aug with the broken eye a few days before. From afar, the beige brick and stained concrete superstructure looked haggard – a collapsed and abandoned attempt at collective social conscience. Beyond it, the docks and the seawall, holding back the ever-rising tide.

It was dangerous to go out there now, onto the sea wall. There were walkways, but it was risky. The tidal motion of the sea beat with an unusual frequency these days, interrupted by constant minor quakes and delaminations in the earth's crust. It wasn't unusual for an errant wave to crest the wall, despite it being built to withstand the worst predictions of climate engineers. Perturbations in the rhythms of the world that would overrun any threshold humanity had set in an attempt to delineate itself from nature.

'I was out there the other day,' she said, idly. She stretched, and finished off the last of her drink.

Col turned to her. 'Out where?'

'We've been hearing a few things happening with the Augs,' Cass said, not really replying to his question.

'Hearing things?'

'Yeah. Well, not hearing. One of my contacts tracks traffic across the Uplink, and there's some weird movement they've picked up. It's lacking some of the, I dunno, encryption and safety protocols they expect to see, so they asked me to check it out.'

'What makes you think it's Augs?' Col asked.

'Not me. My contact thinks so. Says the data looks old, and it's intermittent, which makes it hard to track. If it was someone using the Link and trying to hack into places they're not supposed to, it'd be changing signature, but it'd be traceable. This, though? It just appears at random, then disappears. Like it's someone who hasn't already got access,' Cass said.

Col nodded. 'Hence, Augs.'

'Yep. Anyway, so I went out to the old towers the other day, to ask around.'

A pause hung in the air between them. Cass knew what was coming next, and wished she'd kept her mouth shut.

'Alone?' Col almost murmured it.

She sighed. 'Yes, Colin. Alone.'

'I hate it when you do this stuff alone.'

'*Yes*, Colin. I know you do. But they send you to do your job alone, don't they? What am I supposed to do, just stop sending the scrip for the lease on this place?' She stomped down on the roof. A puff of gritty dust flew across the concrete.

Col sat up. 'Okay, but my job doesn't have me go into situations that might be dangerous.'

'No, but that's the job, right? I'm a reporter. I have to go into situations to find things out. There's risk involved. We do what we have to.'

'Yeah, but they could give you security or something. Private police.'

'You have to go into the Library at two in the morning. Right?'

'Right.'

'Well, the Link could have a night watchman, couldn't they?'

'They don't want to –'

'Exactly. Link don't want to put on night staff, I don't get security. We're resources, not assets. It's cost minimisation. Risk doesn't enter into it.'

That shut him up. He sagged back in his chair, and a short silence passed between them. The argument about Cass's work came up often enough, and she knew that if pressed, she'd bite back with a rejoinder about his dead-end tech position. She didn't want that fight. Not tonight.

As the tension eased, she spoke again. '*Anyway*, I had a lead that someone in that old development might know something.'

'And did they?' He kept his voice carefully level, not wanting the argument either.

'No. All I found was some Aug –' she was about to say *solar-junkie*, but stopped herself, '– on a mattress. Didn't seem to know what I was talking about, but said I should check out the docks.'

Her brother nodded. 'What are you looking for?'

Before answering, she pulled up the notations she had on the job to see whether there were security clearance requirements. Col faded into the background as she searched – she imagined his beat-up old lounge, cut out of the Link while his form was appropriated by the cheap cloth chair he appeared to be lying on weightlessly. He'd lost weight, she noted.

'You been exercising?' she asked, as the security details scrolled past her.

'What? No. Just eating less, I guess.' With that, he vanished for a few seconds, then reappeared holding another can. The tension in his voice had dissipated. 'Alright, so tell me. What are you trying to find?'

Cass recounted the rumours she'd heard about the Augs trying to access the Uplink. Conspiracy channels and chatrooms were constantly full of this kind of chatter – there was always an imminent Aug uprising – but these whispers had come from a source she'd always considered more reputable.

'Some of our contacts have been reporting a huge uptick in the manufacture of server parts and connectors,' Cass said. 'You'd probably actually know what they are – it's just a bunch of glyphs and letters to me – but there's talk that some of the shipments are going to Augs, to use them for... God knows what. There's these rumours, but I don't think this is the same thing.'

Col thought for a moment. 'I agree, I don't think it's that, but they do have us working on something big at work. Sal and I have got to retrofit just about the entire Library. We're throwing out old parts and pushing in adaptors for expansions and all sorts. It's the biggest job we've had since I started working there, almost a complete overhaul of the server structure.'

'And they haven't told you what it's for?'

'No. Had a meeting the other day, but it was just a general update.' He shifted in his seat uneasily.

'What do you think it's about?'

Col shrugged. A gust of wind blew across the balcony and Cass pulled her hair away from her face. Col's didn't move. 'I don't know. In terms of hardware, we're adding bandwidth, which means fidelity or another service that needs huge amounts of data throughput. But I don't know what that means from a software perspective.' He scratched idly at his stubble. 'There's another meeting next week. They might tell us then. Either way, your sources are right about the equipment, but it'd take a lot before it could get into the hands of a bunch of Augs. I don't even think they could use it.'

They could definitely steal it, Cass thought. Things went missing in supply chains all the time. No digital system could deal with all the contingencies of reality.

She noticed him avoiding her eyes as he spoke. He had a secret. She could always tell when he had a secret, but she decided not to push the point. Col was terrible at keeping things from her, and would usually cave with very little pressure. It was one of the things that came with being in a family of only two. To this day, Col was the only person she completely trusted, and it was because of this transparency, built up over a lifetime.

Her job afforded her precious little time to make new friends. Meet other people – other than Augs juiced on solar, or men trying to take over the world from a corrugated iron shack, or violent street gangs – none of whom she wanted to hang around more than absolutely necessary. So, for now, as ever, she'd spend her time with the only person she knew would always have time for her.

She shook her head, ignoring his reticence. 'Anyway. I'll have to get back to you on it; I'm still not exactly sure what

I'm looking at. I've got another lead, might be more help than the last guy I spoke to.'

She told Col about her interaction with the Aug, the addiction to solar energy that was slowly frying it from the outside in. The one she'd walked past in the corridor, haunted with insomnia, no respite from the broken augmentation in its leg. The giddy look of joy on the Aug's face as the surge of power burned through it, and the cold stare of the mechanical eye.

'I don't understand why they do it to themselves,' she said. 'The circuitry burns out or replaces their brain. They have to surgically insert these devices in themselves. It's sick.' She shuddered in a mixture of cold and disgust. The dusk was closing in around them, and her brother appeared to glow. The edges of him remained crisply delineated, another minor artefact of the Link. He'd been listening, pensive expression slowly coalescing into a wry frown. His apparition fidgeted. *Here it comes,* Cass thought, and after a moment he opened up to the secret she'd sensed before.

'Okay. I might have something for you,' he said. 'Hold on.'

His visage shifted and he flicked his hands up and down, scrolling through something Cass couldn't see. His eyes were scanning madly, as though he was suffering a waking REM episode. He winced and ran his hand over his forehead and temple before turning back to her.

'The other night, I went into the Library. I got an alert and had to fix it at some disgusting hour of the morning. On the way, some Augs caught sight of me, and at that time of night, in that type of rain, I ain't gonna take any chances. I legged it.'

He paused to gather his thoughts, as though he were trying to work out how to say something without giving away some detail. 'So, out of curiosity, I got Sal to check the security footage. The cameras were just rolling, 'cause of the rain, see?

Lots of motion. I – I thought it would just be worth checking the security footage. Like a new, I dunno, safety protocol or something. I got Sal to check, and –' he flicked a vidfeed up and onto a false projection in front of the two of them.

He was leaving something out, Cass knew. He only stuttered when he made things up on the spot, and whatever it was formed part of the reason for his reluctance to tell her in the first place. There had been *another* reason that he wanted the footage reviewed. She made a note to ask him about it later.

On the projection, the front door of the Library appeared, weltered with the downpour. The timestamp was early morning. Col came running through the dark and shoved the door open. The camera had enough acuity that it was possible to see through the door to where he stood wheezing for a while before walking out of frame.

Cass turned to where Col lay next to her and opened her mouth to speak.

'No, no, watch,' he insisted. The numbers sped up, as the vidfeed timelapsed. Two lightning strikes strobed and the rainfall had the hasty judder of unreality as the frame rate tripped over itself. Two minutes or so after Col entered, the video slowed down to normal speed again.

In the lower corner of the feed, a shape coalesced into view, a shape almost the exact colour as its backdrop of oil-slick pavement and darkened doorways. Only the texture – the heavy threads of old canvas and prosaic patchwork of the owner's creation – revealed it as clothing. A figure, stepping through the rain into the liminality between the street and the Library.

It crept to the edge of the door and grasped at the gap between the door leaf and frame. It slid its fingers up and down, pushing carefully into the corners. The dim light of the camera and the jitter of the rain made it impossible to see exactly what was happening, but Cass knew. The straining of the tendons along the arm, the determined set of the shoulders. If the door had given, there would have been a lightning-quick transition from struggling to get the door to crack open to making sure it stayed that way.

After a minute or two of frustrated clawing at the door, it turned around. The image froze a few scant frames before the intruder left the camera's field of view. A hood obscured most of the face, but in the blue-grey dinge of the night, Cass could see the smooth outline of a female jaw, lit up with the faint red glow of a mechanical eye.

'It's an Aug –' she began.

'Shhhh,' Col interrupted, gesturing back to the feed.

The image and the Aug disappeared, as did the doorway. A different area appeared. The timestamp had rolled forward slightly. The brick here was caked with mud that had been built up through years of neglect. A fibre cement panel bolted haphazardly into the masonry could just be distinguished beneath the grime.

'This is out the back. That panel covers what used to be the delivery door.'

The mud was thick at the base of the building, and so worn in that even the torrential rain wasn't doing much to shift it. From beyond the camera's field of view came the revenant form of an Aug, looming in the night.

This Aug had no wet-weather gear, and it was hard to make out details in the feed. It seemed to hunch over itself. All four of its limbs were on the ground, bent forward like an ape, the forelimbs far longer than its legs. Its face was a collection of glowing lights, flaring into the cheap safety cameras and obscuring the rest of its head. The metal parts of it were burnished, broken and rigged together precariously.

It was shirtless, and the pale flesh shone white in the frame. It reached the wall of the Library, and with precise, mechanical movement, it drove its forelimbs underneath the caked layer of mud and in between the brickwork and the fibre cement sheeting. When the arm pulled back, a small portion of the cement and mud came with it. Moving a few centimetres, it tried again. It repeated the action, flaking off tiny pieces of cement each time. It didn't seem to tire, or even stop to think.

'I heard this,' Col said, 'from inside, I mean. I knew there was something happening.'

'Were these the Augs that you were running from?'

Col shook his head. 'It was dark, and I didn't get a good look at them. I don't think so, though.'

Methodically, the Aug began shifting and testing every single angle and part of the sheet. It didn't scramble or scrape or rush, it simply pulled, moved, placed, pulled and repeated.

Cass watched, feeling a cold chill in her blood. The Augs were quite clearly trying to break in, and it was coordinated. Planned.

A few minutes later, the Aug who had tried to open the front door appeared and gestured silently to the slowly working automaton. Cass thought she saw a flash of something metallic and flat in its hand. Immediately, the other Aug stopped its work, leaving the rain to wash away the evidence of sabotage.

The co-conspirators turned and swept out of the vid's frame. The dilapidated rear of the library building stood in the rainy murk for a few seconds, then dissolved back into the remains of the sunset that she and Col had been watching before the discussion had started. The light was fading fast now, a velvet sheet cast across the poorly rendered colours of the electric city lights. It was one of the evenings where the richness of the real spoke for itself; a collusion of hues careening around the sky as if to make subtle mockery of the small bright place that humanity had carved for itself in the universe. The siblings stared quietly for a moment, disquiet filling the void between them.

There had always been an unspoken communication between them. Sometimes, they would simply move in concert, the two of them silently standing and walking somewhere as though an agreement had been made. Little things, like the decision to clear the plates after dinner, or an agreement to share a favourite toy. The two of them had an understanding of one another that, to an outsider, seemed almost like mind-reading. The connection had followed them into adulthood. Cass found that contacting Col through the Link was almost as natural as thinking on her own, and she could intuit that same ease in Col.

Without a word, they both stood. Cass picked up her empty drink and made her way to the fire escape, pulling it ajar and worming her way down the too-steep stairwell to her hab. Col jittered, sliding behind her before disappearing and reappearing next to the chaise lounge in Cass's living room. Cass stepped toward her refrigerator, throwing the exhausted stim into the recycling and grabbing another. The mild amphetamine in the drink would make it nearly impossible for her to sleep, but there'd be no sleep for her tonight after what she'd just seen. She did her best work in the small hours of the morning, gnawing away at a problem in the cool and gloom as the world first fell asleep, then woke up around her.

'They didn't look like most of the Augs you see,' she said, after some thought.

Col remained silent.

'Most of them are addicts. The only thing they want is more solar cells to fry themselves with. These ones, though. They were different. They were determined. That one at the back looked almost like it wasn't thinking. Like it was being controlled by something.' She couldn't keep the disgust out of her voice, and in her mind she saw the Aug from the tower. 'So, what were they doing?'

Col took a long pull from his drink. 'I don't know. Maybe they were trying to steal something. Maybe they were trying to break the Uplink node. Maybe they thought it would be a dry place to sleep.'

They weren't just looking for a place to sleep, Cass thought. That was a synchronised attempt at a break-in. That meant they wanted something that they knew, or at least had a strong suspicion, was inside. She tilted her head.

'What's actually in the Library?' she asked her brother.

Col shrugged. 'Not much. A terminal. An enormous wireless relay and more high throughput memory than you could shake a dozen sticks at. Other than that, not a lot. Cabling, I guess.'

'Solar panels?'

'Oh, on the roof? Sure, high-yield ones in an ultra-wideband array.'

Cass thought back to the Aug she'd interrogated. The way he'd darted for the electrodes when she'd moved out of the sun. The blank, cold look of content that had filled his features even as his arm had burned up. The room stinking of rotten human meat and effluent mingled with the acrid scent of melted plastic and the iron taste of corrosion.

She thought of the Aug at the back of the Library. The one in the tower had been desperate, whereas this one had methodical, cold movements.

She pulled herself back to the present with a draw from her stim juice and forced herself to change the subject. She didn't want to waste her time with Col by turning it into a work interrogation.

They sat back into the comfort of Cass's home and told each other old stories that they both knew by heart. But they laughed anyway, and Col slowly became more drunk as Cass began to glow in the amphetamine buzz.

Before Col said goodnight, he turned to her, and there was a quiet loneliness behind his eyes.

'Cass. I know I say it all the time, but if you keep following this lead, just be careful, alright?'

This time, floating in a cloud of stims, Cass didn't get angry, just said, 'Okay.'

Col nodded. 'Hours I work. Hours everyone works. I've only really got you to talk to. And Sal, but that's... I dunno. It's different. Something were to happen, I don't know what I'd do.'

Cass didn't answer. She didn't need to. Col's form glitched and disappeared from view. The lights flickered and Cass was alone in her head.

After a few minutes, she pulled up a series of datalinks on the job she was currently investigating. She built a new connection, labelled it 'Library', and dumped the vidfeed into it. Her eyes twitched, REM-like, and she pulled gossamer threads between the Library link and several others – the words 'solar', 'connectivity', and 'addicts' flitted between them.

She plucked at the threads, then dove into the discussion she'd had with the Aug. She reran every line, every moment, trying to eke out some iota of meaning or information she'd missed before. She tried to keep what Col had said out of her head. Truth was, she was lonely, too. Wasn't everybody?

She fed the vidfeed through several algorithms she'd tested, to try to extract information she might not have noticed. It was several hours later, as the sun was rising, that she went to bed, and her dreams were filled with the sound of automated limbs, scraping at her mind in the dark.

CHAPTER 5

COLIN

He floated in an ocean of smoke. A light, permeable haze that wisped and curled, ebbed and flowed, as a susurrus melted around and about and through him. The smoke was a tide, or a flocking simulation of chaotic motion, driving waves of light and dark into one another, moving and building into great mountains of multicoloured vapour.

The largest mountains of smoke coalesced, crystallised, conformed, and built faceted towers of myriad unknowable colours. These began mired in the fog, struggling to grow beneath the surface. Most never breached, sublimating their solidity and puffing back into the communion of wefting forms.

When they finally rose above, a glimmer of shining gemstone would cut into the rarefied atmosphere, and a maelstrom would form around it. The wind would blow, shattering small pieces off, but the greater part would survive and grow and thrive and build itself into a seemingly impenetrable fortress moving above the rifting tides beneath. The chips and splinters would fall off and become their own subsidiary towers. Each had its own shape, some remaining low and wide above the whirling fluidity, others growing into towering spires.

Eventually, all the towers crumbled. Roiling gases would form a storm, and the turbulence would clash and clamour at the side of the crystal fortress. Sometimes the smoke would burst from within, and the tower would collapse upon itself, or else shatter into a series of new forms. Light shows and colours danced along the prismatic edges, but these new towers in turn suffered from the decay of those that came before, and they collapsed and crashed into the ever more violent sea of smoke and foam.

Col watched, floating, a zephyr in the storm, entirely at its whims. He saw, among the glowing colours of the smoke and crystal world, a darkened, scarlet mote. It danced for a moment, struggling to find itself, before it latched on to something in the vapour. It grew into a viscous clump, a magma-hot granule. Each glowing speck, each particle in the smoke, was smothered as it spread. Soon, it was an oozing growth in the middle of the storm. It killed all motion surrounding it. The chaos that chipped away or infiltrated or joined with the towers halted, frozen, joined into the congealing magma. The growing infection.

Col was caught, able to do nothing but watch the spread. Where it touched a tower it lanced electric veins of murk until the structure collapsed, almost in slow motion, and was subsumed by the ichorous mire. One by one, the towers were touched by the red-black muck, and Col watched the chaotic landscape around him collapse, pulled beneath the motionless gore of the dark, eternal stillness. It grew exponentially, and the endless landscape disappeared. Col pulled and struggled, and a face appeared in the flames. A corruption, some agent controlling the spread and burning through everyone and everything. He knew that the struggle would only drag him down faster, but he couldn't help but push himself further into the void. He couldn't breathe. He couldn't breathe. He felt an immense pressure on his chest. He couldn't –

The breath exploded from him as he jolted awake in his bed. Cold air hit him in a violent rush, and he felt his muscles spasm into motion as the nightmare faded. He felt a tightness in his right calf that turned into a cramp.

Swearing, he climbed from his bed and limped gingerly around, trying to force the contorted muscle back. He was sweating, and staggered with an awkward gait toward his bathroom. He leaned against the basin, breathing heavily, pushing his heel back toward the ground, stretching his calf back to normal.

He stole a glance at himself. Small rivulets were running from his mop of dark hair onto his already soaked forehead. The bags under his eyes were bigger than he remembered, and the grimace of pain from the cramp sank his cheeks in the pale dark light. He looked gaunt. Haggard. Drawn. He'd been gritting his teeth in his sleep, and his jaw hurt.

The cramp had cooled, and he breathed easier. Stripping off, he showered off the stink of sweat.

He didn't dare look at the time before he went back to bed. He didn't want to know how little sleep he had left.

* * *

Col rubbed his eyes again, hoping in vain that the pressure would push away the tired blur, and that he'd feel an alertness that four stimtabs hadn't already instilled in him. He'd fallen back asleep, and had spent the rest of the early hours of the morning napping in fits and starts. His alarm had blared in his mind through the Uplink at the usual time, but the night had felt both too long and too short. He'd sacrificed his usual morning routine for a desperate round of wake-up activities and substances. The shower had been freezing, the music loud, the caffeine strong, and all of them ineffective. He felt, more than anything else, hungover.

This meeting had an air of importance. The silence was usual; the tension was not. The invite list extended both higher and wider across the organisation than the others he'd been called into. Sal was here, as were a number of techs from other departments. In the centre was his director, in her usual panopticon position, staring both straight at him and not at all in his direction. A number of others stood with her, rendered in the unreality. The Uplink drew their faces into sharp relief while their bodies remained obscured in the false light.

Col yawned. *God, I picked the night to not sleep,* he thought, before one of the unfamiliar faces spoke.

'I think that's a quorum. Would you like to begin?'

Colin's director nodded and smiled. When she spoke, her voice expanded into the space with an echoing quality mapped from theatres and cathedrals. Col could picture her at a pulpit, sermonising to the masses.

'Thank you all for coming. Over the last few months, I imagine the majority of you have noted a large amount of work upgrading both system bandwidth and storage capacity.' There was a smattering of assenting murmurs. 'The managerial team across our sector, and worldwide, thanks you for your hard work and apologises for the secrecy so far.

'There have been test studies completed for the work we've been doing behind the scenes, and a few setbacks. These system upgrades have been carried out on the assumption that we would eventually solve the teething issues with these new implementations.'

So, there are still technical glitches? Col thought as the director continued.

'What you are about to see is a series of promotional feeds which will be disseminated through the network over the next few weeks. You, as Uplink employees, are getting a first look.'

Her voice took on a tone of rote-learned flatness that even the Uplink couldn't disguise. 'For the last fifteen years, Uplink has been the premiere social network, business hub, integration platform and source of unprecedented worldwide connectivity. Through the technology that *you* implement and maintain, a safe, reliable and continuously available network has allowed *our* eyes and ears to stay connected –'

Col stifled another yawn. He faded the stream of the meeting room to take a swig from yet another stim, and gazed blearily at his bookshelf. The cloudy white spines of the books glowed at the edges, reminding him of the dream that had stolen his sleep. He was struggling to pay attention to the director as she continued to talk about the history of the Link. He'd heard it before. He knew it. Everyone knew it. Working for the company that had achieved the greatest breakthrough in communications history, one got very sick of repeatedly hearing the tale of the tech giant's triumph over lesser modes of communication. He would have taken a book from the shelf to read, but a warning and countdown timer in his vision prompted him to return to the Uplink.

The director was still talking. 'For years, we've spoken to each other, and heard. For years, we've been present, and been seen. Now we're adding a third sensory experience to the world of Uplink.'

The panopticon smile filled the room.

The white room went dark. Everyone else disappeared, and Col was plunged into an immersive promotional vid.

'The Uplink is getting touch.'

* * *

'All makes sense now, doesn't it?' Sal said.

It was three hours later, and the two of them were in the Library together. Col had watched a careening, disorienting vortex of vidfeeds attempt to describe the *feeling* and *intent* of touch through sight and sound alone. He'd had to stay for the question-and-answer session to receive a datapack, delivered by direct cerebral download. He'd then left the meeting, all without moving from the torn-up lounge in his hab.

'Absolutely,' he agreed, 'Guess we're not doing home days for a while, with this much to install.'

A new box of chips had been delivered. He shunted it over and pulled a low-powered laser cutter from his belt to remove the tape. The inventory used an old kind of smart contract that was intractable once it was signed. Under normal circumstances, he'd have confirmed the contents of the box before signing, but his exhaustion was making him impatient.

Sal pulled one of the chips out, and he flicked a copy of the replacement log over to her. She twitched slightly as she filled her vision with the overlay of what went where, then paused.

'You okay, Col? You look like garbage.' Her tone betrayed genuine concern.

Col laughed, trying to ignore the scratchy feeling behind his eyes and his now ever-present headache. He told her about the nightmare and lack of sleep the night before.

'You're pretty pale,' she said, sceptical.

'Just overstimmed. I'm fine. Really.' He redoubled his efforts on the box of parts in front of him. She didn't press the issue any further.

They worked in silence. Col, rubbing his eyes regularly, laid out the parts for Sal to install. The ability to simulate touch was a staggering technological innovation – yet he was sure it would morph into the same mundanity that all technical marvels eventually became. It would, as with all these things, become work. As for the type of work, he didn't know. Sure, Link pornos and 'immersive' sexual experiences were about to get a huge uptick in marketability, but beyond that, who knew? Nobody knew how exactly people would use this technology. As usual, it would be up to creatives, entrepreneurs, businesspeople and the greater collective consciousness to explore all the new sensory experiences that could be had.

What confused him more than anything, was the secrecy around the so-called 'teething issues' the director had referred to. There had been pointed questions, including a particularly incisive one by Sal, but the directors had dodged it. All he'd managed to glean was that there was something about structure. Increasing the bandwidth required some kind of restriction to the 'shape' of the data. Col didn't understand what it meant. Sal had a better handle on the interface of the Uplink than he did.

The library creaked, and Col's head snapped up. Sal poked her head out to look at him. Both of them were still shaken by the footage Sal had unearthed.

'Just the building drying out.' Col bent back to his work. He saw Sal nod and turn to the stacks, but a few moments later, she came back.

'So,' she said, wringing her hands slightly, 'that noise... it reminds me. The video from the other night – with the Augs trying to break in? It's happened before.'

Col sat back on his haunches, staring across the room at his colleague. Her overalls were grubby and a nervous energy radiated from her.

'How do you know?' Col asked.

'Well, after you sent me in the other day, and I found the video of the Augs, you didn't rescind my access to the feed. You gave me access for 24 hours, so after I'd finished for the day, I kept looking.' Before Col could say anything, Sal pulled him into a dark Link viewing room, where she projected several other feeds from preceding months.

She showed him five other attempts at break-ins. They all occurred at night and in the pouring rain. Each time it was near impossible to make out the features of the Augs making the attack. The lights were disrupted by the rain and the creatures themselves moved in the shadows. But each time it was possible to spot the hulking, apelike form of the hunched Aug from the first vidfeed, skulking and metallic.

'Have you told anyone about this?' he asked Sal.

She shook her head. 'No. Was going to send a digest to you and a few of the higher-ups all at once.'

'Good idea. Include me in it, too, and send the timestamps.'

Sal grinned. 'Hey, good thing you imagined someone in the stacks, or we wouldn't have found out about this in the first place!'

Col blanched. He was still wondering what it was that had caused him to think he'd seen movement in the stacks that night. His current theory was that it was some kind of artefact from the Uplink connection itself, possibly due to the storm.

'Yeah. Actually, do me a favour. Leave me out of the report. Let's just say we were conducting a routine security check or something like that.'

He wasn't sure why he felt the compulsion to lie about what had prompted their investigation, but he knew he didn't want his managers and other people in the organisation to know about what he'd 'seen' in the stacks. As it was, telling Sal had felt like revealing a secret of some kind.

'Sure,' Sal said, giving him a queer look before she ducked back into the stacks to replace whichever piece of hardware she'd been working on before the creak in the building had distracted them.

Col found himself wondering what an Aug would want from this place. It would be redundant in a community where access to the dopamine rush of a solar hit was the most valuable commodity – and they couldn't access the Uplink anyway. *They probably don't even know what's in here.*

But the Augs had specifically decided to scope out and attempt to gain entry to the *Library*, and not any of the surrounding buildings. They'd tried, over and over, to find a way in. It didn't make sense. He looked at the chipset in his hand and tried to imagine what else it could be used for, aside from raw materials or its intended purpose in the Uplink.

He was nearly done cleaning the wiring at the end of a row of multi-core chips when Sal called his name. As he rounded the corner, he noted a look of concern on her face.

'Did you happen to check these three serials?' With a flick of the wrist, she sent a series of numerical strings to him. Fingers twitching slightly, he pulled up the shipping log and crunched the data against all the work he'd done so far that day. It took a couple of seconds, and then he turned back to her.

'No, why?' But he knew the answer. He hadn't been thinking when he'd signed the contract earlier. He hadn't checked.

He should have checked.

Sal pulled out three storage cases from the base of the box she'd been unpacking. The reflective packaging with the same three serial numbers and a scannable code sat inert at the bottom. They were empty.

'Because, if I haven't unpacked them, and you haven't touched them, then they're missing.'

CHAPTER 6

CASS

Apartment buildings rose behind her, a staccato response to the undulating form of grey seawater wearing down the crusted piers. The original docks were barely visible half a metre below the low-tide waterline. Acid-etched marks had been left by lifeforms eating at the surface of the concrete that had once been polished smooth by footfalls. Cass made her way down a new walkway across the dyke that had been constructed to hold back the rising sea. Ships and cranes loomed at her out of the dawn haze. The surface she strode across was a mishmash of marine-grade stainless steel and rockcrete, a dark and cold replacement for the structures that were being eaten away beneath the tide.

She'd sat there once, she remembered, looking down at the submerged structure. Half a lifetime ago, she'd held hands with a girlfriend in a sunrise not dissimilar to this one, passing a flask back and forth. For a moment, the echo of young laughter seemed to drift across the salt breeze, and along with it a gentle memory of teenage smugness. To feel as though a mild act of rebellion made you unique, as though they had been the first people to sneak in somewhere to see the sunrise.

She smiled to herself, and headed further into the shipyard, leaving her innocent sense of taboo behind her. Before long, the open view of the ocean gave way to unfamiliar, sheer-walled canyons of ships astride the new docks. The pale sunlight became crisp and cold, bouncing down off impossibly high, dark walls of container ships. Enormous cranes threw fractal patterns of shadows across the dim. The temperature dropped, and she felt cold radiate up her body. The grating clanked as she walked, singing an announcement to anyone nearby. After a nervous glance over her shoulder, she set up a small geopositioning flag in her Uplink. If she needed to, she could trigger the flag and it would send an emergency alert to her brother. It was a useful security measure, and letting Col know she was using it might stop him worrying so much. Beside her, the ships moved in a slowly dancing rhythm, an achingly sedate replica of the waves running beneath the deck.

The tide was out. That was a good thing. It was worrying enough to come out here, unprotected and alone, without having to worry about the sea rising to swallow her. The sea wall on the other side of the dock was almost entirely out of the water now, covered in striations of green-black tidemarks. It was far enough away that it seemed locked in place as she walked, some permanent reminder that if she were to linger too long she, too, would fall beneath the waves.

A few minutes later, she emerged from the shoulder of the ship and found herself on the corner of a dry dock.

Sometimes I hear things in the dry dock. That's what the Aug had told her. She saw her shadow leap across the stepped concrete hole, and the sun's corona appeared behind the shadow of her head. To the right of the penumbral haze, across the other side of the dock, was a plethora of wiring and conduit that snaked into the wall. She shuddered, and began to walk toward it.

The place looked abandoned. It was the small things. The unburnished grain of the concrete below the waves. The choked, dying brown plants starved of nutrients and burned by reflected sun, struggling through gaps in the new rockcrete. The lapping swish of the waves dancing over the same well-trodden and worn ground on the lower steps.

There was no sign that it had been used in years. But there was a door.

She knocked. It opened.

An Aug stood in the dark behind the doorway, with the telltale ripple of concealed wiring beneath its skin. The wiring ran down one side of its head, protruding from a bald skull. The smile on the face was wide, worn as an affectation while blue-green eyes bore into Cass.

'Hi,' she said, thrusting her hand out to shake, 'I'm Cassandra Mont-'

The Aug put a finger to its lips and beckoned her inside. Cass double-checked her tracker was primed, and followed.

Cass glanced around the dimly lit room she was led into. Small electric lights hung in disarray from the ceiling on black cords, and the furniture was little more than flotsam and jetsam from the surrounds, pushed and bent into vaguely useable shapes. The man took a seat across from her on a stainless-steel bench before tapping at his pockets, pulling out a stimtab and dry swallowing it. She sat opposite, on what looked like an old pier footing, complete with rusted reinforcing rods that jutted from its sides.

Shelves around them heaved with tinned goods and other non-perishables. Behind her was a bench with gas cylinders strapped to the ceiling above it. Rubber pipes ran from them into a crude hotplate setup. When she looked back, the Aug was staring straight at her, impassive, before his face widened again into the same almost-smile.

'Who are you,' the voice was deep, almost guttural, rich with vocal fry, 'and how did you find me?'

Cass took a breath. Through a doorway, another dimly lit room housed a series of storage racks replete with something she couldn't see.

'As I said, my name is Cassandra. I work for – ' She paused. She didn't want him to know she was an investigative reporter. A cover story might lend her more legitimacy. 'I work for Uplink Security, and I'm here to ask a few questions. Do you mind if I get your name for my records?'

The Aug stared for a long time before answering. 'Jake.' The lips barely moved before his features carefully settled back into the same arrangement they'd worn when he sat down. He contemplated something for a while, then spoke again.

'Uplink Security?'

When Cass nodded, his eyes filled with contempt, though the smile remained stoically in place. 'I presume your partner is waiting outside.'

Cass sat stock still and waited for her heart to fall back to a normal rhythm before responding, flicking her fingers to ready the emergency flag. After that, the lie came easily enough. 'They're just outside the gate to the docks. They're expecting me, and you know,' she tapped the side of her head, 'Uplink comms.'

Cass waited, suddenly aware of the amount of extraneous movement in her body when compared with the Aug sitting in front of her. She bounced a knee nervously, stopped, then became hyper-aware of its stillness.

'I'm looking into something,' she said. Jake still didn't move, and Cass tried to hide her relief that he seemed to have bought her lie. The light caught the edge of the series of ugly scars across his head. They were a mottled patchwork of skin grafts, sewn inexpertly and hastily over Augmetic wiring that terminated behind his right temple. Each patch was sewn over the next, calling attention to the augmentations as much as his attempt to conceal them. 'There have been a number of rumours surrounding Aug activity recently. Attempted thefts. Attempts to access the Uplink.'

Jake scoffed. 'Attempts to access the Uplink? We can't do that.' He tapped the side of his head, where the protrusion lay. 'Brain structure, you see. I don't fit in the box the Uplink was designed for. Neither do my... colleagues. I feel as though Uplink Security would know that.' The implicit accusation deadened the air in the cramped cellar. She heard the soft roar of the ocean through the bare concrete. The smile had become more of a sneer. 'Where have you heard these rumours?'

Cass told him, and where she'd been before. About the decrepit building on the edge of town where the Augs coalesced. A sore against an already blighted skyline.

'And he told you to speak to *me*?' His lips barely moved. His body didn't at all. Cass shifted in her seat.

'Not you,' she said, 'It – *he* just said to search the dry docks. I had no idea I'd find you here.'

He grunted. 'And he told you about break-ins?'

Cass shook her head. 'The break-in info came from elsewhere.' She began to describe what she had been told by her brother some nights before, taking care to excise any direct references to where it was that she got the information, and changing enough details as to obfuscate the location.

'After several of these instances, there was a night where the worker' – *my brother,* she avoided saying – 'was performing some out-of-hours maintenance tasks, and heard some unusual sounds. I was provided with the feed footage.' With a flick of her wrist, the vidfeed began playing in front of her, between the two of them. The deep washing sounds of the rain began again, and Cass directed her view to the screen.

Jake stared at her for a moment, waiting as she watched the feed in slow motion and described it to him. He couldn't see it, but he asked no questions, needed no clarifications, and didn't even interrupt by moving. All the while the smile was fixed on his face.

When she was done, he sat for a moment.

'It's interesting,' he said.

'What is?'

'When you said you were from the Uplink Security force – if it hadn't been for the slight movement of his lower jaw and Adam's apple as he spoke, he'd have been standing stock still – 'you didn't show me any identification.'

Cass swallowed. 'Well. No. I didn't have any. It's all on the Uplink now, you know? Here,' she flicked her hand. Nothing happened, but she said, 'My credentials are there. You just can't see them. Same as you couldn't see the vidfeed. It's all on Link now.'

Still, he didn't move. 'Yes. Although this isn't my first time dealing with corporate police. If they know they'll be working with Augs, such as myself, they usually offline the vidfeed onto a tablet. *Don't they?*' He stared at her pointedly.

'Yes, I suppose we usually do, don't we?' Cass's mind raced. *Stupid,* she thought to herself. She'd been too eager to get here, and she hadn't thought her plan through enough. She pulled up the geopositioning flag in her visuals.

Just in case.

Jake stood and walked around the edge of the table toward her. There was a look in his eyes. If she hadn't known better, she'd have called it *hunger*.

'You're here on your own, aren't you?'

'No,' Cass lied again, fighting the urge to hit the geoflag. He was big, and loomed over her as she sat at the table.

'In my experience, that would be highly irregular. You would always have a partner. Someone to help you if you got into trouble. Violent outbursts. Dangerous situations. We're *Augs*, after all.' Jake spat the word at her with palpable hatred, and stepped forward again. The way he said the word gave it away. This Aug, filled with wiring and Augmetics and hardware, hated who he was. He was locked out of the Uplink and he couldn't stand it. He had grafted skin over his augmentations to obscure who and what he really was, turning himself into a chimera.

'And you're not security, are you?'

Cass hesitated. 'No.'

The malice disappeared from the smile, and it was replaced again by the empty stillness with nothing behind the eyes. 'I think it's time for you to go.'

She didn't need telling twice.

On the way out the door, his voice carried out to her. 'If you're looking, there's a warehouse with a green door. Old industrial sector. A fine *security officer* such as yourself might find someone to talk to there.' The mockery and malice were palpable in his tone.

Her coat streamed behind her as the sound of the heavy door hitting its frame rang through the dry dock.

The sun was beaming onto the concrete and steel outside Jake's hideaway. Glare blasted up at Cass as she hurried along, and the bright of the sun turned any shade into areas of high contrast. Each shadow was a hiding place. Jake hadn't followed her, just stood at the table and watched her go, silent and still but for the message he'd yelled after her.

She clambered through the chain link fence on the way out and turned around to look back into the dock. Harsh white sent pinpricks of pain into her eyes. It made it hard to tell if the shadows glowed red with reflections from the side of the ships, or from watchful eyes, following her out of their territory.

CHAPTER 7

COLIN

He wished the nightmares would stop.

That would have made the last three weeks from hell just a little easier. Every day he'd worked through endless action items. Bug fixes, mechanical upgrades and official checklists were required to bring the upgrade online. In between, he'd had to spend an inordinate amount of time trying to invalidate the contract for the shipment he'd received and signed before the realisation that stock was missing. When he finally slept after fifteen-hour days, he was plagued with images of roiling smoke, crystal towers and a seeping magma darkness turning everything to dust. Every night, he'd wake in the small hours in a cold sweat.

Sal was noticing how drawn he looked.

'I'm fine. This upgrade is wearing me out,' he'd say, turning away from the concern in her eyes to the next task on his endless list.

The break-in attempts seemed to have stopped, especially since Colin's management had engaged a member of their corporate police to patrol the library. *We're resources, not assets*, came his sister's voice whenever he thought about how readily money for security and extra personnel could be found when it was protecting property and not people. Sal had sent a compilation of the footage to management, and once Col had alerted them to the theft in the shipment, they'd taken action. Still, Col wasn't sure that it was the police presence that had made the Augs give up. Maybe they'd already got what they needed, or maybe they'd decided to hit another location. Regardless, neither the security systems nor the police had detected any Aug presence since the announcement of the upgrade. Col wasn't sure whether that was reassuring.

All in all, the frantic scramble of the last few weeks had left Col worn down by anxiety, deadline pressure and sheer exhaustion. In the small hours of each morning, he'd watch his alarm timer burn behind his eyelids as he tried to steal a few extra moments of sleep.

Before long, the agitating grate of the alarm sang through his senses. Sighing, Col sat up. He placed his bare feet on the floor and stayed there for a moment, feeling the cacophony of the alarm flood him, saturating him until it became just another part of the background noise. Only then did he twitch slightly to disable it, enjoying the fleeting moment of explosive silence that overwhelmed the room.

This was the day the upgrade would go live.

He slumped toward the bathroom, exhaustion creeping back as water and steam enveloped him. It seeped into his body. When he was finished, he stared into the mirror. The face that stared back seemed a parody of itself. Shadows hung beneath his eyes; his skin was loose and his head seemed almost too big for his neck.

I need some time off, he thought, knowing all the while that his contract stipulated that time off was only for medical emergencies.

* * *

The company's police officers had stood out at first, an ugly reminder of the incident that night. Before too long, though, they sank into the background. He'd never bothered to learn their names, he realised, as he arrived at the inner security door again.

ENTRY 0732H: COLIN P. MONTGOMERY

He had a final round of checks to make before the upgrade went live. The back room, where he'd heard the Aug scraping against the wall, had been cleared of the built-up detritus that had been stored there when it was a catch-all space for used boxes, leftover parts, old equipment and items that needed returning without any urgency. He and Sal had changed that, replacing the mess with an all-new server rack. As he walked through now, it gleamed, even in comparison with the well-maintained mainframe in the stacks itself. The room was now occupied with an overflow server, designed to identify and handle extra system load during high-traffic events. Col had a sneaking suspicion that the capacity required for the upgrade had been underestimated. Touch, for the Uplink, was going to drive a lot of traffic.

A checklist floated in front of his eyes and he noted the matches between socket numbers and data banks. The heaving umbilical was fully connected and ready to spew data to the newly updated distribution array on the roof. Next, Col tested the new bank of relays, the archaic switching system still used for bulk signal transfer. The sharp click of each relay echoed in sympathy with one another, creating a solid *thunk* that reverberated around the Library's gloom.

Sal sat in the main hub, waiting patiently. He nodded at her. She'd held up to the work strain better than him; she looked tired but hadn't lost the weight he had, nor were the circles under her eyes as deep.

'Ready to go?' he asked.

CASS

It was the fourth time she'd been to the warehouse. The first time, she'd done nothing but wait a few hundred metres away for about forty minutes. She'd gone soon after the incident with Jake, but hadn't gone too close. She didn't trust him.

The green door sat resolutely closed. The warehouse was old, and sat in a series of rust-stained contemporaries that lined the pitted street. The sun was beating down on the first day, and the steel and concrete groaned and murmured as heat expansion turned the street into an eerie symphony.

She'd given up waiting and turned around to walk away before she got more sunburned. As she did so, she saw a flash of movement in her periphery. The door had opened, and someone had stepped out, and turned to where she'd stood.

Watching.

COLIN

A timer appeared in his view, counting down. It had a series of sub-timers that demarcated major systems booting up, restarting or otherwise changing state as the system went through the complex process of adding more sensory data.

Sal sat a few metres away, staring into the middle distance with a blank expression. She was watching the same countdown as he was.

The first sub-timer hit zero.

'Overflow is now online. No errors.' Sal's voice seemed far away as Col cross-checked his own set of results. The next timer was a double switch a few minutes away, and it was the one he was most concerned about. Part of the Uplink's core code was being broadcast *into* the neural interface that made human brains compatible with the signals it was sending. Col's understanding of it was incomplete, and he'd asked Sal to explain several days prior. It was 'training' the brain to recognise the electromagnetic broadcast as sensory inputs, which could be mapped onto the person's experience in the real world. The Uplink was about to change everyone's brain. Again.

It made his head hurt to think about it, and his head had been hurting a lot recently.

CASS

Cass had searched all the databases and networks available to find out what the warehouse contained. The results were perplexing. It belonged to a small company that had purchased the warehouse freehold years before. The owners of the company didn't appear to exist, and it didn't ever seem to export. The warehouse drew a substantial amount of power, and there were people that would enter and exit occasionally, but she couldn't find out anything else.

The second time she'd gone there, Cass had approached the building. She was careful this time, and had her geo-flag ready to send the moment she'd arrived on the street. It was early in the morning, and the brackish grey of the building's shadow cast a pall on the front of the warehouse, washing out the colour. A crisp wind blew down the row, and she had to use her jacket to stop dust getting into her eyes.

She knocked firmly on the door, not expecting a lot. To her surprise, there was a rasping noise as something was pulled away from the doorstop, and she heard the unclicking of a number of bolts.

It hinged open a few centimetres, and an Aug's face peered out from the backlit dark. A series of tattoos traced a braided pattern around her eye sockets, failing to cover a ripe burn mark on the right side of her face. The burn congealed and coalesced, but it wasn't the part of the Aug's appearance that was acid-etched into Cass's memory.

The lower half of the jaw was gone. It was ripped away and, in its place, sat a closed mouthpiece of metal.

Cass stared, dumbfounded, for a few seconds, before the Aug slammed the door in her face again.

COLIN

'Any more luck with that missing stuff?' Sal asked. The timer counted down. The upgrade was causing a high-pitched ringing in Col's ears, in addition to the steadily growing whirr of cooling fans and emergency backup drives. Like his alarm, it had begun to sink into the background, becoming a sort of quiet cacophony.

He longed for sleep, but he didn't know when it would come. Once the upgrade went through, his life would become endless patches and bug fixes and more endless hours of nothing but work. He didn't know when, or how, it would end.

He hadn't answered Sal's question. 'No,' he said, over the din, 'To be honest, I've not been looking into it. I've only been trying to get the delivery certificate invalidated.'

Three minutes until the signal towers would begin broadcasting the upgrade to everyone in the area. The room hummed. Col double-checked the warnings on his retina. None from the Uplink, and none from his sister either. She'd told him she was investigating somewhere today. He didn't remember where she'd gone, but she would often let him know that a geoflag might come through if she got in trouble. He hated it, but it was part of her job.

'What do you think they stole it for?' Sal asked.

'Hmm?' Col's attention was pulled back to reality. 'Oh, I don't know. New technology? From the biggest tech company that the world has ever seen? Industrial espionage, probably. I wouldn't be surprised if the Augs had nothing to do with it.'

Sal shook her head, flicking her eyes to the timer as she did so. Not long now. 'Doesn't make sense. The Augs *were* trying to get in here. Doesn't make sense to me that they'd be trying to get in here at the same time as *someone else* stole our shipment.' She was speaking at her normal volume despite the whining screech building up like a capacitor ready for discharge. Col had to concentrate to hear her.

'You think the Augs stole it?'

She shrugged. 'I don't know how, but yes.'

The noise was too much. Col was almost at the point of trying to find a set of earplugs to block out the frenzied screeching pouring from the stacks. He stood up and out of his chair and walked around to try to distract himself. It wasn't working. It sounded like it was building, a discordant waveform that filled the entire sonic spectrum, a physical *presence* in the room. With only a few seconds before the upgrade went live, he wheeled to Sal and gesticulated wildly towards the stacks.

'How are you dealing with that *noise*?' he asked.

Sal looked confused, turned around to the interior of the Library, then looked back at him, concerned.

'What noise?'

CASS

The third time, Cass hadn't tried to get in again. She'd once again held back, watching from a small nook between two warehouses down the street. She'd spent the better part of a day there, and had taken notes on what she'd seen and added them to the file.

Two small trucks arrived, with no brand identifiers or licence plates. Both of them had gone through a chain-link fence on one side and come out only a few minutes later. Cass caught sight of a large roller door, but hadn't been able to get a vantage point of the building as it had opened.

Augs drifted in and out. Every couple of hours, they would arrive in fits and starts, usually alone but sometimes in small groups. They would wait patiently outside the green door, standing with the same kind of stock-stillness that Jake had shown. Cass noted the details of the body modifications on these Augs to try to figure out how long they stayed, but it didn't appear to matter. In the hours she spent there, she didn't see a single Aug walk back out.

As the sun set on a long, fruitless day of surveillance, she realised she still had no idea what was happening inside this warehouse that Jake had directed her to.

And so she was here again, for the fourth time. She knocked on the green door again, and it opened almost straight away. Cass brought up and armed her geoflag. The jawless Aug stood in the doorway, regarded her with a nod, then held up an artificial arm indicating that she should wait there before closing the door again.

When the door reopened after a few moments, the Aug gestured for Cass to follow and walked into the black of the factory building.

The room was small, an anteroom made of cheap ply and, judging by the smell, spray-painted black with old acrylic rattle cans. To the left of the door there was another door, which was being held ajar by the Aug. Cass stepped around a heavy-looking chair with rubbed and faded upholstery, seeing scratch marks on the floor around it, and followed the Aug into the warehouse proper.

The cavern of the main warehouse welcomed her – a repeated truss echoed down the length of the room above her head, supporting a roof system with a range of forgotten factory equipment shackled to it. Dotted here and there were hard plastic skylights which had been worn down from translucent white to a sickly sepia. Bands of sunlight edged through, casting a brown pall onto the floor below. At the far end was an enormous roller door made of rusted steel.

The room itself was subdivided into several demountables and shipping containers, each one as black as the anteroom. They were held on bricks, and cold umbilical lines at the top corners of each were pulled up and away into the roof trusses. Along the roofline, a snarl of thick wiring was held in place with crude steel straps.

There was nobody else around, and Cass wondered when the Augs she had seen entering had left. The silent Aug stalked forward, and Cass followed it. Its gait was strange, and there was an astringent scent in the air. Through the blotted sunlight she could see the structures rising throughout the shed – a shanty town to the left of her, made of dank rags and rusted poles. The dark forms of the black containers were surrounded by mechanical parts, oil drums, broken fibreboard and circuitry stripped of semiconductor. It looked at first glance as though it was a scrap pile, abandoned and forgotten.

As Cass moved through the structures, further from the glowing daylight of the door and into the pale humming light of the transformers in the centre of the structure, she noticed it wasn't abandoned at all. The clear path of desire lines wound through the mess on the floor, with tributaries and offshoots into the piles of garbage. In the middle of the warehouse, near the large door, was a small clearing, a few pallets and a set of racking that was far more organised than everything around it.

Cass looked at the Aug she was following – the replacement jaw was scratched and dented. Part of it, however, gleamed with the high-contrast green glow of a new, or at least newly repaired, piece of metal. It looked like a reshaped bolt. Even in the dark, she could see a series of similar parts at the small edges of the piles.

She checked her geoflag again, and began treading more softly, as though quiet movements would disguise her presence in the gloom.

The Aug stopped in front of her. It gestured at the container, a flat black mass in front of it. A single stainless-steel step led to a door which opened soundlessly while she watched. A flickering LED glow emanated from within.

She looked at the Aug. It nodded. Carefully, she stepped up on the grated steel and into the glowing demountable. It shook slightly, and the light source rippled, tracing outlines back and forth on the opposite wall as she entered.

The room whirred and glowed from a series of flickering lights mounted on a ramshackle framed shelf. She could see a maze of wires, bleached to near-white by the low colour rendering of the LEDs, seeping from the shelving. They wound and twisted and tied together before striking a sharp, ugly juxtaposition across the ceiling grid and into a box in the corner.

She walked closer – her eyes adjusted to the light, and as she rounded the corner she could finally see.

The racks were a mess of memory modules. Lights danced, some in simple binary blips, others in seven-segment numbers, and still others in crude digital displays.

It was a server room.

She let out a long breath. *Holy shit*, she thought. Behind her, the door creaked quietly, and clicked sharply shut. She turned, and the Aug that had led her in stood, electric lights gleaming off its jaw and crisply outlining its wiry frame.

'How did you do this?' she asked.

The Aug couldn't answer. It simply stood, its breath not even a murmur amongst the cooling fans.

Despite herself, Cass kept asking questions. 'Who helped you?'

The Aug took a step toward her.

'Who else lives here?'

Another step.

Cass was panicking now, desperate to try to distract the creature bearing down on her. She triggered her geoflag, sending it to her brother, but it failed. The message sent, but bounced. Something was blocking the signal.

'Where *is* everybody?'

She could have sworn the Aug smiled. Just a moment where the skin pulled upward from the insane mess of its jaw. It could have been a trick of the light. It was only a second.

The Aug ran at her. She had nowhere to go.

COLIN

'What do you mean, what noise!?' he shouted, but it was already too late.

The shrieking stopped. The moment the upgrade went live, it dropped from a high-pitched white noise squeal to an insensible low-bass throb that threatened to vibrate his body apart. His knees gave out on him. The throbbing noise crept from his body to his head, converging itself on the front of his mind and twisting itself into a cluster headache. Knives of pain shot through his skull. He screamed. Sal ran to him. She was asking something. Shouting. He could comprehend the desperation in her voice, but he couldn't hear the words – they were lost in the cacophony. White-hot streaks of fire burned through all of his senses at once, and he convulsed. The timers, connections to remote hosts, Sal's shared workflows and the weight of this new Uplink coursed through his grey matter and threatened to burn it out at any moment if he didn't do something, *anything* to stop the pain.

Sal was screaming at him now, but he couldn't hear. He could barely see. His breath was coming in staccato gasps and he tasted blood. He'd bitten his tongue. The copper taste blurred across his senses, drowning out everything else until it became his entire world. He tasted it in the back of his throat, a red and bronze scent, binding him up into blackness.

PART TWO

We've been out on patrol for weeks now. Standard supply run, but in the last two days security has been far more intense than it was before. I don't know what's caused it, but it's making it hard to find new supplies. Private police forces are locking down food shipments and providing protection details to cargo. Water is still okay, and the desalination kits we have are working.

Other than that, the last place we were able to hit was weeks back: a pharmacy dispensary near the old Library, down in Bern's district. Bern kept half and I sent the other half along with the crew back to the Sanctuary. There wasn't much; we only managed to get one out of the wall. Should have been good for months though. Months at least. Took all the kit, but for a few we dropped on the floor, but then security cracked down as we took on the next lot.

In hindsight, it was a good thing we didn't clue Jake in on this lift — he'd have found some way to get more of the take than the rest of us. The food distro we hit last time — I'm sure about twice as much went to Jake as anyone else, and more than his fair share of the non-perishables, too. I remember; I was on nothing but dehydrated mushroom broth for three days before we got a lead on another shipment. Numbers didn't add up on how much we lifted and how much we had when the rations came back to the Sanctuary. I suspect the maths was better at Jake's end.

Anyway. Couple of weeks after we'd managed to hit the dispensary, a runner came, told us we were down to our last med supplies. Didn't make sense. All we'd sent home was med supplies. It was the only thing that wasn't being watched round the clock. I asked her why.

Ex-Linkers is why. Lots of people not able to access the Link anymore. It's not unusual to get one — every few months we get another Linker, been unplugged for one reason or another. Now though, apparently there's an influx. The runner from the Sanctuary, she's mentioned a dozen in the last couple of days. Big new heap of them, and they need sedating. Sedating with the meds that should have lasted us months.

Something's happened.

- Cynth

CHAPTER 8

COLIN

The information floated somewhere out there, in the void, irritating like an unscratched itch. A cold, insurgent stream of data was at his fingertips, only it wasn't. He felt his mind scratch and claw at the closed door, chasing after it, but the more he moved the further away it grew. The world foreshortened around him. A light appeared at the edges of his vision, and the sensation disappeared, replaced by shouting and noise and the see-saw movement of a vehicle with worn-through shock absorbers.

'Oh god, he's awake,' a familiar voice said, *'He's awake! Hey –'*

'We need you to calm down, ma'am. He's stabilising, we've got him.' A hint of exasperation.

'I don't know what happened. He talked about – he talked about this noise and –' Sal was panicking.

'I understand. Please. Sit. The vehicle is unstable.'

The faces above him were bleary and stained with a white smear that warped his perception and rendered him unable to reconcile with reality. He watched the choral dance between the cold professionalism of the medics and Sal's emotional turmoil. His head thrummed with pain again, and his mind went dark.

* * *

A single lamp hung from a power cord stapled to the ceiling. Stark panelling on the walls, save the one furthest from him. That wall had a series of iron rods and a sheer metal door, once painted blue but now peeling. The rods were connected to each other in a locking mechanism.

It was a cell.

He had no corporeal body. He was aqueous, smokelike, approximating a human form that wasn't his. The smoke fell away and upward in defiance of gravity and danced toward the edges of the cell, only to be snuffed from existence. Puffs and rivulets fled from the body, only for most of them to die as they tried to escape. Each one flew away, only to be stymied or stopped by the containment. But some got out. For every hundred that he saw dissipate into the aether, one would find a crack or crevasse or fault, and sneak through. Tiny puffs of data, turned to sunshine in the dark.

Sunshine. Something in his mind made a connection, and each puff of smoke became a small, bright ray, refracting around the space and turning into the form of someone he recognised.

Cass, he thought. In his dream, she was cornered, caught. Sending something from the space, trying to break her confinement with a message. A signal. A single, bright element.

Somehow, he knew it wouldn't be enough. As the dream faded and was replaced by another, more familiar. The sunbeams were replaced with smoke. It crystallised, grew, was eaten away by red-black magma and torn from the world.

* * *

The last time he'd been in hospital, it had been an acute care clinic for his sister. She'd been sick for a long time, and he was the only one who'd been around. Dizzying memories of screaming inpatients and overworked nurses, and a single cold seat where he'd sat and watched Cass, pale, lying hooked up to life-support machines for hours and days at a time.

Cass. The dream he'd had was fading from his mind, too fast. Trying to remember it was like catching wavelengths of light as they sped through his grasp. Something about Cass and smoke. Or was it light?

His room was silent, the only other bed unoccupied. A series of arcane-looking boxes with biometric readouts, an ancient flatscreen bearing the slick purple-black of a dead channel. It was a serene and orderly room, disrupted only by his own presence.

The lights were dimmed to a warm, soft glow rather than harsh faux daylight, and the window outside was black. Night. The sickly scent of the hospital was still there, burning his nostrils in a way he wouldn't ever be able to forget. As his vision cleared, he noticed a cannula in his left arm, leading up to an IV drip. It had a soft light that blinked every few seconds.

Col lay back in his bed, trying to remember the dream that waking amnesia was stealing from him. It had felt so real, but it was gone, save for an anxiety that he'd missed something important.

Reaching out, he tried to call Cass. She needed to know where he was, and what had happened to him. He closed his eyes, expecting the Link to fade into view. Instead, a splinter of pain shot through his temples. The room stayed resolutely *there,* and the Uplink connection to his sister failed to materialise. He clutched the side of his head, and his vision swam.

Is this because of the Upgrade? He was trying to process what had happened at the Library, but the memory was all white-noise visuals, a wall of sound and a look of concern on Sal's face.

'How are you feeling?' The doctor's voice came from the doorway. It was slightly clipped, gravelly and dogged by tiredness.

'What happened?' Col asked.

'In a moment. I need to run some tests on you.' The doctor was brusque, but not unkind, asking a series of questions without introducing himself. He tapped on Col's various extremities, testing them for responsiveness. He shone lights into Col's eyes and waved a small metal rod a distance away. Col suspected he was checking for concussion, and stayed still.

When he finished, the doctor stood straight again, apparently satisfied with the outcome, and then his face grew serious.

'So. Your colleague, uh –' he twitched, and a flicker of his eyes showed he was searching through the Link for something.

'Sal.'

'Yes, Sal. Sally Cooper.' The timbre of his voice was rubbed raw. 'She got you in here using her insurance credentials. You've got a serious favour to pay back in that regard.'

Too right, Col thought. Getting an emergency vehicle covered by insurance was dubious enough, much less making the gamble that the hospital would allow the name switch for the patient. 'So, I'm here under her name?'

The doctor gave a wry grin, and for a moment Colin saw the care behind the tiredness in his eyes. 'I'm not sure what you mean, *Ms Cooper*.' Behind him, one of the machines beeped. He looked at it, then turned back, unconcerned. 'Sal was extremely worried about you. By the time you got here, though, you were stable. You've just been unconscious. You *are* showing signs of extreme exhaustion, but nothing that's making us immediately concerned. At this stage, we suspect a seizure of some sort, though it's hard to tell. We're recommending you stay with us for a few days, just for observation.'

'Hard to tell?' Col was trying to process what he'd heard.

The doctor nodded. 'Yes. Seizures cause changes in brain activity, but usually those changes are only visible *while* the seizure is happening. It had abated by the time you were near our instruments, so the proximate cause is difficult to identify.' He sighed. 'Before we can do anything else, though, I need your Ident.' He twitched again, and Colin looked at him blankly.

His Ident was a hashcode in the Uplink interlace that held his vital credentials. It was unique and tied to the specific brain receptors of each person that spoke to the Link. No two were the same, and they couldn't be faked – they were more unique than fingerprints, or DNA.

While the doctor waited, Col tried again to access the Uplink. Again came the spike of pain through the front of his mind. His breath came out in a short, sharp hiss, and he grasped his temple with his hand.

The doctor wasted no time getting to Col's side.

'What is it? What's wrong?' A snaking coil of exhaustion crept in under his concern, and Col suspected that the doctor knew exactly what was going to come out of his mouth.

'I can't access the Link.'

CHAPTER 9

The doctor's pupils dilated and his expression went blank. His left hand twitched three times, and he was still again. Col waited for him to finish the Uplink query, as he kept trying to reach out to both Cass and Sal. Each time he tried to reach that part of his mind, a searing pain threatened. Sal hadn't been by yet, but she would have tried to contact Cass, wouldn't she?

He realised he didn't know. Col had talked about his sister, but Sal had never met her, and vice versa. It was strange, he thought, that the two most important people in his life – often the only people in his life – didn't know each other.

'In the last few days,' the doctor's voice was heavy, 'we've had a number of people come in with a similar condition.'

'What do you mean, condition?'

'People unable to connect to the Link. It seems that whatever happened, it's caused some issues. The addition of the new Touch upgrade...' The doctor shrugged, and beneath the tiredness, Col heard a hint of quiet frustration. Maybe even fury.

These system upgrades have been carried out on the assumption that we would eventually solve the teething issues with the new implementations. The words of the director flooded through Col's memory. Was this one of the teething issues? That people would fall out of the Link?

'Will it come back? How did it happen?' Col asked.

'We have some ideas. We think it's a structural issue.'

The doctor pondered how to explain for a moment. 'Think of it this way. Your brain has a bunch of regions in it. You know, frontal lobe, temporal lobe, cerebellum, et cetera. You understand that, more or less?' When Col nodded, the doctor continued, 'Well, no two brains are identical in their structure. It's like a DNA strand. There are crossovers and similarities; *most* of it is the same from person to person, but there are specific differences that make you, *you*. With me so far?'

Again, Col nodded.

'Great. So, the Uplink connects to your brain by fitting its waveforms to that "shape", for lack of a better word. It's really good at talking to the part of your brain that looks the same as everyone else's, and it kind of ignores the part that differs from person to person. It extracts the data it needs from the part of the brain that stays the same between people.'

'Right... but why...?' Col began, but the doctor interrupted.

'So, what *appears* to have happened is that when the Upgrade went live, something changed. That shape used to have quite a lot of play in it to account for people's differences. Since the Upgrade, it seems to have become more rigidly defined. Either that or it has started to encroach on the parts of people's minds that differ from person to person.'

Col couldn't believe it. *Teething issues,* more like *systemic failures.* 'So, what? Everyone's going to just... disconnect?'

The doctor shook his head. 'Not by any means. The vast majority of the population have been fine with the Upgrade. But people such as yourself and others we've seen, who for whatever reason are no longer compatible with the brain shape the Uplink recognises...' He let it hang in the air.

'So, who's affected? Is there a common theme?'

'We have seen some... commonalities, shall we say, between the people who have lost their connection to the Link. There's a high concentration of people with certain mental illnesses. People who have had physical trauma or concussions. People whose thought patterns are abnormal for one reason or another. There are a lot of those sorts of cases, where there's some kind of proximate cause that we're able to identify. But sometimes there's nothing. The Upgrade, it would appear, has simply decided that some people no longer fit.'

Col didn't know which of those categories he fell into, but didn't want to ponder it for too long. 'So, what happens now? I came in with Sal, right? She can Ident me. Or work, they can, I don't know... pull my file, or something?'

'Our regulations only allow identification by family members. Though Ms Cooper is currently paying for your stay, she isn't eligible to positively Ident you. And despite you working for the Uplink, we can't use your records there to positively Ident you either.' His features remained calm, but he couldn't keep the angry edge from his voice. 'I'm sorry.'

Col reached out to the Uplink without thinking to get his sister's details. Pain shot through his head again. Cursing, he tried to recite her contact from memory, then waited as the doctor reached out.

'Hmm. Nothing. She must be screening contact.'

Col's heart leapt into his throat. He still couldn't shake the feeling that she might be in trouble.

'We'll keep trying. In the meantime, do you have any other family members who can Ident you?'

Unbidden, an image of he and Cass, much younger, in a different hospital, came rushing back. He'd stayed and held her hand, and it was one of the many times as a child he'd wished for a grown-up to come around, to help and take away the responsibility for looking after his sister. The Uplink had been an escape, but there had still been food to find, clothes to steal, and figuring out how to be an adult, years too early. No, they had no other family.

The doctor looked as though he was about to say something else, then changed his mind. 'I'll leave you to it for now. Later today, I'll need to take some tests, but just rest now.'

'What happens if you can't Ident me?'

'Using Ms Cooper's details was a stopgap. When she went back to work, the Link flagged that she was in two places at once. With all the new people who have recently lost access to the Link...' he gestured to the door, '...we're already taking some unusual measures. Until we're able to get people positively identified, by family members or, in your case, hopefully by reconnecting you to the Uplink, we've been given a grace period.'

'A grace period? Of how long?' In the corridor outside an alarm went off, and the doctor turned his head sharply.

'Only a couple of days. If we haven't figured it out by then, we can't keep you here. I'm sorry, I have to go.'

H sprinted away toward the code alarm, leaving Col. The room light dimmed, and Col could see the deep blood-red of the first hints of sunrise coming off a cloud. It looked like the magma and smoke of his nightmares coming for him.

He tried one more time to reach out and send a message to Cass. He was gentle, but the feeling came back. The urge to scratch an itch, and the fingertip-scraping feeling of trying to touch something just out of reach. It felt as though it was on the inside of his skull, and it made his eyes water. He reached out again, and the itch crept toward his heart. The feeling of reaching for something that was no longer there intermingled with a desperate, rising panic. He couldn't call his sister. He couldn't call Sal. He couldn't work. He couldn't pay for anything. He couldn't do anything if he couldn't access the Uplink.

He couldn't shake the overwhelming feeling of *wrongness* in his body. Col found the image of his sister twisting through his brain with the doctor's words.

How have I ended up locked out? The Uplink always worked for me, Col thought. *It worked for me until the Upgrade. I never had a problem with it before then.*

He realised that wasn't true. For a couple of months now, he'd had headaches. He'd been tired, worn down, sick. The headaches occurred when some part or other of the Uplink interface was active, and the amount of work he'd been doing on it to prepare for the upgrades meant he'd been in a near-constant state of tension. He'd thought it was just the work, but Sal hadn't seemed as worn down as he did. She was *tired* from the crunch, sure, but she hadn't lost weight or become as drawn as he had.

He punched a call button on the side of his bed, and after a moment a nurse poked their head into the room.

'Sally Cooper. Can you contact her?' Col asked.

* * *

Sal was standing at the foot of the bed, eyes shining out of a face creased with worry.

'Don't scare me like that,' she said. 'How long are they keeping you in here?'

Until they confirm they can't bill me, he didn't say. 'Couple of days. Observation, you know. Going to see if they can bottle lightning and run the MRI off me if it happens again.' He lifted his hands to the side of his head and made a mocking explosion motion.

'Do you remember what happened?'

Col told his side of the story. The growing whine that turned to pain and the total overwhelming of the senses as the Upgrade went live. The half-remembered dreams he'd had while he was under. The itch of disconnection.

'And you? What did you see?' he asked.

'You were acting strange, really strange,' Sal looked down at the floor. 'At first, I chalked it up to nerves. We've worked so damn hard over the last few weeks, I know I was nervous. Anyway, after the first set of timers, I asked you a couple of questions and you ignored me. Didn't stress me too much, but then you started talking too loudly.'

'The noise.' Col nodded.

'Then you got real agitated and started moving around. You asked me about the noise and everything got wild. You just *dropped*. Passed out, twitching and muttering to yourself. Something about smoke, and crystals.' She fidgeted with her hands. 'Col?'

Colin turned to her.

'Are you alright?' Her usual brashness was gone. Her brow was trying not to furrow. There was a twitch in her cheek, and he was hit with the realisation of just how worried she'd been. He nodded, too enthusiastically, to reassure her.

'Yeah, I'm okay. But there is one thing you can do for me.'

He told her about Cass. About the geoflag, and the way the hospital staff hadn't been able to contact her. 'I'm probably worrying about nothing, but can you reach out to her? See if she answers?'

A few moments of twitching, then Sal shook her head. Col felt the grip around his insides tighten. Where *was* she?

Sal stayed for several hours. She sat on the end of the bed and they chatted, leaving as much room for comfortable silence as talk. The ball of tension in his chest almost unwound simply by having her nearby. Only the part that worried for his sister remained. As she was leaving, he called her back.

'Hey Sal, can I ask a favour? Or a couple?'

'Shoot,' she said, turning back to him.

'Can you keep trying to call Cass? I want to know she's alright.'

She nodded. 'And?'

'Tell me something. What's the Upgrade like?'

Sal laughed. Actually threw her head back and laughed. Behind the sound was a hint of desperation. The sound of a deep breath before an underwater plunge. 'Oh, *man*. You're missing out.'

* * *

It was a clear night, or possibly an early morning, when Col woke up, radiant fire and crystals running through his sleep. He could feel a chill through the closed windowpane. The sweat on his forehead ran down into his eyes, and he wiped it away without thinking, bumping the fluid cannula in his hand. His breath came in short, sharp gasps, and he gulped the cool air to calm himself down. Once the hyperventilation had eased, he noticed the bed across from him.

It was no longer unoccupied.

The small frame of a woman was under the covers, and a pair of large black eyes watched him from beneath a shock of red hair. The woman didn't say anything, but her gaze followed him as he got out of the bed and walked to the basin to wash his face.

Her eyes glinted like flecks of crystal in the pale light of the night, following him as he sat back down on the edge of his bed. He rubbed his eyes.

'Sorry,' he mumbled, 'didn't realise you were in here.'

'It's okay,' her voice was low and soft, 'I've been asleep too long anyway.'

He looked at her, but there wasn't much he could see of her between the pale light of the evening and the infrared wayfinding lights on the floor. She lay beneath the flimsy coverlet on the bed. Her face was in shadow.

'So, what are you in for?' Col asked quietly. His voice hit the walls of the room flatly, ringing hollow in the space.

The woman didn't respond immediately. She took a moment to process the question, then spoke in the same near-whisper as before.

'I can't get into the Uplink.'

CHAPTER 10

'Wait. You've lost access to the Uplink as well?' Col sat up. The low-quality bedding on the hospital gurney crackled. The lighting in the room detected the movement and changed from navigation lighting to the same warm night-lighting he'd seen when he first arrived.

He could see her properly now. She looked as drawn and frail as he did, with very little muscle mass. She was shorter than him, shorter than his sister and thin to the point of malnourishment. For a fleeting moment, he thought she might have been an Aug solar-junkie, but no. She had no Augmetics, and her arms didn't have the crisscross markers of solar burns. In the deep shadows of her eye sockets were pupils black as night. Her face was framed by some of the most shockingly red hair Col had ever seen. It danced, almost gravity free, like fire, framing a pale face that remained cold and withdrawn despite the warmth of the room's lighting. She was so light she barely disturbed the bed with her slight frame.

'It seems so.' Her voice was deeper than Col expected, with a slight resonance that echoed through his bones. When she smiled, it took him by surprise. She still seemed afraid and out of sorts, but there was a quiet confidence about her.

'I knew something was going to happen, you know. It's all I'd heard about. But then there was this noise, and then the light turned to dark and everything disappeared.' She shrugged, and the moonlight reflected off her hair. 'Anyway. Then I woke up here.'

A string of incoherent thoughts burst from Col. 'That happened to me as well! I mean, I was working *on* the Upgrade, so I'd known about it. When did the noise start for you? Who brought you here? How –?' but before he could keep going, she put a hand up to quiet him, laughing softly.

'Whoa. Okay, settle down. So we went through the same thing, from the sound of it.' The corner of her mouth twisted sardonically. 'Funny. I figured I'd be alone.'

Something about the way she said it made it sound like *alone* was all she'd ever been.

'How's that?' Col asked, but she kept talking as though he hadn't spoken.

'It was this, I don't know. A ringing, sort of buzzing noise that started all around me and built and built. It was electrifying! It was like every single part of me was being drawn into something. It felt like life and death, calm and catastrophe at once.' With that, she turned back to him, and her eyes bore into his. Before he had the chance to collect his thoughts, she asked, 'Same for you, I guess?'

She stared at him, and Col had the uncomfortable feeling of being studied. Of being assessed for some flaw. He averted his gaze. 'Yeah. Same for me.'

'You said you worked for the Uplink?'

'Hmm? Oh, yeah. I mean, it's not glamorous or anything. I'm just a tech, swapping out hardware and doing software upgrades and maintenance.' When he said *hardware* she'd cocked her head inquiringly. 'Oh, not Augmetic stuff, like implants. We don't interfere with your mind, that's all done wirelessly, you know. Just, the data's gotta go somewhere, right? It goes to my work.'

'What do you mean, doesn't interfere with your mind? It still interferes if you're connecting wirelessly, right?'

Col thought for a minute. 'Yeah, true enough, I suppose. But it's different.'

'Why?' she pressed.

A silence. 'Oh. I don't know. I guess it's not surgical or anything? It's a passive process. It doesn't hurt people.'

At that, she laughed. It was a gentle sound, but there was a soft kind of mockery behind it. 'You're sitting in a hospital bed, and you're thinking that the Uplink doesn't *hurt* people?'

He didn't know what to say. It was just a fact of his life that the Uplink was, and always had been, a benign influence. He'd never noticed if something had gone wrong because he'd never been on the other end of it, but now? The Uplink *had* done him harm. It *had* hurt him. It *had* cast him out. He and the people in the hospital he'd heard about, and now the woman he was sharing a space with.

He considered that he now lived in a world where the Uplink wasn't a force for good for him. It wasn't, as of this moment, a force for *anything* for him. He was just not a part of it; a creature swimming in a different stream from everything he'd known. He and this woman, who was watching him quietly as he considered what she'd said.

'I'm sorry, that was rude of me,' she said, and she smiled a wide, friendly smile, without any of the trepidation she'd shown before. 'Asking you questions like that when I haven't even introduced myself. What's your name?'

'Col. You?'

'Ariana,' she said. 'My name is Ariana. Nice to know you, Col.'

* * *

When Col awoke the next morning, the faded blue curtains around the bed were drawn. Before him stood two nurses and a doctor, in scrubs that blended in with the soft cocoon around him. The doctor wasn't the one he'd seen before, but she was no less exhausted. Each staff member seemed on the edge of burnout. They spoke in quick, clipped tones and jittered in and out of the room, hands and legs shaking faintly. Typical signs of stim addiction from hours and days of scant sleep on untenable schedules.

It had been three days since he'd been admitted, and he was becoming more and more concerned about Cass's continued lack of contact with the hospital. When he'd asked, nobody had tried to contact him at all, not even Sal.

Sal was probably swamped, having to deal with a post-Upgrade workload, but still. Not even a contact to check in on him? She had seemed concerned when she'd visited, but it was as though he had disappeared from her mind the moment she walked out of the door.

All of this had been ricocheting through his mind as the doctor and the rotating circus of staff bounced him between tests. It was a shot in the dark, they said, *they had no idea what to look for*. They'd been looking at everyone who'd come in, trying to identify a commonality between them.

Ariana must have been getting the same treatment. The curtains were open, but her bed was empty.

'Unfortunately, unless we happen to catch someone *in the process* of falling from the Uplink, we're really just guessing,' the doctor said, as Col's attention was drawn back from the empty bed. 'It's a specific set of impulses that had to happen, and we don't know what they are, so we can't try to reverse-engineer them.' She flitted one hand in front of her face, sending data across to one of the nurses next to her.

'How is that possible? Don't you have the schemas?' Col was nonplussed.

The doctor shook her head. 'The schemas used for the interface with the Uplink are proprietary. They can't be used by anyone but Uplink.'

Col groaned. The staff asked him more questions, then wheeled him back out of the room for another round of tests. They fed him dyes, ran him through machines, poked, prodded, questioned him and found nothing.

* * *

Hours later, he was back in his room, talking with Ariana again. After a full day of frantic, stimmed and sleep-deprived hospital staff, Ariana seemed preternaturally still. She was sitting up on the edge of the bed, her legs hanging down without touching the floor. She spoke plainly to him, and looked into his eyes, while they spoke. He realised how long it had been since anyone had simply looked at him as he spoke to them, and vice versa. There had always been so much more going on. A constant stream of data flitting across the Link, distracting from what was in front of him.

'They still haven't heard from your sister?' Ariana seemed curious. She looked stronger than she had the day before, but still frail. As though she'd fly away with the wind and disappear. Still, she was sitting up, and appeared interested in what Col had to say, which was refreshing after a day of being talked *at* by doctors. 'What's her name?'

'Cass. And no, they haven't heard from her.'

'You seem worried.' It wasn't a question.

'Yeah. Because of her job, right? She's got a... dangerous job.' He suddenly found himself unable to continue. Speaking it aloud would make the possibility real. He looked at the ground, aware of Ariana's dark eyes watching him quietly. 'I just hope she's okay,' he whispered to himself.

Ariana let the whisper dance through the still hospital air for a few seconds. 'I guess getting back to the Link will help you find her, right?' she said, and behind the softness of her voice there was a hunger that surprised Col. The discussions they'd had so far had made it seem like Ariana was fairly unaffected by her disconnection from the Link. She was ready enough to smile or joke about it, even as Col was frantically trying to understand what had happened. Yet here it was, a small hint of desperation, still quiet, and held beneath the surface.

'If I can get back into the Link, it'll be much easier to find out what's happened, I think.' Col told her about the geoflag that had been set up. As soon as he was back in the Link, he'd be able to find her.

'Well, I hope they figure it out.'

'Me too.' Col said. 'What about you? You got any family waiting for you in the Link?'

Almost before it was out of his mouth, he realised he must have made a mistake. She looked away, no longer meeting his eyes. Her hair flickered in the poor colour rendering of the cheap hospital lights. After so long being still, her leg began to bounce anxiously, and she clutched her arms to herself.

'Whoa, I'm sorry!' Col said, 'I'm sorry if I said something wrong, I didn't mean –'

'It's fine.' Her voice, so smooth before, had become pointed. A warning. Col waited, confused, for a few seconds, unsure what to say next. Where before there had been a convivial conversation between two people who had nothing to do but get to know one another, now there was the leaden stillness of an awkward silence. Colin wasn't sure what boundary he'd broached, and so he stayed silent until she stood abruptly and walked around to the other end of the bed and lay down. She pulled a blanket over herself and turned away from Col, leaving him in the blue-dark room. He remained perplexed and as the bustle of the hospital hall waned into the quiet of the midnight hours and he finally fell asleep.

CHAPTER 11

When Col woke up the next morning, Ariana was gone again. In her place was yet another doctor flanked by two medical staff, the familiar formation. The doctor's face was an apologetic mask, a pre-emptive defence against what she had to say. The two medical staff were bigger than the previous nurses and aides Col had seen. He suspected that part of their responsibilities involved strong-arming patients out of the hospital if they didn't take unpleasant news well.

The doctor started talking, but Colin was distracted. The bed next to him lay empty, and he couldn't help thinking that he'd made an awful error in asking about Ariana's past. *Stupid,* he thought. She'd been the only person to hold a conversation with him that wasn't about his diagnosis, and he'd pried into her family life. He wouldn't even get to apologise to her. She was gone, and the bed already looked as though nobody had ever been there. The same as his was about to look, he realised, tuning back into the doctor's words as she mentioned Sal.

'– been noticed that her details are being used here at the same time as her Ident is being logged at her place of employment. Unfortunately, that means –'

'Hold on, sorry,' Col interjected, holding up a placating hand. 'Back up, what's happening?'

This doctor, like the others Col had seen, bore an exhausted kind of sympathy behind the unyielding words. 'I'm sorry. We were using Ms Cooper's credentials as a stopgap. Those are no longer valid, as she's been recorded using her Ident at work. And as you're still unable to access the Uplink...' She let the implication hang in the air.

We can't do any more for you, was the upshot of the discussion, *and you have to leave*. And that was it.

Less than a week after his admission to the hospital, he was back out again. To the careless streets, with no answers, no Uplink connection and an invoice far beyond his ability to repay.

Col was frogmarched out by the two medical staff that doubled as ad-hoc security guards. He was too numb to resist, shocked beyond words that in less than a week he'd gone from a precarious but ongoing employment to being escorted out of a hospital and left to rot. He was left alone to face the realities of a world that no longer fit around him. He'd found the gap, the jagged hole of indeterminate width and infinite depth. On one side was security, and the other? Only time would tell. The question that kept spinning through his head was *what the hell do I do now?*

His lack of connection to the Link still gnawed at him; he could practically *feel* the signal passing around and through him, but there was no way to access it. He'd stopped trying to reach Cass. The stabs of pain struck thick and fast every time he reached out. The raw data was there, and as impossible to grasp as a wave on the ocean or a ray of sunshine.

The concern that he'd been able to hold at bay in the hospital returned with force as he reached the end of the block. Before, in his bed, he'd been able to reason that his affliction was temporary, as limited in scope as it was unusual. His confidence had faded, but he'd not given up hope. He worked with technology, he knew how advanced some of the systems on the Uplink were. Surely it was just a matter of the hospital staff finding the right button. Overlay the patterns. Find the faults. Now that he was out, he had none of that confidence.

Unease built within him while he stood on the quiet pavement beside the black concrete walls of the hospital. People wandered around, and he watched them twitching, flicking their hands to communicate over the Uplink. The tech that had been his job. The tech that had been his world. The tech he'd lost. The generated world of advertisements that would usually play across his retinas where they found a blank surface had vanished. The normal cacophony of colour and sound surrounding him was replaced by the silent warmth of lime and aggregate heating in the sun. The silence was overwhelming. It beat against him.

He turned down an empty back alley, finally out of view of the hospital entrance, and nearly ran into Ariana, leaning heavily against a bare concrete wall. He jumped in alarm, and she grinned as she recognised him.

'You too, huh?' she said, flicking her head back to the hospital disdainfully.

Col tried to gather his thoughts. Of course, Ariana had been ejected as well. She was in the same situation as him, unable to connect to the Link and unable to pay or provide the details the staff required. She must have left just before he woke up; maybe they had broken the news to her in a different room. Looming in front of all that, though, was the conversation that she'd abruptly ended the night before.

'Hey, about last night, I just wanted to say –' he began, but she interrupted him, waving away his concerns.

'Don't worry about it. I just... don't ask me about my past. Okay?'

Col agreed, and then the two of them stood in awkward silence for a moment. Rather, Colin felt awkward. Ariana, on the other hand, was staring expectantly at the point above the blank concrete where a dizzying array of colours would be displayed had they been connected to the Link. Col followed her gaze, and then kept going, looking down the alleyway to the street beyond, a desolate thoroughfare to a den of cramped lounges and stimrooms.It was all empty – the blank walls of the capsule apartments didn't dance the way he was used to, but the world was blanker even than that. In the Link, when he walked down a street, there weren't just ads and services piled up on one another, flying into your retinas faster than your mind could reasonably process, there was also *everything else*. Wayfinding, signs, coloured lane markings and overlays for traffic zones would be flooding his senses. Staring down a street canyon like this used to be overwhelming, but now?

It was *empty*. Devoid of any data save for the brutality of bare concrete. The callous impermeability of hostile architecture normally unseen beneath the layer he used to interact with the world.

'Hey. Col, you there?' Ariana was waving a hand in front of his face and blinking at him expectantly.

'What? Yeah.' He focused back on her.

'I was saying, we're kind of in the same situation here, huh?' She was as still as she'd been the night before, watching Colin intently and waiting for his reply. She didn't act like Linked people did, constantly flicking and twitching as they manipulated whatever was going on behind their eyes. When Ariana spoke to him, she was speaking to *him*, and nobody else. Nothing distracted her.

'Yeah, I guess we are,' Col agreed, trying and failing to return Ariana's attention with the same steadfast stare. He was still feeling the urge, the senseless pull to switch his attention between tasks lest one of them even hint at boring him. His eyes flicked from Ariana to her shadow, to the street, to the alley and back in rapid succession. The twitch that had been his life. She kept talking.

'You and me, both trying to get into the Link. We're in the same predicament, like I say. It makes sense to me that we work together, you know? Seems like we could find out more about what's happened if we don't do it alone.' She leaned back against the wall again. 'You don't agree?' Col's apprehension must have shown on his face.

'It's just... Before I do anything, I need to find my sister. I'm not sure why they couldn't get in contact with her. I'm not sure what Sal knows, or doesn't know.' He met her gaze, finally holding it for more than a scant second or two. 'Want to help?'

Ariana was nonplussed. 'I don't know your sister. I'm not sure how much I'll help just tagging along.' She thought for a moment. Col tried not to fidget.

'Let's try this. If you work on how to get to your sister, I'll do my own thing.'

'Do what?' Col pressed.

'Oh, I'll be around. Just finding things out. Need to know more about this new world we're in. Knowledge is power, Colin.' She tapped the side of her head.

That doesn't tell me what you'll be doing, Col didn't say. He'd already annoyed her once by prying into her private life. She'd offered to work together, so why not?

He waited a few seconds, to let the awkwardness dissipate. 'Okay. First things first, I'm going to talk to Sal.' He didn't know why he felt the need to let her know his own plans, except that at the moment she seemed to be the only person who cared if he lived or died. 'Find out why she didn't get back to me when I asked her to contact Cass. That'll be easy enough, I just need to get to the Library.' *How will I find it?* He relied on the Uplink for navigation more times than not. That wasn't an option now.

'Great. Talk to your friend. I'll figure out where I'm at, and we can talk again in what, a couple of days?' Col nodded, and Ariana turned and began to walk away down the alley toward the concrete canyon.

'Ariana!' Col called after her, and she raised an eyebrow in response. 'Where are we meeting?'

Ariana laughed, as though she hadn't realised that without the Uplink they wouldn't be able to coordinate their movements. They figured out a time and place, and she walked away again, disappearing around the corner, leaving Col to contemplate a world bereft of the information he needed to navigate through it.

CHAPTER 12

It was the sea wall. That was how he could mark his location. It was a touchstone, a beacon and a landmark to him. After several minutes walking around in a daze, wondering how he was going to find his way back to the Library to speak to Sal, he saw the causeway rising at the edge of the city. The cranes in the docks loomed out of the morning haze next to it. He could map where he was in relation to those two points, and he realised the Library wasn't far away at all. He plunged into the labyrinthine walkways between the buildings and highways, pouring himself through the overcrowded streets like liquid, rising occasionally above the sputtering stream to reorient himself and find the sea wall again.

As he became just a particle in the flow of the crowds through the streets, he wondered why he'd been so quick to agree with Ariana. It was good that they were trying to help one another, but he didn't know anything about her. Her reaction when being asked even a basic question had been to rebuke him. She'd only come back to talk to him when she realised she'd needed him. He wasn't sure what to make of it at first, but as he blundered blindly down the streets, he decided it made very little difference. Any information she got to him would be useful. If the end result was that they both got back to the Uplink, then what was the harm? He didn't need to *trust* her.

Col ducked down the same cobblestone lane he'd walked down several weeks earlier. As usual, this part of the street was mainly deserted but for the evidence of Aug activity. Instead of being the void in the night that it had been before, the Library was identifiable by its boarded-up windows and anachronistic architecture. It still sat out of place with its surroundings, a disfigured and ageing hulk among the sharpness of the sheer cliffs that surrounded it.

Near the corner, he breathed a sigh of relief. Since he'd reported the break-in, Uplink-sponsored private police had been posted outside on rotation. He walked up and hailed the woman on guard.

The policewoman looked him over, not recognising him and clearly not convinced by his appearance. He didn't recognise her either. They changed the staff every few shifts, and he'd been away for days. The official line was that this would stop external staff from becoming overfamiliar with the building systems, but like everything else, it left Col without a personal relationship with the people he worked next to.

'It's an auto-Ident system. It should recognise your Uplink code.' She shrugged noncommittally, then turned back to her patrol.

Col followed her. 'I know, I work here. Or at least I did. I need to talk to Sally Cooper; she should be inside. I can't get into the Uplink anymore, and the system relies on –'

'I'm sorry, I can't Ident you,' the guard said more firmly. 'I don't know who you are. Now, please, leave the premises before I am forced to escort you away.'

Col fought to keep calm. 'I told you, I lost my access to the Uplink. I can't provide my Ident to you, but I work here, and I need to talk to –'

'Sure you do, buddy,' the guard replied, looking him up and down. Her cool demeanour cracked and a slip of contempt showed through. She set her stance, and placed a lazy hand on a holster at her hip.

'Look, I've been in hospital. When the Upgrade happened, I was brought in by Sal. She works here, but now I need to –'

The taser was out of the holster and jammed into his side so fast he couldn't react. Bright, sparkling pain rushed through him from the contact point near the kidneys, followed by a thump like someone had hit him with a block of cement. His vision went black and erupted in stars. When it returned, he was on the ground, and the policewoman was standing over him, brandishing the taser and looking at him like he was a piece of trash.

'Fuck *me!*' Col swore, 'What the fuck was that for?'

'You say you work here, come back when you've got an Ident. Ain't my job to make sure you do yours. Now get out of here, I don't need any more of your sort getting funny ideas.'

Col raised his hands placatingly, side still dancing with the aftermath of the electric shock. He scrambled away as fast as he could and started back down the way he'd come, feeling impossibly small in the chasm of the street.

Your sort, he thought. Did they think he was an Aug? The Library, his place of work, once a relief from the pummelling of advertisements and a symbol of his connection to the Uplink, sat mocking him. He hurried away from the building, not sure if Sal was even inside and not wanting to push his luck with the trigger-happy policewoman. As he walked past a grubby window, Col caught a glimpse of himself. The dark shadows under his eyes had faded, but not disappeared. His hair hung lank and unkempt, framing the loose skin of his face and the quiet undertone of desperation in his eyes.

He passed the cobblestone lane again. Tech-junk was piled in a corner, and at the base of it, with cables hooked to a solar panel sticking out of its arm, was an Aug. It looked up and stared at him. Hazy, empty eyes. The look of someone with nothing left to lose.

Col turned away. Whether from the taser or the Aug's empty stare, he shuddered. He needed to find a way to get in contact with Cass or Sal. He walked a few more blocks, then stopped. In the distance, he could see the sea wall. Despite being built to hold back extreme tides, it still had moments of failure. As he watched, an errant wave, a coincidental overlap of force, pushed over the top of the wall. The sea was near-black and foaming, and he could see it glint in the sun as it breached and washed over the causeway. All the safeguards humankind had come up with, and it was still not enough to hold back a lack of forethought.

* * *

If he couldn't wait for Sal at the Library, he'd have to wait by her hab. She lived about 40 minutes from where they both worked, so he decided to try to find her there before he went back to his own hab, hoping that she'd have heard from Cass and he could stop worrying.

He was sitting on the stairs in front of the hab block that Sal lived in. The pale, empty sky had disappeared as rainclouds had descended, heavy and pregnant with rain.

He sat, one leg outstretched, the other cocked to rest his foot on its side on the step below. The balustrade he leaned on was old and needlessly elegant, with inadequate thought given to maintenance and drainage. Rust streaked out of finely detailed holes, burnishing the stark, white steps with ugly, tea-coloured stains that ran into the grey waste that should have been a garden. It was a repurposed building. In times past, it had held entire apartments with only a single family in it. Huge amounts of room for so few people. In the intervening years, as space dwindled and property premiums increased, the interiors had been torn out and replaced with capsule habs. Single-hotplate kitchenettes and enough room for a single bed. If you were lucky, your capsule would line up with an existing window, and you'd get natural light into your room.

Sal hadn't been lucky. Her hab was lit with cheap, harsh bulbs, and barely had enough room to stand next to the kitchen. He wondered how he'd like living in a place without even a hint of the outside, and stared around himself into the concrete mire, cluttered with people.

Nobody looked at him. Col watched their faces slide past, as though he was a gap in space. A nothingness, little more notable than the surrounding infrastructure. Their hurried pace, cold expressions, and empty eyes skimmed past the man on the sidewalk who had nothing more to do than to sit patiently and wait. Whenever the Link projected something into their visual field, their eyes went blank. Col hadn't noticed it at first, and had felt fleetingly unsettled without knowing why. It was as though all their actions and reactions took just a few moments longer than they should have. It was quick enough for his vision to gloss over, but his brain felt the disjunct.

When was the last time he'd done this? The last time he'd been in a single location, simply sitting and waiting, without being explicitly in motion to get somewhere else?

'Col!' Sal barrelled toward him shouting, barely slowing down enough to run up the steps, and absorbed him into a hug that made them collapse back. Col laughed.

'Good to see you, too.' She held onto him for a long time. He could feel her fingers flexing ecstatically on his clothing.

Sal pulled out of the hug. The bags were still under her eyes, but she seemed bright. Col wasn't able to tell if it was stimtab-induced or natural. 'Good to see you out of that damn hospital! That place was way too depressing.'

Col pulled himself up and brushed himself off. 'Where have you been? Nearest I can figure you knocked off work two hours ago.'

Sal didn't answer, just turned to the door to give her Ident. A chime sounded, along with a cold, sharp click as the magnetised door disconnected. Col stepped into the cool darkness of the hallway.

The walls were almost entirely blank but for a series of blue-light strips that ran horizontally along the edges of the floors, walls and ceilings. The door to Sal's hab slid open to let her in, but began to shut before Col could follow. He gave a yell. She turned and waved a hand to open it properly until he came through.

Col rushed into the hab and squeezed into the small space next to the kitchenette. Sal leaned against the bed, and then sat down to give the two of them a marginal amount of personal space.

The room was long, a rectangular prism, two thirds of which was taken up by a bed, and most of the rest by the kitchen. Had he looked, he'd have seen a smattering of storage spaces built into the walls for clothes, food and cleaning equipment, but the long single bed dominated the room.

'Stimtab?' Sal offered, opening up the cooler sunk into the edge of the counter.

'Uh, sure.' Col took it, snapping the edible reagent on the top of the package, waiting a couple of seconds, then putting it in his mouth. A cool, sweet taste that the packaging assured him was berries hit his tongue, followed by a ripple of bitter cold and a profound sense of wellbeing. A tingle of electricity coursed through his body, and his mind sped up. He took a deep, conciliatory breath to calm himself after the initial rush of amphetamine, and allowed himself to settle around the glow.

'Big day?' he asked. The hab was dirtier than the last time he'd been here. Clothes were strewn about everywhere. The kitchen counter was hidden beneath cardboard cutlery and ready-meal wrappers. Behind the smell of grease, there seemed to be an undercurrent of a familiar but unplaceable scent. Salt, maybe.

'You have no idea. Well, you do. I'm having to do your stuff, as you're not at work. For obvious reasons.' She blinked, and her eyes refocused Col, 'Plus, you know that stolen stuff?'

'The stuff I was trying to invalidate the contract for?' He'd forgotten about it. The existence or otherwise of a high-bandwidth card had been the least of his problems recently.

'Yeah. Contract. That one. Since you went off-grid,' she grinned, 'the other parties involved in the contract are pushing back. Saying that everything on their end was signed off as normal, and that if the hardware was signed for and then rescinded by you, then *you* must have stolen it. Here, I can sh– never mind,' she said, and her arms returned to her side after making an attempt to flick everything over to him as she would normally do. Col was getting used to people forgetting about his disconnect from the system.

Col sank onto Sal's bed as well, and the strange smell hit him anew. It was sweat. The salty tang of a gym, only just starting to seep into the fabric of the space. It smelled like a locker room, or like the stale afterglow of sex. Sal wasn't looking at him, once again sinking into the slightly trance-like state of the Uplink. He tapped her on the shoulder, and she came back to him.

'Hey, sorry. I was trying to look at the information around that contract for you.'

'I can deal with that later,' Col said, 'I'm here to ask about Cass.'

Sal's face darkened. The distracted look disappeared, and she was sharp when she turned to him. In the room fully for what felt like the first time.

'I'm sorry, Col,' she said, 'I've been trying. Really.'

Col looked to where the window should have been. Outside, there were scant rays of sunlight, and somewhere, his sister. Col felt his chest contract.

'Can you try again?' His voice was hoarse.

Sal nodded, and her face went slack. Col stared around the room, trying to stop his heart hammering. Somehow, he knew what the answer would be.

'Nope. Still nothing.' A razor-thin edge of concern. 'God, Col.'

'Yeah.'

She hesitated. 'What about her work? She's a journalist, right? Have you contacted her company?'

Col shook his head.

'It's gig work. She works alone, and the only contact she has with the feeds is when she sells them a story. They keep their sources from communicating with one another. Keeps them competitive is the idea. I don't think she even has anyone you could call a colleague. She doesn't talk to anyone else because of the workload. She doesn't have a girlfriend at the moment.' He let it hang there. He was out of ideas.

Col would have given anything for Sal to come and embrace him in that moment. Hold him, tell him things were going to be alright. Touch him. The connection that was now commodified, a product of the Uplink he wasn't able to find in the real world. Famine through oversupply.

Col looked at Sal; she didn't look back. Her arms twitched slightly. Her eyes were hollow, unseeing. Col snapped his fingers to get her attention, and she jerked.

'Sorry. Was looking at –'

'Doesn't matter,' Col said, annoyed. Cass was missing, and he couldn't hold the attention of his best friend for more than a few minutes before she drifted back into the Uplink. Had it always been this way? Had he, too, had been a quietly twitching automaton disconnected from reality?

A long moment stretched out between them.

'Anyway,' Col cleared his throat to break the silence, 'looks like I won't be welcome at work for a while.' He told her about his troubles at the Library.

'They tased you? Really?' Sal seemed shocked.

'Yeah. Thought I was some Aug, you know? Trying to sneak my way in, or whatever. I can't Ident myself now, so –'

'Wait – you can't Ident yourself?' she interrupted.

'Oh, yeah. Seems obvious, right? But you need your Ident to get anywhere, and your Ident is tied to the Link.'

Sal whistled low. 'Okay. Take it from the top. Tell me everything that happened in the hospital.'

He did, and she sat, asking questions and swearing at all the right times. Even telling the story seemed to release something in him. By the time he got to the security guard again he was laughing, even if there was still a dead, cold weight inside him whenever he thought about the reality of the situation. Sal couldn't fix the problems he was having, but it felt good to talk to someone who cared. It eased the anxiety, if only for a little while.

Until he eventually had to go home, and the dread closed in as the door to her hab block sealed itself shut behind him.

* * *

Navigating by one landmark made it extremely difficult to get around, but at least he knew the way from Sal's hab. His walk, initially relatively upbeat, had turned to a desultory trudge through the near-empty streets, back past the dispensary that had been ripped out of the wall weeks prior. He could have used a stim, but you either needed an Ident or a crowbar to get those from a dispensary, and he had neither.

He needed his physical pictographic Ident. His ledger card. Even an old portable app device might work to prove he was who he said he was. They were things that, until mere weeks ago, he'd long supplanted with the Uplink. Without the Link, and without his Ident, he had rapidly become *persona non grata*.

Just some Aug, like the one he'd just seen at the Library, empty eyes staring into his. He tried to reason that *that wasn't him*. Sure, he knew that there were Augs and people who weren't able to Link. He saw them every day, but they weren't like him. Being shut out of the Link was one thing, and mutilating yourself with robotic 'enhancements' was another. If they wanted to, they could use the cards and the apps and the proper Ident – but instead they slept in the gutter and pumped solar energy into their blood so they could lay in a torpor and bliss out of their own existence.

No, that wasn't him. He'd find a way back in, get on with his life.

A gnawing sensation hit his mind again as, without thinking, he tried to reach out to Cass. He wanted to know whether she'd ever seen his Ident cards around his hab when she'd been there. Cursing, he rubbed at his forehead. He couldn't reach Cass. His kidney and side still hurt from the altercation at the Library, and he limped as he descended the set of tar-blackened stairs at the rear of his hab.

Who the hell was that policewoman, anyway? He'd barely asked three questions when she'd jabbed him in the side, all choler and fury, sending him sprawling. If he'd had access to the Link, he'd have been able to call her in, submit a complaint about the behaviour of the staff on site. She might have been reprimanded, maybe even lost her job. Now, though, there was no avenue through which he could mete out justice. He was out, she was in, and she was the one with her finger on the trigger. A discussion of legality was, at that point, moot.

He had arrived at his hab.

The exterior wall was sheer, vertical, blank and concrete, as all the rest of the complexes around here were, the block only broken by small joints in the panels. It had begun to drizzle on the way back from the Library, and Col found himself once again huddling under his coat, walking up to his door and waving his...

'Fuck.' He hung his head. His hab, like most of its ilk, relied on an active Uplink identification to confirm access. God, he was an idiot. He should have asked Sal if he could stay with her. He should have *realised*. He'd been telling her about being shut out of the Link, and he hadn't made the connection.

He'd been rattled, too busy thinking of his home as the one safe place that he could seek refuge from what had happened to him. *He couldn't even go back to Sal's now,* he thought. She didn't have a window, and you needed an Ident to work the intercom. Some kind of anti-Aug measure.

'*Fuck,*' he swore again, and the unfairness of the situation drowned all other thoughts. With a fury so sudden and surprising that he didn't quite understand where it came from, Col punched the steel outer door of his hab. His hand pealed into bright stars of pain, and he stepped back and stared up at the building, rain pouring into his eyes.

'God *dammit!*' he screamed, holding his hand and wondering if the water on his face contained tears or not. He stood staring at the door, wondering if he could possibly jump and climb to the top with only the scant handholds the breaks in the concrete would provide, when someone spoke to him.

'Best watch yourself.' The voice belonged to a man holding two waterproof card wraps in one hand and a metal pipe in the other. Seeing the makeshift weapon, Col put his hands up.

'Oh, come on, man,' he said, stepping back and away from the door. 'I live here, I'm just trying to get home. I've had a shit of a day.'

'Yeah? You live here, huh?' The man looked up at the wall. 'You normally get in by scaling the walls?' He was moving toward the entrance, herding Col away as he did so by brandishing the pipe.

'No, man. Normally through the front door, but my Ident –'

'Oh yeah, your Ident. Go on, tell me about your Ident.' As he said it, the front door registered the man and opened automatically. He remained outside, fending off Col.

'Yeah, my Ident. I… there was the Upgrade, and I can't access the Uplink anymore. Please, I'm just trying to get into my hab, I promise –'

The man stopped even pretending to entertain what Col was saying as soon as he realised Col couldn't access the Uplink. He swung at Col, who jumped out of the way. 'Can't access the Uplink? Well, I've got a good idea. Clear out of here 'fore I get inside and hit up the building security. They're pretty good at dealing with your kind.'

'No, I'm not an Aug, I just –'

But it was too late. The man had shut himself inside, and the door slammed shut with a resounding thud. Col stood, staring at it, and the empty, hopeless eyes he'd seen so often in Augs began to make sense to him.

Once the shock cleared, his mind seemed to crystallise, and what he had to do became clear in his mind. To help Cass, he had to get back into his house, which meant he had to go to the distribution centre to get a new physical identity card. They did make them, for secondary and safety reasons, so he was sure he would be able to get one. He dashed away into the rapidly darkening shades of evening. The sea wall loomed ahead, his low-rent navigation device. The sun was sinking into the water, and the rain was settling in for what Col knew was going to be a long night.

CHAPTER 13

The walk from his hab to the distribution centre for the Uplink was as wet as it was miserable. Ducking in and out of main streets, trying to avoid crowds, he quickly fell into a rhythm of hunting for deeper shadows in the dark grey of the evening. The rain grew heavier after the sun went down. The sun that he'd always associated with Cass, that bright spot he held for his sister. As he dashed through the downpour, he worried about whether this was the right move. Should he be relying so heavily on returning to the Uplink to find her? Surely once he made his way back online, she would respond if she contacted him?

The other possibility – that she had truly disappeared, maybe even fallen from the link the way he had – was one he didn't want to think about. As he peered down an alleyway, trying to decide whether a pile of trash was inhabited by an Aug or not, thoughts of her filled his mind.

The two of them were often able to understand each other on almost an instinctual level, even without the Uplink. His emotions were transparent to her, and hers to him. He'd heard of similar things with twins; pseudotelepathy, almost, that led to a kind of intuition. As far as he knew, none of those connections had been proven by science, but he knew how he felt when his sister contacted him and how he felt when others did, and he knew which was easier. More natural. It was a warm embrace, compared to a cordial handshake. One more time, he tried to reach out to her, but again there was nothing but the ringing sting of the broken connection.

He wasn't far from the distribution centre now, if he'd gotten his bearings. The rain danced off the street. On one side, the smooth walls of the hab blocks were broken up by an immense vehicle stacker, a metal armature on rockcrete slabs, extending into the night. Col looked up and felt the chemical rain tingle on his face. The stacker was a place of shelter, but he might not be alone in there.

He decided to risk it.

At the centre of the stacker was a lift core and a set of open escape stairs. The rockcrete was slick with oil and water. The constant din of rain echoed around Col. The stairs were two flights to a level, and he climbed them to the landing halfway. He hunkered down in the corner and pulled his wet coat around himself.

The rain was a white-noise blanket and the car stacker's structure groaned and cracked as it cooled in the evening air. Every time a sound burst through the rain, Col started, hoping it wasn't the sound of some Aug gang out on the prowl. He began to shiver and wondered if Ariana was having the same difficulties as him. Had she been beaten, denied entry to her home and forced to find a hole to batten down in for the night? Or had she fared better? They had arranged to speak to each other again the day after next. Hopefully by then he'd have his identification, if nothing else.

The white noise of the rain continued, and after an age Col fell into a fitful, shivering sleep.

* * *

The rain wore itself out early the next morning, and Col woke unharmed in the stairwell. The cold of the rockcrete had formed a knot in his back, and he was stiff and sore and hungry. He staggered back down to the ground floor and outside. His nighttime navigation had served him well, and he saw the glass shopfronts of the distribution centre.

There was no name, as he'd expected; signage was all done in the Uplink now, but he could see the scraped-off outline of the building's original sign: GENERAL SAVINGS AND LOANS. Though the building was barely a hundred years old and refurbished relatively recently, it had a disused air. It wasn't far from a damaged section of the sea wall that was battered by unpredictable waves as the tides rolled in. The distribution centre was a tired-looking construct of upcycled plastics and cement panelling with chipped corners. An automatic door groaned open as he approached, and he was met with the stale air of a badly maintained conditioning system.

Two employees were facing one another in the centre of the room, heads and arms twitching. They stood at a singular dais, the only remaining concession to human comfort. The centre had been relieved of the customer seating, semi-enclosed dividers and operable walls that had once split the place into a hive of offices and co-working spaces. Col took three careful steps, crossing the threshold.

'Please select a service from the console, and be seated until a representative can assist you.'

The disembodied voice startled Col, and he tripped on a hastily applied square of cheap carpet that had patched over a strange lump. The split cables and a divot in the fibres showed where a service machine had once stood.

One of the workers stopped twitching and turned around to face him.

'I've got this one,' she sighed, speaking to the man next to her. He nodded vaguely, or maybe it was just another neural response to whatever he was doing in the Uplink.

She wore no nametag, and when Col got close enough to her, he could see in the poorly maintained light of the room how tattered and frayed her uniform was. A thick layer of acne scarring splayed across her chin.

'Hey. I'm, uh, looking to get a physical wallet for all of my currencies, and a physical transit pass.'

'Sure thing. Just push through your Ident on the Link.' The drawl at the corner of her mouth was a permanent affect, nearly a physical thing, ennui as accent.

'I can't,' Col said.

'What?'

'I can't push my Ident,' Col explained, 'I've lost my access to the Link. During the Upgra–'

'That's fine,' the drawl interrupted, 'we just need a pictographic Ident and we can sort a manual one. I'll just need to get the scanner.' She silently made a series of flicking motions, and the male employee turned to her.

'Oh. I need a pictographic Ident?' Col said.

'Yes.'

'What happens if I don't have one?' He could feel an upwelling of frustration in his throat. He hadn't needed one for years, and even if he'd still had one, it would be at home, which he couldn't access *because he didn't have an Ident*.

'Sorry – need the card and Ident to go with it.' The apology in her tone was plastic and reflective, something rote-learned in lieu of having to deal with the emotion of work.

'Right. Can you not look me up in the database? I remember having to send a pict.'

'Oh, yeah. Used to be able to do that. System was deprecated a few years ago. Something about server overflow space.' Her attention was still elsewhere.

'Can I, I don't know, sign for it or something?' Col pressed after a few seconds of silence.

'We don't keep signatures on file, sorry,' the girl said. 'It's one of those things. People usually just use the Link.' Almost before she finished talking, she started to twitch as she dropped back into the Link to do whatever she'd been doing before Col arrived.

'Listen,' he said, slowly and calmly, 'I really need to get access to my money. I really need a transit pass. Somebody's life may be at stake. Is there any way I can do that here? What steps do I need to take?' He felt as though he was talking to a machine.

Col's impassioned plea slipped through the recognition systems of the low-level employee. What was she supposed to do? A heaving sigh dropped away the last of her professionalism. Her face fell, and an otherworldly exhaustion seeped into her posture, the same he'd seen on Sal's face prior to the Upgrade, and on the doctors who had been forced to kick him out of the hospital. The crinkled clothes matched the crumpled young woman underneath.

'Look, I dunno, man,' she sighed, and for the first time an edge of sincerity crept into her voice. 'I just know *my* stuff. There's the Link Services Centre, they might be able to help?'

Col nodded. 'Where's that?'

A flicked wrist, and a sweeping gesture with the right arm. 'It's just up –' She pointed to empty space between Col and herself, then paused. 'Oh. Sorry.'

Once again, Col was on the receiving end of information that couldn't be shared. 'It's okay. Describe it.'

It wasn't far, in the same set of near-abandoned shopfronts that clung on to life near a food distribution centre.

He thanked her and walked back outside. Looking back in, his reflection partially blocked the view of the two young people; they'd turned back toward each other, twitching inscrutably, the fraying remnants of a smiling face.

The sun crashed furiously onto the pavement outside and the glare stung his eyes. He stayed under the eave as he hurried to the next block. Around the corner, he spotted the ubiquitous logo of the Uplink, incongruous in the setting of the real world. Col was a little shocked to see that it was a physical sign, not just some ideogram that relied on connection to appear. It spat from a black wall that had faded to grey, bathed in the soft blue-green light of the signage. It was the sole entrance along the shopfront; the rest was a smorgasbord of ply, tape and faded apologies to long-departed clientele. In their place, an empty village. The Uplink sign lorded over a street manned by automated cleaning robots and security cams, and the soft whistle of an unfelt breeze.

Of the dozen or so workstations behind the screen, only one was staffed, surrounded by ageing and broken seating covered in dust. A smile affixed itself to the face of the customer service representative as soon as Col walked in.

'Hi.' Col said, walking to the desk instead of taking a ticket.

'Good morning,' The voice was sugar, poured over rancid oil. Far from the dishevelled and abandoned appearance of the two young employees in the distribution centre, the human face of the Uplink remained crisp and neat. The man's hair was fixed in an unlikely windswept curl. His single-button blazer stretched over a faux-linen shirt. Everything about the man *reflected*, from the toothy smile to the gleam on the shoes. He sat in his role with a disarming comfort; a mirror to push away any attempt at incursion to the machinations of the Uplink.

The man beamed back at Colin as he explained his plight, and his reply had the rounded tone of a rote response.

'Of course! The Uplink service would be happy to help. I'll guide you through the process today. First of all, what is your name?' The smile stayed firmly affixed to the syllables as they cruised, slippery, through the air. Col tried to contain his exasperation.

'Mr Montgomery, it looks as though we have a profile that matches the information you've provided.' The voice was like glass. 'I *will* have to go through a process of identification, however, and as you can't access the Uplink it will need to be four-factor. You've provided one factor already by knowing your name and other personal details. Do you have your pictographic Ident card?'

Breathing deeply, and clenching one fist in an attempt to push down the rising sense of panic, Col said that he didn't. That he'd come here *because* he didn't.

'No problem, sir. We'll just have to find some alternative identification. Each account has a secret password, which you would have set up the first time you were registered with Uplink. Do you know what that is?'

'Secret password?' Col was nonplussed.

The smile didn't falter. 'Yes. It was supposed to be something important to you.'

It was hard to dig back that far for a scrap of irrelevant data. These days, Uplink connections were confirmed via biometrics. Initially there had been some pushback, something about privacy, but not so much anymore. Convenience, apparently, outweighed privacy.

Back when he'd set up his account, he'd been living with Cass in a youth hostel. The hostel owner had put them into a private room due to their young age. 'Too much strangeness goes on in here for your little eyes,' she'd said, in the quiet, rasping voice that had terrified Cassandra. Col had hated it there, but it was the only place open to them while they'd scrubbed dishes and hustled as couriers to keep themselves fed.

While their eyes had been saved, their ears and sleep had not. Nights of raucous partying and reckless promiscuity had echoed through the walls to the two orphans. Col remembered sleeping the mornings away while hangovers cured in adjacent rooms.

He gave the name of the hostel. If anything had been his code, it would have been that.

The man's smile managed to widen. 'Absolutely. Now, I'm sending a confirmation to your App deck. You'll just have to –'

'I'm sorry, I don't have an App deck.' Col interrupted.

The representative didn't hesitate. 'Okay then. No problem! We have an alternative pathway here.' Only a series of muscle twitches in the left arm gave away to Col that a value had been switched in the script, which was directing the man down a different verification pathway. The man's eyes were neither smiling, nor directed at Col, but at an empty space somewhere slightly in front of him.

'Okay, here we go. Mr. Montgomery, can I have your address?'

Col gave him his address, and then his previous two addresses for further confirmation.

'Excellent. So, we've got your personal details, name, date of birth and gender Ident. We've got your secret password,' the rounded tone was slipping, and the man seemed to be talking more to himself than Col, 'and we've got the address, and the historicals...'

The anxiety eased in Col's chest. It was going to be okay.

'I just need one more thing... can't connect to the App deck...' More twitching, and the smile faltered slightly as he manipulated menus. It quickly came back.

'Alright! We can get around this!'

'Great!' Col's heart leapt.

'Just need the contact of your next of kin.'

'Oh?'

'Yes. Looks like we'll need confirmation from...' Twitches, and the eye flickered back into focus straight onto Col, 'Cassandra Montgomery.'

Col sank his head into his hands.

CHAPTER 14

'I'm not sure what I'm supposed to do now,' Col said. Ariana listened sympathetically. 'I mean, I can't go home. I can't get even a temporary Ident. The security at the Library won't let me near the place. I don't know what to do.'

They were in an abandoned shopfront. From the empty display cases and broken chairs and tables, it used to be some kind of food shop. He'd slept rough again, and had been chased out of the stacker in the middle of the night, sent away by security into the unmarked dark. Initially, he'd tried to go to Sal's place, but people eyed him suspiciously when he waited out the front, so he'd searched elsewhere until the haunted sounds of the night city receded. It had taken a while to get to their meeting point that morning, but he'd found her sitting at a rickety table, red hair floating, wry smile on her face. The table rattled this way and that as his weight shifted, and he fussed with it as Ariana watched on quietly. Her pale features seemed to fill the drab room.

'What about you?' he asked, 'How have you been getting on?' His hair hung lank and black over his face, and he was grimy from the rain and two nights sleeping in disused stairwells. Ariana, though, looked as fresh as ever. He didn't know how she'd found a clean place to sleep.

'I've been... okay. Trying my own things, you know? We really need to find our way into the Uplink; you can't be sleeping out in the cold like this. The distribution centre did nothing? And what about the Library?'

Col left the table alone, and pulled his chair back in. He shook his head, 'Nope. Wouldn't let me near the place. I asked two, maybe three questions and then, bang.' He mimicked the sound of a taser, pushing his hand into his kidney where the cop had got him. 'No way I'm going back to try talk to Sal. They think I'm some Aug.' He turned to her, 'What about you? I couldn't even get into my house, hence' – he gestured to his appearance – 'but you look alright.'

Ariana looked at the empty display case, 'There's a place I can stay. Let's just say it has its downsides, but at least the weather doesn't affect me there.'

Before Col even opened his mouth, she followed with, 'And I'm sorry, but space is limited. I barely fit in there.'

Col tried to hide his disappointment. Last night hadn't been as wet as the first night, but it had been colder. His jacket was thick, but it didn't cover him completely, and he'd been forced to shift the jacket to successive extremities as they'd gotten cold in turn.

'I don't know what to do, Ariana,' he whispered.

'What do you mean?' Ariana asked. Not for the first time, Col noticed how little she seemed to worry about what was happening around her. Her demeanour remained slightly sardonic and aloof, as though everything they were going through was some kind of cosmic joke, and she knew the punchline.

'I mean *I don't know what to do*. I've tried everything immediately practical. I can't get into my house. I'm barely able to navigate the city. Shit, my *neighbours* are treating me like some solar-junkie Aug. I don't know what arrangement you have, but I don't have it. I'm... I'm in serious trouble here. And I still don't know what's going on with Cass.'

'Worry about yourself first. Then worry about your sister.' Ariana leaned forward toward him, and her dark eyes bored into him. 'The first priority, for both of us, is to figure out our way into the Link. Your sister will be there when you get back.'

'What if she isn't, though?'

'What do you mean?'

Col tried to think of some way to explain the connection he and Cass had always had. That, somehow, he *knew* something wasn't right, that she'd have found a way to contact him. But it came out all wrong. He tripped over his words for a minute more, then finished with 'I just think... I think I need to do something to find her.'

'What, now?' Ariana was nonplussed. 'What about the Link?'

'What about it?' Col felt himself getting frustrated.

'How are you supposed to do anything without the Link? Figure *that* out, or you'll be useless to Cass even if you do find her.' She said it with such finality and resonance that Col was almost shocked into agreeing with her.

'She's my sister, and she's been missing for the best part of a week. I'm having a hard time right now, but I actually give a shit about her, too, and I need to know she's okay,' he snapped.

'Oh, sure, whatever. Do it your way then,' she bit back.

Col rounded on her. 'Look, I know you have this devil-may-care attitude, but I'm worried. Really worried. I know she was looking into some pretty dark shit before the Upgrade went live, and the longer I wait in customer service lines to fix whatever's gone wrong for the Link in my head, the more I worry about her. Do you get that?'

'I do, but –'

'Do you? Because you're being pretty callous about my sister's welfare right now. Have you even got anyone you care about? What would happen if your family disappeared?'

As soon as he said it, Ariana shut down. Just like when he'd asked about her past in the hospital, she went quiet and started staring into space. Col breathed out, realising that he'd made a mistake. That he'd prodded something that Ariana didn't want touched.

Tension hung in the air between them for a few minutes. Col stood and took a few steps around the ravaged room. The glass at the front of the shop was broken and boarded up. Someone had scrawled some kind of inscrutable graffiti on the back of the panel, long ago. The paint bled and faded down the grains of the swollen ply. He stared at it for a few minutes, then turned back to Ariana.

'Look. I'm going to go find my sister. Okay?' When she nodded, he continued, 'I'm going to go to her hab. See if she's there. If she is, I'll find out what's up. If not, I'm going to look for her. Once that's done, I can help with the Link, okay?'

Ariana nodded again. *Okay,* he thought, and turned to walk out the door. Before he left, he checked with her. 'Two days, same time, same place, right?'

She looked at him, confused for a moment, and then gave him a third nod; the sly smile was back on her face. He walked out the door, located the sea wall, and started the long route to Cass's hab.

* * *

The sky had grown heavy and dark, the oppressive purple-black of an oncoming thunderstorm. The light of the streetlamps seeped into the dark, leaping no more than a metre or two from the bulb before dying into aetheric nothingness.

Glancing up the street, he let a group of people walk past, twitching in that same frenetic way, before he made his move.

He planted a foot onto the reconstituted plastic bracing of the fence outside Cass's hab block, then vaulted up to grab the top of the wall. He used his momentum to swing up and over and released at the top just in time to notice the small rock garden he was about to fall into.

He swore softly and rolled away from the stones before dusting himself off and gingerly touching a scrape on his knee. Gazing up at the apartment block, he could see the rooftop fans of the broken air conditioning unit that they sat near to watch the night sky. He looked across to the fire escape at the edge of the building. It spat out near a plascrete drainpipe not far from where Col had collapsed over the fence. Several such drains made their way down the building, but Col focused on this one. It passed just by the lowest section of the fire escape. Checking once again that there was nobody watching, he gripped the side of the drainpipe and began to climb.

'Cass?' he whispered into the darkness, after he'd scrambled through the window she kept half-open to climb onto the roof. He'd already said her name as he'd knocked on the pane. The window frame had creaked as he put his weight on it, blocking the wide shaft of cold light as he'd climbed in.

Standing in the gloom, Col could see just two things – the deep purple of the outside sky, and a bright red LED on a security system older than either Cass or himself. He panicked. The alarm blinked at him, silently reaching across the Uplink to whatever security force Cass had paid to watch the place.

His footsteps echoed as he hurried across the room. A sharp relief of flooding light spilled across the floor as he hit the main power switch. Col blinked, waiting for his eyes to adjust, standing in the haphazard not-quite organisation of Cass's hab. Nothing was out of place, but in the brightly lit silence of the night, it seemed wrong.

Col and Sal had studio habs, but Cass had been lucky enough to find somewhere with a separate bedroom and study. A pile of dirty clothes lay in the corner nearest her bedroom. The standby lights for the appliances winked. The snick lock was closed, but the deadbolt remained open. A soft breeze through the open window rustled the coats on the wall rack.

He made his way to the study. The surface of her desk was a computer that she used to take notes, and the top of it was a glowing screen. As he got closer, he could see the image of nodes connected by glowing wires. He touched the surface of the desk, but nothing happened. He swiped. Still nothing, but a thin film of dust danced off the display and left a shining trail. He reached for the glowing power key on the side of the desk and pushed it.

IDENT N/A - DENIED

A sharp, exhaled breath. He was getting too used to reading things like that.

The warning disappeared. The screen glowed, and only the last set of inquiries were visible. '*Query - aug interv.*' took up the centre of a number of floating nodes and connectors. An apartment number for a set of high-rise flats caught his eye. The rest of it Col could barely read. His head was starting to hurt again, and the text was too small. This was a backup display; usually Cass would be interfacing with this using the Uplink. He caught the word 'solar', along with 'stockpile' and a shrunken version of a handwritten note.

He patted his pockets, looking around for something to write on, but couldn't find anything. Swearing, he tried to memorise the address, then frantically ran his eyes over the small section of the desk screen in case he'd missed anything. With access permissions, he could have jumped to the parent node and understood what this set of addresses represented, or he could have found which one had the more recent date on it.

Col stood up and stared out the window to try to throw off the ache in his mind. The ink-black of the night sank into a kaleidoscopic series of streetlight colours. In the distance, a hulking tower sat, squat, dark and low on the horizon.

'I was out there the other day,' Cass's voice sprang to the front of his thoughts. The address in his mind mapped to the location of the tower.

It was as good a place as any to start.

He closed the window and ducked away, watching the baleful light of the blinking alarm as it kept calling for security. He didn't know how much time he had, but he waited as long as he could. Willing, hoping for Cass to appear. To let him know it had been a mistake, that she was okay. That the abandoned hab was just because of a late work call or something. He wanted her to be there.

She wasn't.

* * *

That night, as he slept fitfully in a corner at the edge of a culvert, he was plagued again by nightmares of sullen smoke and an all-consuming spark. When he woke, jacket soaked in sweat and limbs shaking, his mind was afire, pounding against his skull. He lay in the dark, and a form of a solid colour beyond any real description stuttered into existence. It shuddered around the geometry of the space with an immense weightfulness that outgrew its surroundings. Col closed his eyes, but it was still there, and a colour that was also a sound started in his brain. It was formless, a cymbal crash of convalescent chaos that broke into his mind. He had no choice but to watch and hear as it tried to form a stuttering panoply of sound into comprehensibility. It seemed to last forever, infinite colour and an echoing blast. He couldn't make it stop, but slowly and finally, it coalesced. The form still broke around the edges of reality, but the sound that wasn't sound scattered away the frequencies it didn't need until a mantra began repeating, in a dialectic that bore only a passing resemblance to human speech. But speech it was. It was a voice. It was saying a word.

A name.

His name.

Cass's voice, calling across the Uplink.

CHAPTER 15

CASS

Cass could see the old metal filaments of the lightbulb that was throwing scant light around her cell. It had an orange halo, a weak glow that faded into something just shy of darkness by the time it reached her on her canvas stretcher bed. She couldn't discern any of the details in the room from where she lay. The pattern-seeking, less evolved part of her brain had spent the first week jumping at faces in shadows. Mocking hints deep in the steelwork of her cell.

Her ankle still hurt where she'd sprained it after waking up. There had been screaming. Yelling. Violence. She'd lashed out, kicking and punching and throwing herself into the walls, all the while screaming through the Link, reaching out to Col, to anyone. She hadn't noticed the injury until much later, after the adrenaline had faded. Eventually, her thrashing had broken the plastic cover of the hanging lightbulb and smashed it. She'd been plunged into a darkness more complete than she'd ever known. She'd stopped moving, trying to make sense of the void as terror had crept down her neck. Terror of oblivion, of being held forever in this hole of chaotic nothing.

Deep breaths and a few curse words directed at herself had calmed her down, and she'd felt her way back toward the cot she'd tossed across the room. She'd picked it back up, fumbling as she righted the light aluminium frame. She'd lain down on the stretched canvas and caught her breath. As she listened to the silence disappear into her breath, an itch began deep in her brain.

She had kept trying to call out to Col, but the connection never got through. The effort would press heavily onto her, building around the edges of her mind. Something was actively blocking the signal getting out. She'd feel the familiar cold breach as a connection sync co-opted part of her brain, only for it to immediately falter and fail and leave her in the dark again. She felt as though she were a cloud threading its way through the edges of a metal box. Every now and then, something would penetrate through some unseen gap, but then it would be cut off, releasing nothing but tiny bursts of incoherent noise into the void outside.

She hadn't realised how much energy it took to create and maintain a connection to the Uplink. Normally the extra effort could be mediated with an extra stimtab, but not in here. In here, she felt as though she were straining to bridge a chasm separating her from the rest of the world. She threw her consciousness out over and over again until the effort became too much, and she collapsed, sweating, onto the canvas cot. She held her hand in front of her face and couldn't see it.

She had to pee.

The urgency built up slowly, but before long her panic was overridden by simple biological need. Holding onto the cot with one hand, she rolled to the ground and used her other hand to undo her trousers. She relieved herself and hauled herself back onto the cot, trying to ignore the fact that she was going to be trapped in a dark room with nothing but the stench of her own piss for company. Silence returned, and time took on the wefting, warping feeling when every moment held an eternity.

She was scratching the side of the cot with a fingernail when it happened. The soft *scritch scritch* and the feeling of pressure against her nailbed was keeping two of her senses occupied, which helped keep her head clear enough to think. The noise of her nail disappeared beneath a loud, clanking echo and a silver stripe of blinding light.

The door squealed on heavy, dry hinges as it opened. Cass held her hands in front of her face as a white-hot spear of light forced her pupils to contract. Sharp footfalls barely registered behind the sensory overload, and then a voice spoke. It was a soft sound, and it took a few seconds for Cass to realise that the murmur had been a question directed at her.

'Huh?' she muttered.

The speaker was a slender form in the doorway, haloed by light. 'Can't leave well enough alone, can you?' it said, snorting at the broken lightbulb and the stain on the floor. The shape beckoned, and a second silhouette appeared. 'Clean up her mess, and find a new light.' The second shape nodded and withdrew.

Now that her eyes had adjusted to the light, Cass could see through the door and into the room outside. A network of fine interlaced wires ran along the top of the wall. From this distance, it looked like a dark cloud against the building's structure.

'It's a scattering array,' the voice said. They were silhouetted against the light in the doorway. Cass couldn't make out their features, but saw that their hand was clasped around a device of some sort.

A scattering array, Cass thought. *That explains why I can't reach the Uplink.* Wherever she was, they didn't want anyone to know she was here.

* * *

That had been days ago. Two dead-eyed Augs had lumbered in, replaced the light and cleaned up. She'd been forced against the wall for the duration. After they left, her jailer had closed the door again.

The light stayed on permanently. A sliding door was inset into one of the wall's panels. It led to a water closet and a small basin. No shower. An Aug opened the door three times a day to push through a plate of near-tasteless mush. At first, she ignored it, but before long, her hunger got the better of her. The constancy of the room and the inadequacy of its lighting dragged Cass down into the same kind of glum hopelessness as her surroundings. The delivery of food became her only means of measuring time. Occasionally, her food would come with a package of some other item. A small toilet roll, or tampons, or wet wipes. Her original terror at her capture gave way to a kind of weary malaise as it became clear that the Augs were going to keep her captive for quite some time. Exactly how long she didn't know.

She stared at the walls. One of them had a patchy, orange pattern. A leak had rusted part of the steel interior. Cass marked the edge of the stain by sticking a wad of wet toilet paper to the wall, wondering if it was still growing. She laid back down on her cot and turned away from it, trying to sleep.

She redoubled her efforts to reach out via the Link. Each time, she was blocked by the scattering array. She'd try for fifteen minutes at a time, or until she felt like her mind was filled with static and foam. Then she'd lie on the cot and recharge. Sometimes she'd drift off to sleep. Other times, she'd simply stare at the ceilings and walls. The watermark didn't move.

She found it easier to reach out to Col through the Link than to others. She wasn't sure why, but the noise in her head ebbed lower when she reached out to him. The feeling of clawing her way out of a box with fingers made of smoke was still there, but wisps escaped more regularly. Small puffs of data fled her cage and flew off into the night, screaming through the Uplink's servers in search of her brother. After a while, the strain of trying to contact anyone else proved too much, and she began to solely focus on sending small data packets to Col.

Her captors either didn't notice or didn't care that she was trying to contact the outside world. They were Augs, and Cass reasoned that they wouldn't have been able to tell she was doing anything. Either that, or they trusted the scattering array and were happy to let her wear herself out by bouncing off it harmlessly.

After a while, even this became a ritual. Cass's mind turned into a blank slate, an idle process. She waited for the watermark on the wall to move below her makeshift marker.

Each time the door opened, Cass did her best to glimpse her surroundings. She looked past the ceramic and plastic Aug hand that slid her food tray in and tried to memorise as much as she could before the strip of light disappeared again.

Sunlight was being filtered through a series of skylights in a steel-framed sawtooth warehouse roof. Covering the caustic rust and detritus hanging from the steel trusses was the scattering array. The filaments were fine, like netting, and glowed copper orange where they weren't deep black. The thin steel skin of the factory continued down and married thoughtlessly with the dark grey concrete. Slick patches of oil and faintly sparkling patches of long-embedded metallic swarf were visible in the clean areas of the floor; the rest covered in mechanical trash. Behind where the Augs placed the food, Cass saw a heavily trafficked area, a set of desire lines converging on the buildings' periphery just out of her view. The exit. Or *an* exit.

The days of inactivity meant even the smallest movements made her atrophied muscles cramp. After the next meal was delivered, she hydrated gradually. She drank a mouthful of water at a time, feeling the liquid warm in her mouth before swallowing. She got onto the filthy floor and stretched out, relishing the complaint from her muscles as they released.

After several more meals, she was ready.

She had no timekeeping mechanism but estimated when the door would open again. She finished off the last of her water. The lack of showering had left her hair in a greasy mess. The filth of her own dead skin and the stale air of the cell hung off her. She crouched next to the wall nearest the door.

The faint fog of ennui from the last week was thrown into sharp relief. Every breath she took seemed to kick the chill out of the room. The air in her throat screamed at her, and the thumping rhythm of her heart echoed in her ears. *They would hear it*, she thought. *They'd have to hear it. It was so loud*. A flush rose to her face, and she tried not to panic. Had she drunk enough water? Her mouth was coarse and her tongue stuck to her teeth.

The door opened.

The Aug wasn't fully in view before Cass jumped up and sprinted toward the light that was burning her dilated pupils. She crashed into it and sent the plate of food flying. Cass was hit in the face with the container of water and watched it fall in slow motion toward the ground. She slipped in the wet grease slick and nearly fell over herself. Instead, she simply slid as the Aug reeled and tried to grab at her. It screeched something, and Cass sprinted for the door that she knew had to be there.

The Aug pulled a device from its pocket and gave chase. The light in the room was yellow and cold, the deep blue night outside the skylights sent no warmth into the warehouse. As Cass ran past her cell, a pair of shipping containers held together by crude welds and fibre cement boards, two more Augs pounded after her. Adrenaline pumped through Cass's ears, and the Aug from the doorway peeled off to let the other two catch her. She had the jump on them, but they were gaining fast. She could hear their footsteps growing louder behind her.

She dodged around sections of floor that still glistened with untamed oil, and sprinted toward the door nearest her, away from the large garage door that remained closed. She could see the copper scattering array and felt its Uplink-blocking effect pressing against the inside of her skull like a lead weight at the end of a frayed string. She winced and pushed further toward the door, barrelling into it and grasping the handle. To her shock and surprise, it was unlocked.

The copper trace between the door and wall sparked short blue arcs of electricity as she burst out into the night. The grease and glimmer of the concrete indoors was replaced by acid rain–etched roughness and exposed aggregate. As she took off again, she heard the thud of the Augs hitting the door. The pulsing, crushing weight that was stopping her from reaching out with the Uplink was gone, and she screamed a message out to Col.

Her mind opened and she felt the caress of the Uplink wrap itself around her as she sprinted across the pavement, but something was still wrong. Colin didn't connect, and her vision was obscured by a ghost of smoke and mire. She reached out to touch it. Her hand glowed with warmth and the faint feeling of a breeze on her skin, but the connection wasn't there. The ghost took a faintly human form.

'Col?' Cass called, confused. She tried harder to reach out to him and called again, 'Col! Colin?'

The grey shape shifted and groaned, filtering across Cass's vision like a broken dream. She tried to touch the vaporous arm but couldn't reach. She called his name repeatedly, each time with more urgency, as she careened across the concrete and bitumen at a dead run. He didn't answer. The Augs behind her were gaining. She was running out of breath, but her voice continued to ring out, unanswered, into the shape in front of her.

'Colin!' she cried, first in fear and then in pain as she hit something that brought her to a halt. She collapsed onto the ground. A scorching pain nettled her body, and she waved the amorphous form from her mind's eye. A chain-link fence, three times taller than she was, swam into vision. The rips on her skin cried out. She'd grazed her thigh as she fell. Looking up, she saw the razor wire at the top of the fence. As she tried to stand, she was grasped from behind. The hands were rough, strong, and entirely inhuman. The hot breath of the Aug was in her ear and she struggled against it. Its legs were far stronger than hers, and it simply lifted her into the air as she thrashed uselessly. It turned her around, and she jerked in surprise and recognition. Weeks before, she'd seen a vidfeed of *this* Aug breaking into the Library.

Its breath came hot and rasping past the broken mask that held blank eyes. It held her up with two makeshift and broken mechanical arms, too long for its body, vice-grip claws holding her torso. She screamed at it, but it didn't respond. It simply stood, bracing itself with too-small legs and staring with glowing red lights that served for eyes.

She almost blurted out something about the Library when she noticed the second Aug. It stood behind the first. Impassive, uncaring and identical to the Aug that held her. They both waited patiently as the Aug that had been delivering her food walked calmly toward her. Cass panicked and redoubled her efforts, calling Col's name uselessly into the smoke. The shape ebbed and faded, then drew together in the night. The outlines became not more rigid, but more recognisable. The grey-black cloud formed into the shape of a man that could have been her brother.

'Colin!' she cried as the second Aug pushed a needle roughly into the meat of her upper arm. The shape of Col deformed and wisped away. She screamed his name once more before her voice slurred, her vision faded, and before long she saw nothing, said nothing, knew nothing.

CHAPTER 16

COLIN

Col was pulled out of his reverie again by the acid sprinkle of the rain. Yesterday had left him feeling somehow thinner. Insubstantial, like a story told in half-drawn sketches. He could feel his own reek eking from his clothes, and his stomach had gone numb after days without food. His nightmares were changing, and beginning to infect his living reality. The chaotic noise had given way to Cass's voice, and he didn't know what to make of it.

Cass, or the apparition of her, had disappeared, and for an hour he'd made himself sick trying to reach out to her again, but whatever connection had happened had been fleeting and insecure. All he was left with was the pain, the sharp cry that told him that no, the Uplink was no longer available. After a little while, he wasn't even sure it was real. Maybe he'd still been asleep, having some kind of vivid nightmare? He didn't know, but he'd been on the move as soon as dawn came, following the sunlight like he'd tried to follow his sister's voice.

He was standing outside the Aug-infested hovel Cass had visited shortly before disappearing, hoping that something inside might have some answers. When she was here, she'd been looking into the rumours of Augs trying to break into the Uplink. He recalled her saying that she hadn't found much, but she'd got a lead to somewhere else from one of the Augs inside.

The crumbling concrete barely concealed bricks that were on the verge of tumbling from their decayed limestone grouting. The entrance was inset from the street front, and dark. The remains of the entryway lights were shattered and broken on the ground. If he'd bothered to check, Col was willing to bet that he wouldn't find any of the copper or ferrous wiring left. Augs would have stolen it to rig themselves and their Augmetics, or wired it to a solar array. The door hung from broken security-grade hinges. The walls were covered in impact marks, cankerous sores on the building left after repeated break-in attempts. Col thought of the dronelike Aug in the vidfeed from the Library and felt his skin go slick in the cold.

Sweat was rising on the back of his neck, and the world shrank from him. The opening to the building was mocking him, leering at him to frighten him away from entering.

Glass crunched underfoot as he reached the threshold.

* * *

He cursed the broken lift shaft in the disused lobby and made for the stairs. The sounds of Augs permeated the space. A feeble, dingy ray of sunlight was streaming through the windows, and he saw Augs twitching and groaning in ecstatic throes on the east side of the building, or fighting over which of them got the prime placement for their solar arrays. Col's breath was heavy in his ears as he trudged up to the floor he'd memorised from Cass's computer.

The walls were covered in graffiti: age-old curses and lewd pictograms and declarations of lust for solar and lamentations of burnt-out souls and unquenchable hunger in sardonic writ. Individually, they were raving cries for attention, carving out their own eternity on the concrete. Together they became a storied though illegible history, leafed through but never read. An unfiltered, colloidal mess which constructed the meaning of the space more than the physicality of the walls. It became more than the materials, more than the colours, more than the place, more than the words themselves. It became a silent scream for help. After several days outside the world of the Uplink, with nothing to see or read, the scrawls were almost welcome to Col. The information, the connection from afar to another piece of humanity – even if it probably was an Aug that wrote it. Within the scrawl, nearly subsumed, was a printed number that told Col he was on the right floor. The fire safety door had been broken off long ago and the architrave had been torn and widened, leaving a mess in the blockwork. A whirring and a clanking dominated his ears as he walked into the circulation space of the level. It was coming from his left. Not wanting to find out what it was, he turned to the right and began looking for the room he'd seen in Cass's screen.

Most of the doors were open, and the rooms were full of Augs who had plugged themselves into the solar panels that littered the floors. Some were scrambling for a spot in the morning light. Most of them simply crackled softly, with blank expressions and worn faces, limp and carefree. Col looked away, trying to avoid seeing the Augs climbing over each other. Most of the room numbers were ripped off, with only decaying strands of gunk remaining, adhered to old glue.

The door to the room he was looking for was closed. No sound emanated from inside. Col knocked, first tentatively and then more firmly. When he went to knock a third time, a voice from the hall drifted to him.

'He won't answer. He don't talk much these days.'

The voice was nasal, bearing the accent of the dockworkers from around this part of town. Extended syllables and rounded edges. Exhaustion seeped through every word. The whirr of a constantly thudding false leg drove the Aug toward Col. The corridor seemed to shrink as it drew closer. The remnant of a cheap, canvas-soled shoe padded with every other step. The mechanical leg was affixed somewhere at the hip, underneath what looked like a hessian sack.

The Aug's voice dripped with fatigue. 'Go on then, go in. Old mate won't mind, he don't say much no more.'

The leg drove him inexorably onward. Col pressed himself against the door and tried to shrink into it. The Aug kept coming, until Col's world filled with the hulking frame and hopelessly broken countenance. Then as quickly as it had arrived, the Aug was disappearing down the hall. The servos in its leg growled and complained for the lack of lubrication. The Aug's exoskeleton had been jerry-rigged with devices to ferry fluids and power around the ageing metal. Its skin was pale, fleshy, covered in red marks where the cheap sack that stood in for clothing had chafed. Col waited until it had staggered out of view before pushing the handle down and entering the room.

The stench of death hit him like a fist.

He gagged and reeled back out of the room, slamming the door shut behind him. The clang echoed through the space and became just another catastrophic noise in the maelstrom of the Aug hovel. He took a few deep breaths, steeled himself, and pressed the door open once again.

The crisp smell of carbonated and cauterised flesh perforated his nostrils, along with a sick scent of decay. Behind it came a series of other assaults to his senses. The iron scent of dried blood. Urine, faeces, and other bodily odours that had sunk into the fabric of the space and become a part of the walls. The bitter tang of the cockroaches which were beginning to swarm over the corpse. It was hanging half-on, half-off the mattress that was well beyond its service life and had become a near-solid coalescence of the offal of the man who had lived there. Its original whitish colour had been stained a rich tapestry of muted yellows and browns.

The terminals were still attached to the Aug's hand, where solar wires were running underneath his skin and into his neck. The arm was a blackened mess. The soft tissue and meat of the arm was gone; in its place was char, a slowly crumbling mass. Grey soot lay underneath it, evidence to the fact that its decay was incomplete; it was seeping out of the cracks of itself. Every now and then a spike of red-gold would appear at the periphery as electric heat continued to flow through the scant remnants of flesh. The rest of the body was cold and pallid, except where the oxygen-starved blood had pooled and left a blue-black stain on the skin.

But for all that the Aug was dead, it still moved. The cold, blue stare of its augmented eye roved around the room. It hissed and buzzed, moving in erratic circles. The aperture opened and closed, expanding and contracting a sheen of blue light over the dead skin in a syncopated rhythm.

Col swore under his breath. He'd never been this close to a dead body before, and he was having trouble processing what he was seeing. The eye twitched and swivelled, and Col watched as it careened blindly. He squatted on the ground, trying not to touch anything in the squalor.

It hadn't been *that* old. Worn down more through circumstance than age, the lines on its face were concertina folds of substance abuse and exposure. Col would have put it in the mid-sixties, maybe younger. It was hard to tell while the smooth calm of death fought the horror of the machine embedded in its face.

Looking away, Col began to properly take in the room around him. The wiring that spread from the Aug and around the room took up most of the space. Obscured underneath it at the edge of the bed, there was a small collection of items. A silver and black pen, a small metal cup and a wooden pencil box. Scrawled into the corner of the wall were abstract images drawn with shaking hands in faint, sketchy lines. A small reminder of the Aug's humanity.

Col rose from his crouch, stepped over a small clump of wiring, and took a few steps toward a small cabinet in the backmost corner. It was obscured beneath the grunge, peeking out from beneath filthy rags that had served as clothes. Maybe there was something in here that his sister had been looking for? Using the leg of a broken stool that was lying on the ground, he pushed aside the clothes to reveal the sole drawer in the cabinet. It squealed a small cry of resistance as Col pulled it open.

Inside, there was a paper folder, which Col lifted out and opened. He tried his best not to think about the fact that he was rifling through the possessions of the man who lay dead not three metres away. It wasn't something he wanted to do, but several days of being beaten and sleeping in the rain had softened his morality. If it helped him track down Cass, it'd be worth it.

The folder's contents couldn't have been more different to the catastrophe of death around him. The sheets of paper were arrayed neatly, labelled carefully with dates and what looked like names. Each of the files bore silty thumbprints and frayed corners. Aging sticky notes adorned some pages, with scrawled handwriting that Col couldn't read. He leafed through it, pulling out a page at random. It was in portrait orientation, with a signature and date from some 30 years prior in the bottom right corner. An older version of the same Uplink logo he'd seen in the abandoned mall was in the top left of the foolscap page. 'Uplink: Connecting People', it declared. Col skimmed the typed memo. One of the rows had been highlighted in something that had probably been fluorescent green at one stage, but had bled and faded until it was little more than a sickened khaki mark on the page.

It was a communication between the Uplink Corp and the Aug. Col put the page back and pulled another one. This page was brown and orange, almost the same colour as the mattress, and it had a sketch on it. Colin had to rotate the page a few times before he realised that it was a sketch of a brain. Arrows connected strange, scrawled handwriting to certain sections of the image, and a crude boxout contained circuitry diagrams. The writing was in black ink and near illegible. Over the top of this was angry red pen, smudged as though scrawled hurriedly by a left hand. It was the angry scribble of someone who had just realised that the methodology on the sketch wouldn't work. It drew his eye, and it was a moment before he noticed that the sketches were on the same worn-out letterhead as the first page.

Col breathed out, and looked around himself. He slid the paper back in the file and scooped everything out of the cabinet. The old Aug on the mattress wouldn't miss it. At least, that's what he told himself as he wondered how his life had come to this. The file felt heavy and awkward in his hands. It was old and nearly falling apart, cardboard stretched by the unfurling of time. He looked back at the dead Aug, the dead man.

'Did ya know 'im?' The voice came from the same place as the rhythmic clanking in the hallway. He'd done a full rotation of the building since Col had entered the room. Col nearly lost his grip on the file, jumping with fright when he heard the man's voice.

'No. No, I didn't. Did you?'

The Aug shrugged, then had to readjust himself as the unexpected movement threw off his walk. 'He was just one of us, y'know? Some old cobber, stuck outta everywhere. Been here longer than most, maybe.'

'Did you know his name?'

The laughter was more a wheeze than anything else. It eked out of his chafed chest, a hollow pitch that intermingled with the percussive stepping. He drew level with Col but didn't stop. Couldn't stop. Col turned and walked with him.

'What's funny?' he asked.

'The name. His name. I'm not so sure he knew it 'imself toward the end.'

Col proffered the file he'd taken from the room. 'Do you know what this is? Or what it's for?'

The man's head turned, but his eyes barely registered the folder. 'Not my business, what he kept in his place. You'd have to ask him.' The high-pitched whine of his wheezing laugh returned.

Col walked silently at a pace with the Aug for a while. The rhythm sank into him, surrounding him, becoming a wordless mantra. When the stairs came, he didn't turn to descend. He walked along with the man-machine, and for the first time felt an affinity for the Augs. As they once again passed the room, he spoke again.

'My sister was here,' he said simply.

'Eh?'

'A few weeks ago. She visited him' – he jerked his head – 'and now she's missing.'

'It wasn't 'im. He was a quiet one,' the Aug said, and his tone had a different edge. A world weariness, not just physical tiredness, had crept in.

Col stayed silent. He hadn't even considered it, but he didn't think it was likely now that he was here. In the man's voice was the brittle tolerance built up from a lifetime of accusations. 'I don't think it was him,' Col said quickly, 'I just need to find her. Did you see her? When she came?'

The tall man relaxed slightly, as much as his metal frame would allow, and he asked about Cass. Col described her, and he nodded.

'Yeah, she came through here. Well, I reckon it was her. We don't get too many visitors, so I'm guessing the lady I saw walkin' through was her. Couple weeks ago.' He thought carefully, and his expression went blank. Col saw a memory chip on his neck brighten up. 'Was a weird day. Cloudy. Had rained the night before but when she arrived the sun came out.'

The sun came out when she arrived. Col almost laughed. The sunshine and his sister – apparently it wasn't only him who had made the connection.

'Yeah, that's her. Do you know where she went after that? I haven't heard from her.'

The man's eyes leaked, whether from exhaustion or emotion, Col didn't know. It was the mechanical giant's turn to look confused, and he tapped at his head with his arm. 'Can't you... you know... Linker?'

Col's laugh was mirthless, a low, bitter chuckle that rolled across the detritus and bounced against the concrete. He shook his head.

A look of surprise. 'Oh, no Link for you, eh, cobber?' the Aug grinned. Genuine this time. 'Okay, well. Here's what to do, yeah? I dunno what's happenin' with your sister, but if she spoke to old mate in there, he mighta sent her to one of the Sanctuaries.'

'Sanctuaries?' Col asked.

'Yeah, Sanctuaries. Bunch of 'em round. Help out people like us. We don't fit, and there's more of us every day. Gotta make something of our own. Something that's ours, y'know? Let's see.' The big man thought for a moment. 'There's Bern, but I think they're full up at the moment, and I dunno if your mate even knew about 'em. Haven't heard from Jake recently, and I don't really like him much. Fella always gave me the creeps. Clem? He's a bit small-time, probably can't help.'

The Aug considered for a moment, then nodded, almost to himself. He told Col an address in an abandoned office in town. 'Ask for Cynth.'

'Thank you,' said Colin fervently.

'Hey, no problem, cobber. Hope you find your sis.'

On the next walk around the interior of the old tower, Col found the stairwell and made his way back down to the street below. He walked back out into the dusk haze and found himself wondering if the tower he'd left behind could be less savage than the city he'd just walked back into.

CHAPTER 17

Another night of shallow sleep and dreamlessness followed. Col had found that in just a few days, he'd developed a knack for finding the kinds of hollow spaces in the world where he could, with some kind of certainty, bed down for an evening. His mind adapted from dealing with the Uplink's invasion of noise and sound to being able to spot security, safe corners and escape routes with remarkable ease.

Cowering and trying to sleep, he was woken by the howl of a crowd of people ripping through the dark. He wasn't sure if it was in pain or rage or joy, but in the dark, in the cold, alone, it was a threat. The feeling of safety that he'd managed to create evaporated in a bare moment.

Almost unbidden, the conversation with the lumbering Aug from the tower came to his mind. A sanctuary. A place for people to go when they couldn't go anywhere else, sounded like exactly the place he needed.

Trying not to disturb the night, he stood and walked from the alley. Dawn was still hours away.

* * *

The lights on the train were blotted out by a heaving press of bodies. Each person stood, grasping the ceiling-mounted handrails like picts of rainforest animals he'd seen on an old vidfeed. The air conditioning was badly maintained. Col felt like he could barely breathe. It had been a long time since he'd been around this many people. Every part of his life had been small spaces, digital rooms and the unreality of the Uplink. Only Sal and occasionally his sister saw him in real life.

Col was convinced the other commuters were avoiding looking at him, suspecting him of being disconnected from the Link. Or was he imagining it, and simply noticing their blank expressions again?

He'd caught the early rush for the day shift. High-vis, rugged clothing and heavy-duty boots adorned most of the passengers. To his surprise, there were also Augs. Here and there, huddled among the work crews, he saw a mechanical arm or an Augmetic torso, attached to people who, unlike the others, stared around the carriage attentively. They looked like he imagined he did, discomforted at having to share their space with so many people staring into nothingness.

Col didn't know how he was supposed to find Sal, much less Cass. Since the time he'd caught her on the commute home, Sal had been impossible to find. He didn't know what shifts she was working at the Library. Contacting her wasn't a priority, compared to the pressing need he felt to find his sister or get back into the Uplink. Besides that, there had been something *off* about their previous interaction. Distracted, maybe, by the new joys of the Upgrade. Not that it mattered. The Uplink was his primary means of contact with her, and that was gone now. Aside from happenstance, it was unlikely he'd see her. Still, he wondered if something had happened to her while he'd been away.

Sighing, he looked at the file he'd taken from the tower. He was uncomfortable holding it, like he was outing himself as some kind of pariah by making public his reliance on paper and physical storage. It was as though he was expecting someone to reach out and take it and demand to know its provenance.

Again, he was struck by the lack of displayed information around him. Without the Uplink, he couldn't see the advertisements that would burn themselves into his retina on the upper edges of the carriage and floating against the walls between the stops. That much was obvious and expected, but there was also a lack of safety information, general directions, or data about the train and the loop itself in the carriage, or even on the platform. The screens that he remembered from years ago were all switched off; Linkers were able to see the relevant information as text tags in their vision. They received directions to the correct platform through navmarkers on the floor. He'd had to remember, as the Augmented people around him presumably did, where to go. Stepping onto the train platform without a ticket and having to divine which line would take him to the address he'd been given had been yet another stress to add to his growing list. All efforts to ask for directions from the commuters had left him with cold stares at best and hostility at worst. Eventually he'd found the right station through inference and vague memory, then had simply sat and waited, unable to find out when it would arrive.

There were no seats, and he found himself with a clear view of the window as the train accelerated into a tunnel. All at once, the outside world seemed to vanish, and the glazing became a mirror. A choleric, acid-etched face of lines and furrows stared back at him, and he whipped around to see who it was before he realised it was *him*.

He'd lost weight. Cass had said it to him before she disappeared, but he hadn't noticed how fast he'd been shedding it. Long, heavy lines dragged his skin down over his cheekbones, past shadowy eyes that barely held a spark in them. His clothes were as filthy and ragged as the folder in his hand. Stubble pockmarked his face. His hair was a worried mess, clumped and tufted. The train sped beneath a series of bridges, giving his reflection a ghostly appearance as it sank and flickered between foreground and background. One minute unerringly present, the next vanished into the infrastructure and high rises and cold industry of the city. His reflection sank into the background, a zephyr in a storm. He didn't notice the slowing of the train until the static puppet of the face that he barely recognised was projected onto the concrete gangway outside the station where the train stopped. He was staring at the way the cleft of his jaw had somehow disappeared beneath his jowls, and yet his face was thinner than he remembered it ever being. Solid and static as the background.

The train had stopped moving.

He pushed through the crowded car, managing to squeeze onto the concrete platform just before the doors shut again. This platform, like the carriage and station he'd left from, was completely bereft of textual information and signage. At the very edge of the unused part of the platform, there was the last portion of yellow paint that demarcated the safety line for passengers. Behind Col, there was a powder-coated steel sign that barely showed the station name, rusted through and now a different colour than when first pressed into service from some long-defunct factory.

Half a dozen other passengers in front of him had alighted and were already walking down the gangway to the street below. Before long, the crowd and the train had disappeared, along with the high-pitched whining rumble of the magnetised tracks, leaving only a soft howl from the growing wind through a rusted chain-link fence. Col wended his way down two streets, trying to remember the instructions he'd been given by the man in the tower. Before long, he was alone in a desolate, abandoned housing estate. Grids of windows in rehashed faux-brick frontages stared from every side, and dead plant life brushed his ankles as he sat on the edge of a concrete garden bed. The soil was poisoned. The concrete had been poured, and then its chemicals had leached into the plants. They had been suffocated in by lime and acid rain. Now a stunted simulacrum of the designer imagery the residents were sold watched the skeletal man as he sat down and tried to get his bearings.

Col breathed in. The air around here stank. The salty tang of the ocean combined with the powdery taste of decaying infrastructure. The folder sent up a small puff of dust from the wall of the garden bed as he placed it down beside him.

He was lost. The Sanctuary was somewhere, but the street wasn't right. This street was empty and desolate, and had clearly been abandoned for some time. The windows in the housing estate were ravaged by the elements. Faded sheets draped over a balcony. Curtains, torn and twisted, hung askew, billowing the chill wind through long-forgotten facades into homes rapidly abandoned for a reason Col would never know.

He shuddered in disquiet, working at reorienting himself. He realised he'd turned a street too soon, and then left instead of right. Only two direction changes, but enough to disappear.

Sanctuary. A sanctuary for Augs, and he was going there willingly. He had to admit that the Augs had been the only people to treat him with any dignity since he'd lost his access to the Link. He thought of his face, sinking in and out of the background on the train, and picked up the folder next to him. Several pages fell from it and onto the grimy footpath.

The top page was a diagram of a human arm, cut off halfway down the forearm. The radius and ulna were showing, along with a complex wiring diagram and a code snippet in some deprecated language Col couldn't read. On the bottom of the paper was a sketch of an Augmetic hand and half a forearm. Where the diagram ended, there was a compact set of concentric discs, into which arrows from the radius and ulna of the human arm fit. Several badly preserved notes were scribbled over the page, with hastily drawn pointers connecting the two drawings.

> *Silico-Steel amalgam should replicate nervous structure. All – tests ha– shown pos– reuptake.*

An arrow pointed from this note to a hatched circle covering a portion of the mechanical arm replacement.

> *Bone fusi– – plate. Timeframe?*

A crude sketch of a clock and a heavy underlining of the question mark. Pointing to the raw end of the broken arm with the radius and ulna exposed.

> *Integrat– MLA into chipset embedded. – should avoid – xternal training req–*

This one was a note on its own, and the most perplexing to Col. MLA, he assumed, stood for machine learning algorithm. It was an old technique which had been refined over the years, and which the Uplink was perfect for, because of its distributed power core and ability to build from minds, or real networks. This seemed to predate the Uplink in its current form – these documents featured the older version of the Uplink logo, a rubbery, glossy look fashionable with the other high-end research firms of the time. Machine learning back then was… was it something that a bionic limb would need? He didn't know.

Distracted from his immediate need to find the sanctuary, he looked at the next sheet down. It was a scrawled diary. The dates and years were blacked out, as was the signature at the bottom of the page. Crusted brown markings of age danced across it, leaving faded spots where the writing was illegible.

> ▇ ▇▇▇▇▇ ▇▇ – *Artificial arm isn't working. Sometimes, at random, I'll be able to force it to spasm, but it breaks again almost immediately. My fingers will close, and open again hours later.*
>
> ▇ ▇▇▇▇▇ ▇▇ – *Night sweats. Again. I've been having them every night for the last – ——— weeks. When I've taken my temperature it's been above – —— ut I'm trying not to be too concerned. Doctors seem to be confident.*
>
> ▇ ▇▇▇▇▇ ▇▇ – *It looks like my arm is beginning —— ——— —— ——— ———*
>
> ▇ ▇▇▇▇▇ ▇▇ – *I keep losing weight. I'm still eatin —— ——— - ——— — I'm still getting thinner. I've got a new nutrition plan. My new — ——— — that it might be because the Augmetics are consuming — ——— ———.*
>
> ▇ ▇▇▇▇▇ ▇▇ – *well, it took longer than expected. This morning it looks like I've gained*

'What are you doing?'

A shadow had crept over the page as Col read. He looked up and a fiery blaze appeared around Ariana's head as she blocked the sun. She leaned against the other end of the blockwork wall that Col was sitting on, looking vaguely annoyed at having found him scratching through old documents in an abandoned street. Col carefully bookmarked the old piece of paper and slid it back into the stack where he'd pulled it from, then looked at Ariana, bemused. Her face was in shadow.

'What are you doing here?' he asked, 'And how did you find me?' A slow clenching hand had gripped his heart, but he didn't quite understand why. The odds of Ariana showing up *here,* of all places, at the same time as him, made him wonder who this woman really was.

Ariana simply smiled.

'Come on,' she pressed. Her body still blocked Col from seeing the sun. 'We need to find that Sanctuary, and it'll be night before too long. You don't want to be out here after dark.'

'Wait,' Col said, 'how do you know about the Sanctuary?' He stood up and stepped back from her. He watched puffs of dust and decayed lime dance between the two of them. Ariana eyed him incredulously.

'Are we going to find this place or not?' she asked.

'Not until you tell me how you found out about it,' Col said, 'and how you found me here today.'

Ariana rolled her eyes. When she focused on Col again, her smile was laced with contempt.

'Come on, Colin. What are you doing? You're wasting time. Look at you, you're not doing well. We need to look after you, and the Sanctuary can help.' Her voice had taken on an almost preternatural smoothness, as though it wasn't interacting with the world around it.

Col took another step back, and Ariana walked toward him. She still blocked the sun, and for a moment her hair created a halo of fire around a black shadow. He didn't know what to make of her. She seemed to know more than she should. And what did he even know about her?

She'd shown up at the hospital and before he'd known it, she had become a part of his life. They'd met precious few times, but she was the only person he knew of that had gone through the same thing he had. And they wanted the same thing, didn't they? She was trying to get back into the

Uplink, he was trying to get back into the Uplink. She'd said she'd lost access to the Uplink, right?

Except no. He looked at her, and her exact words on the night they'd met came back to him. She'd said *I can't get into the Uplink*. He'd assumed she'd meant *I've lost access to the Uplink*.

What if she'd *never* had access to the Link?

He tried to think of something he knew about her. He'd told her about his sister. About Sal. About the Link, his job, his history. He'd told her about all the things he was doing to try to find Cass and get his access back, but what had she offered in return?

Every time he'd asked about her past, she'd gone quiet. She never shared any more details about herself. She never let him know what her plans were when they were apart. He'd assumed that her history was none of his business, and he'd inferred that she would be doing the same kind of searching as he was to get into the Link. But she'd never *told* him. He knew nothing about her except the colour of her hair and the depth of her black eyes.

Trying to remain calm, he asked himself if there was any way she could have found him. He'd spoken to the man at the apartment tower; he'd worked his way to this place. He hadn't spoken to her in between. Hadn't seen her.

He started to panic, and the smile on Ariana's face turned sardonic as she watched him reckon with something he wasn't ready to admit.

'You in there, Colin?' She was mocking him now. 'We'd better go, it might not be safe out here much longer. You look tired. Thirsty, too. You need the Sanctuary.'

Col gathered himself, turning first right, then left, then right again as he oriented himself with the memory map he'd made in his mind earlier. Without responding, he began to run down the street with the file in his hand. Ariana followed him, and her hair flashed red against the sunlight as it bounced from the sea wall. The word *psychosis* sprang to Col's mind. What was happening to him?

The pavement beat a steady rhythm through him as he ran away, but Ariana kept pace with him, still smiling and barely showing any effort. He turned the corner, the fiery air of the street lighting up his lungs as he sprinted the last few hundred metres to the Sanctuary.

If he hadn't known it was there, he'd have gone straight past it. The dust on the ground was sparser, and the concrete better taken care of than the surrounding suburb, but otherwise it looked like an abandoned office block, boarded up like the rest of the suburb. Behind him, Ariana was giving chase, but seemed unconcerned with keeping up with him, apparently content to simply force him onward. To push him. When he looked closely, he could see movement behind the tinted glass of the Sanctuary walls, people stepping in and out of view. From where he stood, they may as well have been ghosts.

He fell against the door, a semi-concealed panel made of frosted bulletproof glass, and knocked as loudly as he could. He could hear scuffling and whispered, commanding tones. Several pairs of feet pattered away as Col stood panting, waiting and trying not to panic. The paint was scratched and torn from the handle. The door leaf was held on a set of retrofitted hinges. Behind the darkened windows were solid metal bars, anchored into the concrete and brickwork.

The door clattered with the sound of a long sequence of locks coming undone, then swung open silently. A woman stood in the doorway. Col didn't notice any obvious augmentations at first, but there was a small, boxlike protrusion sticking out above her collarbone at the back. It had several differently shaped sockets in it, and a set of wires ran like veins under her skin from the connection. Col looked up to her face and saw a pair of sharp eyes hidden behind a greying fringe.

'Yeah?'

Col swallowed, trying to catch his breath as he spoke. 'My name is Colin Montgomery. I'm a – I was sent here by... I don't. Oh god, I don't know his name. He's in the old housing estate near the industrial zone. Can't stop walking. He told me to ask for Cynth. Please. I need to get in.' His eyes darted around, trying to focus on the woman in the doorway but failing, looking around for Ariana instead.

The woman didn't hesitate. Without any further questions, she opened the door fully and moved aside, gesturing for him to enter. Col hugged the folder to his body and turned around to see where Ariana had gone, but there was nobody behind him.

PART THREE

The other leaders and I met the other day. All the Sanctuaries within the city limits, coming together to discuss our latest news. Well, I say all of us. There's only four of us left. When people start an enterprise like a Sanctuary they have the right idea, but they burn out. Don't realise what it actually means to do the things we do, you know? When you haven't got access to anything, you haven't got access to <u>anything</u>, which means you gotta get it from places you <u>don't</u> have access to. I remember the realisation when your desire to help people like yourself, burned out and having the worst kind of go at life, has led you to breaking into the back room of a dispensary to steal medicine, presumably from others who also need it.

It's not a thing you like. It's a thing you get used to, becoming a thief and a crook and a criminal, but only so you can feed and house and comfort. Some of us can do it, you know? Deal with the constant, low-level fear of being found out. Of being taken and judged for trying to do what you're sure is the right thing, but which falls between law and morals. Only a few people can do it, and it's fewer than how many we need to do it.

Took a lot of effort to get the four of us together. More trouble than the last few times. When I was speaking to Bern beforehand, he mentioned something strange.

Apparently they're seeing Linkers in places we'd normally not. I asked what he meant, and he just shrugged. Old buildings, you know? Parts of the world that Outcasts have been able to co-opt and find a space of their own.

Before the Link, everyone had to go somewhere to do whatever it was they did with their day. Then after, those places fell into disrepair and disrepute. Once you could build a virtual office in the Link, real offices became too much of a burden for companies to maintain. So, you end up with a whole raft of buildings that just sat empty and unused.

Well, those places were _our_ places. For a long time. They're all bombed out, no elec, no heating. They're as shitty a place as you can expect to find, but it's where we usually go to find Outcasts. Fresh ones especially. They find these places and tend to hunker down, try to figure out what's happened to them. It's where I was, couple decades ago, sucking down solar and frying myself from the inside. Then they found me.

Bern found me, actually, him and his partner. She's dead now, and he's getting on, but they drew me up, unhooked me, then put me in a dark box until I stopped screaming for sunlight. That voice is still there, and it'll never go away, but I keep her quiet now. The terminals on my arm got duller as my mind got sharper.

Seeing Bern is always welcome. The quiet comfort of trust and the first time I remember feeling it. Clem, who runs the Sanctuary out west, is friendly and cordial, but I don't see him often.

And then there's Jake. His Sanctuary, such as it is, isn't far from mine. He makes you feel _observed_ in an uncomfortable way when you speak to him. Like he's taking measurements of some bacterial growth, and when he speaks, there's always an undertone of condescension.

When we met, we could see the strain on each other's faces. Except his. Jake stood straight and calm while Clem, Bern and I felt as though we were leaning against each other for support.

Apparently, instead of Outcasts in those hollow places, the places left behind from before, we were now seeing Linkers. I hadn't been on a search since the dispensary a few weeks earlier, but Bern and Clem both reported instances of Linkers, awake but unseeing, staring into the void, lying on the ground or sitting against a wall.

I'd heard the same from my runners, though in truth I'd only sent out one group in the last little while because in a much larger way than had ever happened before, the Outcasts were coming to <u>us</u>.

I mentioned this and got a general nod of assent from Bern and Clem. We'd had several dozen ex-Linkers find us in the last few weeks, usually directed to us by some well-meaning Outcast that knew about us. At this stage, we still think it's because of whatever's happened to the Linkers. They're pushing into the empty spaces, to do whatever it is they're doing, and Outcasts are coming out of the woodwork because they've got nowhere else to go.

Bern mentioned that he'd heard of a systems upgrade that may have gone wrong, and I'm inclined to believe him. It seems too convenient to see this kind of new Outcast behaviour at the same time as the Linkers are starting to change how they interact with the world.

In any event, we need more supplies. More food, more medicine, more clothes, more of the basics that a Sanctuary needs to do the things it does. Between us, we discussed some target locations.

I say <u>between us</u>. It was between me, Bern and Clem. We were trying to understand what was happening, and trying to deal with the impact it was having on our supply chains, our Sanctuaries, and our decision process. Jake, though? He went quiet after we started talking about the Linkers. While we talked about possible supply chains to get food and clothing, Jake simply waited, hard eyes staring at the three of us, as though he was weighing up something in his mind.

For over an hour, as we discussed the problems we were having, he never said a word.

— Cynth

CHAPTER 18

COLIN

The walls were covered with scrawled text in markers and pencils and charcoal and everything in between. Notated sketches, lewd remarks, stuttered conversations and graffiti. Much of it was incomprehensible, but Col recognised it as writing even if its meaning eluded him.

Col felt the sweat wick off him as he followed the woman into the depths of the Sanctuary. He was trying not to think about Ariana's sudden disappearance. Despite knowing what it meant, his mind wouldn't let him consider it, and so he watched the walls.

After being deprived of information from the Uplink for just a few days, the sight of so much text arranged in haphazard abandon, and so close, unnerved him. Gone was the blank nothing of the outside world. The words spilled through him faster than he could process. The walls shrank around him and the memory of Ariana's voice ran through his head. The corridor narrowed until he was sure that the woman walking in front of him wouldn't be able to fit. The words loomed and forced their way like an unchewed mouthful down his throat. His breath and heartbeat mingled in his ears, and he glanced to either side and saw glinting eyes following him from open doorways. None of them were Ariana's, but somehow they all were. The rooms were small. Glum, moody spaces that only existed to allow those inside to stare him down and judge him. He turned back to the silver-grey of the back of the woman's head.

His breathing sped up and formed a complex syncopation with their footsteps on the floor. He watched the woman's feet and tried to walk in step with her, tried to distract the front part of his mind. She wore a roughly cobbled pair of leather work boots and loose-fitting cargo pants that swished as she walked. Col watched and listened to the rhythm of the two sounds, the swish of the fabric and the thud of her feet on the bare concrete floor. They danced with his heartbeat and breathing: *swish-breathe-thud-heart-heart-swish-thud-breathe-heart-swish-heart-thud*. On and on and on down the unending hall while the febrile scrawl screeched down at him. The woman turned right and held a door open. Col was near apoplectic, trying to build a world for himself where Ariana's disappearance meant anything but what he knew it meant. Where had Ariana gone? Why had she left him alone? Why had he thought it was a better idea to come here instead of looking for Cass? He looked at the woman he'd followed in. Was her smile kind or mocking? He couldn't get enough air. The woman's face was in sharp focus but the world around her blurred. Her lips moved. She was asking if he was okay. When he didn't respond, she grasped his arm and pulled him roughly into the room.

The door slammed behind her, and she pushed him down into a charcoal-coloured iron chair. Col's ears were ringing, and she spoke again. Her voice clanged through Col's mind.

Do you know where you are? he parsed, seconds later. He didn't respond, instead bouncing his knees nervously. The cold chair bit into his back. He couldn't get comfortable. Tremors started in his hand.

'Do you know where you are? How you got here?' the voice repeated. Col looked up. The woman's face was all jeering angles and contemptuous lines of wrinkles. The corners of her mouth were twisted. Her eyes bore into his.

'Look around,' she said, 'tell me what you see.'

The room blurred around him. He couldn't identify any of it. He was stuck. He was trapped. He couldn't get away. The room was too small, and Ariana –

'Tell me what you see. Say it *out loud*.'

Something in the tone cut through the screaming in Col's skull. His frenetic movements slowed. She spoke again.

'Tell me what you see. Say it, one item at a time. Breathe in between each word.'

Col looked. 'Table. A big table. Writing, on the wall. Concrete floor. Unpolished,' he breathed, 'laundry tub? No, washing-up basin. Against the wall,' – the next breath came deeper, easier – 'an old, an old wardrobe? Next to the sink. Looks like – is that *real* timber?'

His breath was back. The twitching in his leg was subsiding. His muscles relaxed, and adrenaline began to flush out of his system. The sharpest edge of the panic attack was subsiding, but it threatened to rise up again and overwhelm him the moment he began to think about Ariana. Instead, he kept looking around, naming the things that he saw. A plethora of mismatched crockery was neatly arrayed in an old magazine stand that had been reappropriated as a dish rack. As his breath slowed to its normal cadence, he turned back to the woman.

The smile was kindly, turned up in the corners hopefully, and the jagged lines of the face were in aid of a hospitable, handsome appearance.

'You can stop naming things now. Just breathe.' The fluting cadence of her voice danced across him. 'That's it. You're okay.'

She squatted down next to him, watching carefully. Her white hair drifted over her face, and she pushed it away with a pitted and age-scarred hand. On the back of her wrist, Col could see the connection points for a solar cell. They were faded, rusted. The surrounding flesh was pink and healthy.

'My name's Cynth. I'm the matron of this Sanctuary. Pleased to meet you.'

Col was trying to get his bearings. Had they walked downstairs to this parlour? Or were they on the ground floor and away from windows? Behind the ancient timber wardrobe, the scrawled scratch marks and graffiti splayed across cracking concrete and remnants of wallpaper. The roof sagged, and lighting came not from ceiling luminaires but retrofitted posts. Crisscrossed chair legs nestled beneath the stainless-steel tabletop. It was onto one of these chairs that Cynth lowered herself. She clasped her hands together and waited patiently as Col worked his way up and out of the well of reactive darkness that had gripped him. He tried to speak, but she put up a hand. The terminals on her wrist glinted dully in the warm light.

'It's okay,' she said, 'take your time. There's no rush.'

Col breathed in and out again, trying to centre himself. Ariana was gone, and he pushed the thought away. That was something he'd have to confront later, but there was still an itch at the edge of his mind. He'd had something else with –

He jerked around as he realised that the folder was also gone. His heartbeat started to rise again before he saw the dilapidated cardboard file leaning against Cynth's chair.

'You dropped it on the way in,' she explained. Col hadn't noticed. 'Don't worry. Your belongings are still yours.' Her voice flowed with a soft sibilance that bled innocuously into itself. Col fought against his desire to relax further into it.

'I just – can I have the folder? Please?' he said.

Cynth held it out to him without hesitation. Col snatched it off her, then felt guilty.

'Oh, god.' He put his head in one hand and stared at the ground. His breath and heart were speeding up, and he grounded himself again by paying close attention to his surroundings. His thumb was hurting from gripping the folder.

'How are you feeling now?' It had been a few minutes since Cynth had last spoken. When Col finally raised his head and nodded, Cynth moved to the door and let someone else in.

There were only a few small Augmetics on the person who walked into the room. Replacement ears, sleek grey blocks with small strips of blue light at the top. They were barefoot and wearing loose-woven, long-sleeved clothing. They carried a small sack made of patchwork pieces sewn together.

They held their hand out, and for a moment Col was confused, before gladly shaking it, standing as he did so. He could feel the rough edge of their fingerprint against the back of his hand and calluses on the palms. He shook firmly, and they held as long as he did, before the welcoming look on their face gave way to an enquiring one. *How long were you planning on shaking hands for?*

Col let go with a start. Aside from a brief hug from Sal a few days ago, this was the first time anyone had touched him without ill intent in days. He drank in the feeling of skin on skin, appreciating it in a way that he hadn't before. The Uplink had provided the world with touch, only to take it away from him.

They smiled and placed the hand they'd just been shaking on their chest. 'Rory,' they said.

'Col.' Rory turned on a heel and indicated for Col to follow. Cynth stayed in the room, and Col felt her eyes on the back of his head. He held the folder in his hand.

Rory led Col to a communal bathroom. Lockers lined both walls, and a set of mirrors ran down the centre, with basins and work surfaces. An assortment of towels in various states of repair were folded neatly to one side of the room. There were many more either hanging up or splayed on the floor.

'Sorry about the mess,' Rory said, 'Got a lot more people in than we usually do.'

'Oh?' Col wasn't sure what else to say.

Rory nodded. 'Absolutely. I'm usually helping Cynth with the admin internally, but at the moment half my job seems to be laundry.' They laughed, 'It's not much of a Sanctuary if you can't get a clean towel, you know?'

Col supposed that was true enough. 'Why so many new people?' He suspected he already knew the answer. The lights around where Rory's ears should have been lit up as the sound of Col's voice hit them.

'We don't know exactly, but it's this upgrade. Some Linkers... it didn't work for them, I suppose. Same as happened to you. Same as happened to a bunch of people when the Link went live.'

Rory pulled the satchel off their back and tipped the contents onto the countertop. Toothpaste. A wooden-handled toothbrush. Soap. A stick of deodorant. They indicated a shower cubicle in the side of the room.

'All yours. I'll be outside to show you to your room afterward.' Rory gave him a thumbs-up and walked out to the corridor.

Col looked down at the file he still held in his hand. He went to place it at the end of the counter, then thought better of it. He stuffed it at the end of the row of basins, in a cupboard with a loose hinge, then made his way to the shower.

The warmth of the water hit his body. Far from the cold acid hiss of the rain in the city night, the water was luxurious and homely in a way he'd never experienced before. He felt the dirt and stink wash off him, replacing the grime of the outside world with the synthetic scent of the cheap soap in the cubicle. He closed his eyes and subsumed himself.

When he finally finished, he wrapped a towel around his waist and found Rory in the corridor.

'Can I have a razor?' He pointed to his face. Rory nodded and handed him a simple straight-edge scalpel.

'Sorry,' they said, 'sometimes we get people in here and we worry they're a danger. To themselves, I mean. So, we tend to keep sharps away from new Outcasts initially unless they ask.'

Col thanked them and returned to the mirror, digesting what he'd just been told. He'd only been out of the Uplink for a relatively short time, and he was already desperate and afraid, without even considering Ariana. His skin was pale, and he could see his ribs through it. His beard was patchy and coarse, and his skin sagged. He'd always been thin, but this was new. He looked half-starved.

His skin was still supple from the shower, and he watched the youth return to his face as he shaved the wastrel beard away.

When he walked out, he was dressed again, in a similar set of loose-fitting linens to Rory's. Rory smiled at him, then led him down the hall.

'Better?' they asked.

Colin almost cried at the simple kindness of the question.

The bedroom was as makeshift as the rest of the Sanctuary. Crude metal brackets held sheets of aging marine ply in place at the floor and ceiling. Light and murmured noises crept in through the cracks between the boards. Col hid the file under a steel table next to the door.

The bed was steel framed with a thin mattress and bedclothes cut from the same patchwork fabric as Rory, and now Col, wore. It groaned as Col sat on it, and sprang back quickly as he stood back up when Cynth entered the room.

'I need to talk to you, or someone. My sister is missing, and I –'

'You will,' Cynth interrupted him. 'You'll talk to me. Once you've rested.'

Col started to protest, but Cynth spoke over him.

'You're exhausted. I'm willing to bet that was your first shower in a few days.' Unconsciously, Col ran his hand over his freshly shaven face. 'You're lost. You're confused. You're upset. It's understandable, and it's normal. This Sanctuary is a safe place, and you're in good company. Most of the people who find their way here are in a similar place to you, and when you get up, I can explain more. But first you're going to rest, and then you're going to eat, and then we're going to talk about that' – she gestured to the file – 'and your sister, if that's what you want to talk about.'

With that, she left the room with Rory. It wasn't dark with the door closed; the space was lit from the gaps in the ply board at the top and bottom and edges of the room. It left the impression of a cube of light, with the bed in the middle.

Colin lay down and tried to calm himself. He was still trying to ignore the implications of Ariana's disappearance. Cass was still gone, but for some reason he'd followed the advice of the Aug in the tower to come to this place.

He hoped Cynth wasn't lying to him.

CHAPTER 19

The dusk was clotted. Muted. Cotton wool had been thrown over the horizon and blurred the line between the ground and the air. The hue of the sea blurred into that of the sky. To his left sat a desalination tower. It was sharp against the horizon. Inarguable. Unapologetic.

Col was trying to clear his head. He'd made his way from the Sanctuary to the causeway above the seawall to get some air. Below would have been a beach, some time ago. On extremely low tides, he supposed it still was, but nobody went there. The causeway was mostly deserted. Ahead of him, he could see a pair of Augs talking in one of the small alcoves that dotted the sea wall. Rusty echoes of sharp words drifted toward him as he trudged.

It had been several weeks since he'd entered the Sanctuary. The place, hidden and secretive though it was from the outside, was the first place he'd found that could relax even a little. He was expected to do a certain amount of scutwork, contribute to cleaning and cooking and the ongoing machinations that made a place like the Sanctuary work, but other than that he was left to his own devices. Cynth had even said to him that he was free to leave if he wanted or needed to, though he wasn't sure where else he'd go. So, he'd stayed, with the other Outcasts – he was still getting used to not calling them *Augs* – forming a community in the hole they'd built in the world. For people like him, that had lost their access to the Link, or people like Rory who'd never had it.

He'd learned fairly quickly that even mentioning the Link would get you ignored in the Sanctuary. The first night he'd been there he'd tried to ask Rory about it, but their eyes had gone dark, and they'd just said they didn't want to discuss it. It was a faux pas to talk about trying to re-enter it. So, his efforts had been reduced to the hours he could spend out of the Sanctuary, trying to understand what it was that had happened to him. He'd tried dispensaries, he'd tried to find a communal health service, he'd even gone back to the distribution centre again. This time, as soon as he'd mentioned he couldn't get into the Link, the facade of professionalism had dropped, and the threat of private police had left him scrambling to escape the place as fast as possible.

Seawater crashed against the sheer concrete wall, sending a rhythmic spray up at him. He shuddered and pulled his coat tighter to his chest. The tide was coming in, and the waves threatened to breach the walls.

Ariana, whatever she was, haunted him. She hadn't appeared again but that, somehow, made things worse. Having found out what she was, or at least the nature of her, he wanted to understand how to be rid of her. It felt as though she was now simply dormant, and she could appear again in his mind, to try to do whatever it was she did. Trick him? Change him? She'd been pushing him around, but he didn't understand *why*.

As he got nearer to the Augs, the gurgle of the sea dropped deeper along the concrete wall. The crash of the waves quelled slightly. He was lost in his thoughts, and didn't consciously recognise what had happened. His subconscious, however, was attuned to the soundscape around him, and the falter in the rhythm disquieted him even if he didn't know why.

Sal had disappeared. He had gone back to the Library, watching from what he thought was a safe distance, but he found he wasn't able to see the entrance without the taser-happy security forces seeing him. He'd waited outside her home, but all he'd ended up with was a cold ass from the concrete. The hours she worked were erratic, and if they were out of sync by even a minute or two, he would miss her. Half the time she'd be working on code from inside her capsule anyway, so it wasn't a given that she'd even head outside. After a week, he'd given up. He couldn't find it in himself to wait, watching the empty, twitching eyes of the people that walked past him.

'Linker!' One of the Augs was waving a metal hand to get Col's attention. The lull from the sea was beginning to dissipate, replaced by a guttural roar that spoke with the ocean's gravity. Col looked up to see an enormous wave about to hit the base of the sea wall, a freak harmonic set to flood over the side of the causeway.

'Grab a hold!' the Aug shouted as the water erupted onto to the dock. Too late, Col grabbed at the handrail beside him, but the immense press of hydraulic force knocked him backwards off his feet. He automatically gasped for breath, and spluttered as he was buffeted along the harsh bitumen. He felt the water rush past, then ease before falling the other way and drawing him back across the causeway. His foot got caught on something, and he recognised the feel of the cylindrical steel handrail. He shot his hand out and grasped at it, only just managing to hold himself around it as the wave tore at him and receded back into the ocean.

His legs were hanging over the sea wall, while his body was contorted around the handrail post. His mouth and lungs were filled with water, and he was wracked with wet coughs. He felt the hard grasp of fingers too strong for a human hand, and he was pulled back from the precipice and thrown roughly on the road.

'You 'right, mate?' the Aug asked. Col kept coughing, and turned his head to the side. Through salt-stung eyes he could see four feet, three in battered shoes, one built from broken servo motors and rusted metal. The pair of human feet had heels off the ground, crouching next to him. The mechanical hand that had grabbed him dropped into view.

'Yeah Kris, he's 'right,' said a second voice. Col spat out a mouthful of water. He made to roll over, but the unforgiving hand held him there.

'Stay on your side there, Linker,' Kris said. 'Don't go swallowin' the water. It's poison, yeah?'

Col nodded, and squeezed the words *thank you* out in a wordless gasp.

'No worries, mate. Best get up soon, though. Get down off the causeway, y'know. Tide's coming in and there's a bit more of that on the way. Worth makin' sure you're not in its way again when it gets here, y'know?'

The second voice sounded concerned. 'Ca'rn, let's go. Leave the Linker, he's good.'

Col breathed, and it hurt, but came a little easier. With a struggle, he sat up and wiped his eyes. The dusk was deepening quickly now, and the ocean was black, with crisp highlights on the top of the waves. He coughed again. His ribs hurt.

'You 'right?' the Aug asked again. Col nodded and gave a feeble thumbs-up. He saw the second Aug jerk his head in a *let's get out of here* motion, and they turned to go. After a few steps, the one with the mechanical hand turned back.

'Don't stay long. World don't care if you ain't in it.'

* * *

Early the following morning, Col jolted awake from a dark and dreamless sleep. The room gasped into view around him and threw his senses into sharp relief. His mind raced to catch up, but the room was uncanny and wrong. A strung-out ray of mid-morning sunlight limped through an open window – but his room in the Sanctuary had no windows.

The floor was a thick carpet weave, but as he turned his head it was the bare concrete, and now tiles. The sunlight, the sunlight that shouldn't be, crashed in a brash cry of contrast onto the foot of his bed. As the rest of his world coalesced around him, the shaft of sunlight stuttered. It pulled away, flickering and pulsing, and the room fell backward into the uniformly lit blandness of his room in the interior of the Sanctuary. Immediately, he tried to reach out with his mind, to see if this was a re-connection with the Uplink.

Cass?

But no, this was something different. As soon as he tried to extend his mind, he felt the familiar itch pushing against the front of his skull. It made him stop reaching before the pressure gave way to pain. As he watched and the sunlight faded to a constant uniform glow, a stain appeared on the wall. It was the colour of rusted metal, and it puckered onto the plaster wall like oxidised lichen. The rust pulsed and sputtered, and water began to sweat from the stain. It began to bead, starting from the centre in globules that gave a sickly sheen to the surface. Before long, the centre of the slick patch warped the otherwise uniform light around it, reflecting hemispherical rainbow patterns around the room.

Col threw his sheets off and walked toward it, hypnotised by the incursion into the room. The roar of the water from the causeway filled his mind and subsided. He gripped his arm where Kris had held it. The water kept expanding outward, and the centre of the rust patch began to drip. It ran in slow rivulets to the floor, where it sank and stained the bare tiles with the rust-coloured murk of the wall. The trickle ran faster and faster, and the wall began to leak from everywhere. The water formed a patina across the surface that shimmered and twisted. Col reached out to touch it. His hand slid through the water, and he watched it dance around his arm, carving a teardrop-shaped rent in the drizzling curtain. He ran his hand up and down, watching the warping, wefting shapes that the water threw up. It was a torrent now, and he could feel the wetness of the water, and the dryness of the wall.

The dryness of the wall.

A pressure on the front of his mind screamed at him. This wasn't real, but it *felt so real*.

'Ariana?' he called into the dark, wondering if the woman he'd hallucinated was building the world around him into a nightmare, a reminder of the dark moments as he'd been dragged over the edge of the causeway that day.

He could feel the water, see it flowing over his hand, but the wall behind was as dry as it had ever been. Something pushed on the inside of his head, and he winced as he struggled to reconcile the dissonant perception. The pressure built until it released like the snapping of a brittle twig, leaving him standing dumbstruck as the water began to rise up his bare feet. The impossible, lapping, liminal line between the wet and dry, the crisp delineation of the water – it crept up his feet and began to fill the room. It made his mind scream. He watched the azure liquid pool ever higher.

A stream erupted from some unseen porosity in the wall, foaming and flecking, crusading down a waterfall. The water level in the room rose, and Col turned to move to the door. It was like running in a dream; he was gripped on all sides by something he saw but did not feel, inhibiting him from reaching the closed door. He tried to cry out, but nothing happened. His mouth refused to open in shock or terror. The water rose to his hips and he lost all ability to move. He could feel the torrent on his skin, building into a maelstrom that was rising ever faster and higher. Before long, he was standing rooted to the floor, holding his head above the roiling surface, desperate for air, but it was no help. He was submerged, and his vision blurred and took on a rusted azure tint. He held his breath.

Stop it! Ariana, stop! I can't breathe! But he couldn't speak, he couldn't get words out through the inundation.

This isn't real, he told himself, and opened his mouth to take a breath of the air that he knew was there. Immediately he was overcome by the sick feeling of suffocation, of immersion within and without. He panicked, gagging silently as the water that wasn't there invaded his lungs, expelled the scant oxygen within and began to choke him. It held him in place. Dull pain turned into a spike in the chest, which turned into smoking desperation as he fought to draw every ounce of oxygen from his final breath. Fire burned inside him, screaming to escape, a raw wound. His vision began to blur and darken around the edges, and he saw a flame turn into Ariana's face, with the same contemptuous smile she'd worn the last time he saw her.

The flame leapt from his bluing lips. It tore through the water, setting it afire. The room erupted in a chaotic blur of orange-red dancing forms. Where the water had taken several minutes to overtake Col and subsume him, the fire consumed the water with shocking immediacy, and just as the false liquid that bore no moisture, the flame bore no heat. The water didn't steam as it disappeared into the inferno. The flame, bereft of its unlikely fuel source, disappeared along with it, leaving Col reeling in the room as his consciousness and ability to breathe returned.

He coughed and sputtered and fell on the floor, expelling the last few mouthfuls of the not-water from his lungs. Before his eyes, he watched it spread among unreal carpet filaments, darkening them before being engulfed by small fireworks that stung his eyes.

He breathed heavily, concentrating on the feeling of the carpet beneath his fingertips, concentrating on the texture and the pattern. He forced it away and beneath it was the cool concrete he knew was there.

Real.

This was real. The room was dry. Dark. The sunlight he'd seen wasn't real, and neither was the drenching water nor the flash of flame. The floor was clean but slightly dusty, and tiny holes and rough patches worn by age and time were all through it. The rusted spot on the wall was gone, and the walls were still cold and dark. Yes. This was his room. This was real. This was right. And Ariana was gone.

He was almost sure of it, but then the light in the room shifted, and a flickering set of forms coalesced around him. They blurred and bent the light, but never resolved. He had the *sense* of a shape crystallising, an entity. Reaching out through an Uplink connection he'd thought he no longer had.

'Who is it?' He spoke softly, trying to blend his voice into the soundscape of the building. The insurrection of whatever sound he was hearing became a separate thing, one he could neither latch onto nor ignore. The crystallising form was *almost* a person.

Col, it said, *can you hear me?*

'I hear you,' he murmured, 'how do you know my name?' He followed the voice around the room. It wasn't Ariana; this was someone else, more familiar. The fractious and near-invisible form broke the edges of the lights at the boundaries of his sanctuary. Looking straight at it made it disappear, like a glass bead in a vase of water. He crept around it, casting askance glances in its direction.

Whatever the shape was, it was following him.

Reach out to me.

It wanted him to reach out through the Uplink. Col shook his head, 'I can't. I can't. What do you want? Who are you?' His mind began to burn. He pressed his hands to his head and felt the burgeoning connective ticks of the Uplink again through the pain.

Reach out, it said again. The words weren't sounds so much as *ideas* pressed like cold iron into his brain. This time, though, they had a timbre. A warm, smooth impression.

His mind was beginning to tingle with the thought that something might be going wrong with him again, like in the Library when all this had started.

Col.

'How do you know my name?' he demanded.

Reach, it demanded, pressing urgently on his mind to make him understand. The disjoint in the room careened slightly as the thing's intent, which had started in fits and jumps, became firmer. It had become a forceful push into the burning itch at the front of his mind.

He gave in. With the stagnant part of his mind that had been unable to connect with the Uplink since the accident, he reached out to whatever the entity was.

The glowing white edges of the room leapt into the darkness of the space until almost the entire room resonated with false brightness. The crystalline figure in the centre shattered the brilliance into myriad rainbows, which bent and flashed in the space in front of him. Slowly, the refracted light turned into shapes and colours, which burst and made the white surrounding the rest of the room shrink. Col put his arm up to hide his eyes. When he looked back the white nothing in the room had gone, and the rainbows had pulled and warped into the shape of a woman. He couldn't pick out everything in the features and clothing, but what he saw was enough. Familiarity crept over him. A connection.

His sister.

'Col!' Cass screamed, then another flash of light. Col jumped forward, reaching out to grab her, but it was too late.

She was gone.

CHAPTER 20

CASS

Cass woke up groggy.

The sedative they'd given her clearly hadn't been delivered with any care for the aftereffects. The inside of her mouth tasted rancid, and it was a few minutes before her body responded as she tried to move again. The room around her blurred into vision. She was back in her cell. Once she could move a little, she tried to sit up, rising only a few centimetres before something brought her to a stop.

She looked down at her wrists and groaned. Handcuffs held her to the bare aluminium sides of the cot.

Fear bit at the back of her throat as she realised that the escape attempt had only made things worse. She began to pull against the handcuffs in the vain hope that the sides of the cot would give way before her wrists or her strength did. The cuffs pressed, and hot spikes of pain ran through her wrists. Eventually it became too much, and she lay back, allowing the fire to reduce to a dull ache that spread through her bones and overwhelmed her fear. Her wrists were raw and slick with either sweat or blood, but she couldn't look down properly to see.

The sole, dangling light globe hung limp over her, and she could still see the watermark on the wall. She searched for the wad of paper she'd left there before her escape attempt. It had been at the base of the mark before, but she couldn't see it. She squinted, wondering if it was just the poor orange light and her restricted view. Or maybe it had fallen from the wall entirely.

She started searching in the watermark and there it was. The mark was moving. Expanding into the space to join her. For a moment, the spot on the wall reached out, as though it was Colin calling to her and trying to find her. It was only for a moment, and as she wondered at the sensation reality snapped back, and she was just looking at the damp mark on the wall again.

Relaxing away from her restraints, she lay back in the gloom and tried to reach out to Colin. Her mind pushed, and this time *something* happened. Before she'd only been able to send inchoate snapshots of data untethered to meaning. This time she found that the connection request got through, even if it was incomplete, a stain filtering through blotting paper. An insensible caricature of her intent.

She continued to push out toward her brother, to let him know where she was, until eventually the dull ache in her bones became all she knew, and she drifted to sleep.

* * *

Harsh light woke her as three Augs entered the room. One was smaller than the others. Only a series of scars on the right side of her neck and down her arm betrayed her as an Aug.

The other two lurched into the room behind her, and a bleak sense of familiarity sank down over Cass. The hot breath against her. The flickering vidfeed of a creature outside her brother's library. Hulking metal frames where their shoulders had once been. Their legs were gone from the hip downward and replaced with the backwards knees of a jackal, writ in proportions that were too short for the torsos they supported. Their arms, in contrast, gave them the appearance of elongated metal gorillas. Hunched sentinels, watching her through a faceful of wires and lights that obscured what remained of their features.

The third Aug clicked her fingers contemptuously. The other two growled, an unreal binary noise that scraped against the inside of Cass's ears. They stalked off to stand guard at either side of the door. The third walked toward Cass, and she began to sweat. Her skin flushed with blood and her breath came in sharp bursts, as though affirming her humanity against the automatons in front of her.

They had food. It was a small container holding a plate of green-grey slime and a cup of water. The Aug placed it at the base of the cot, then made her way to the handcuffs, undoing them before stepping back.

Cass sat up and rubbed her right wrist with her left hand. She stared at the Aug. It stared back, then shifted its attention to the plate. It gestured for Cass to eat. She considered for a moment. The food had a greasy sheen, as did the water. She looked back at the Aug.

She placed her foot on the tray. With a slow, deliberate calm, she pushed it, until all at once the cell rang out with the clattering noise of spilled food and broken crockery. All the while, Cass stared the lead Aug in the eyes. Behind it, the two creatures she thought of as the Sentinels bristled. The Aug held up her hand to silence them, holding Cass's stare. The moment dragged.

Finally, the Aug shrugged. She touched something in her hand, and the Sentinels lit up. Loping forward on their overlong front limbs, they arrived at the cot faster than Cass was able to process. They grabbed her limbs and held her in place as the third Aug handcuffed her again. Cass didn't struggle this time. She knew their strength.

As soon as they were out of the room, she reached out to Col, and checked the watermark on the wall.

Something *was* happening when she reached out. There was still no response, but the mess in her mind would resolve into something like a connection confirmation. The same wasn't true of anyone else she tried to contact; those failed and left a sandpaper itch on the inside of her head. With Col, it felt more like digging through a tank full of mud, trying to touch the glass at the bottom. Each time she tried, she scraped away a little more of the muck.

She looked at the wall. The watermark had grown again. Was she imagining it? Did the mark on the wall grow as she felt closer to contacting her brother?

She slept, and woke, and tried again, and then the Augs would come to feed her and the process would repeat. For days, the process repeated. Each time she reached, it got a little easier. Each time she woke, the watermark had spread a little further. She dreamed of waves spilling into the room, a wicked maelstrom dragging her to safety, only to wake as the waters receded once again in cold silence.

She didn't know what time it was, but she reached out to Col, more from habit than anything else. This time something happened, and the shape on the wall changed; a hole appeared and a few drops of the water on the other side spilled through. She saw the ghost of Col's form, burbling and white edged. It wasn't a full connection, but it was close.

'Col, can you hear me?' she whispered, despite her solitude. The wraith-like form mouthed something, but no sound came out.

Come on, she thought, then out loud, 'Reach out to me.'

The form danced around her sphere of vision and moved further away. She followed it as best she could to maintain contact, straining to hold on to the mental connection as she did so. The shape tried to talk again, then held its hands to its head.

'Reach out,' she urged. Something hardened, and a series of ripples fled from the edges of the watermark on the wall. They danced through nothing and struck the wisps of Col's form, and he began to thicken, growing viscous and firm.

The impression of the words *I can't* echoed through the Link. Cass reached out and grasped them, the touch of the idea translating to words in her mind.

Something was working!

'Col!' She was too loud. She risked a glance at the door.

How do you know my name?

She was transmitting her Ident on the connection request. It should have been there, on his Link. He should *know*.

'Reach.' *Come on, Col. I need you.* The effort was making her tense her arms. The restraints bit into her wrists. She was tiring out. The days and weeks of little water and less food had sapped her strength. Despite this, Col's form began to coalesce. Its liquid edges disappeared, and the white tank vanished to become the room Col was standing in. It blended with her own cell, and together they condensed into a shell of warm flat surfaces and cold edges. Col sat in front of her on a bed she didn't recognise.

As the form became more cogent, the door at the end of the cell opened. Her brother and the bed floated in front of her, still obscured by a vague rippling affectation. The whirring clank of the two Sentinels shattered her perception. Their metallic frames prowled into view, and the buzz of their voices screeched in alarm at the sight of her staring blankly into space, wrists pulled up against the edge of the handcuffs on the cot. The third Aug rushed into the room after them, throwing her tray of food to the ground. It motioned the Sentinels forward.

Cass pushed out with her mind in a desperate attempt to breach the block in the Link. Col's features sharpened and began to glow, but she still couldn't see her brother's face. She pushed again, trying to send something, *anything* through that would get him to understand, but nothing was working the way it should. Everything was stifled and muted. The Aug pulled a syringe from a pocket on its vest, and Cass thrashed again. *Not the needle, not again.* The Sentinels lunged forward. Cass tried to escape, but she had nowhere to go with the restraints holding her down. She saw the needle glow in the air, lining up with the shine from Col's connection. The enormous arms held her still once more, and the Aug pushed the needle into her neck. Everything started to fade, far too fast.

'Col!' she screamed. Her brother was gone, and the last thing she remembered was two human eyes and four glowing bulbs staring down at her.

CHAPTER 21

COLIN

'Cass? *Cass!*' Col spun around, trying to force the connection to come back. There must have been two visions. There was no question in his mind that this second one, when he'd heard the sound of his sister's voice, was real. She had reached out to him, connected, and disappeared. He searched the fried part of his mind he used to connect to the Uplink, only to find a burning itch again. He tried to reach out to someone else. *Sal*, he thought, and pushed his thoughts toward her instead of his sister. The itch changed. It switched from a soft insistence to a burning pain, and he clapped his hands to his forehead in the dark and closed off the connection attempt.

The inundation was a nightmare he knew he'd have to confront eventually. Ariana lurked beneath that image, haunting him like fire beneath the waves, but he pushed the thought aside.

He knew it wasn't any good to call her name. Cass wasn't there, and the connection was dead. His yelling was as futile as it was cathartic and pointless and painful. He screeched her name into the dead air.

The rest of the repurposed office building had fallen still and silent, listening to Col's cries. The flimsy walls flexed as the door opened, and white light poured through the aperture. The hooked end of a crude metal arm gripped the door handle. It wasn't a high-tech Augmetic, nor did it resemble the detailed diagrams in the file Col had found in the old man's hovel. The hook was welded to a complex series of pistons and actuators which were for the most part frozen with grime and detritus. Only the joint in the elbow still bore the oil-slick shine of well-maintained machinery. The man eyed Col cautiously.

'You alright?' His expression was open, concerned.

Col's throat was sore. How loudly had he been shouting? 'I think I need to talk to someone.'

The man didn't respond, just stood back from the door and extended his arm, hook and all, motioning for Col to head out. The corridor, which weeks ago had loomed violently at him, was now benign. The graffiti still scrawled the walls, but it seemed less oppressive.

His guide didn't speak, simply walked on and eventually stopped outside another room made of the same cheap ply board as Col's. The door scraped a well-worn arc in the floor of a makeshift anteroom where Rory worked quietly at a desk. Their head was down, as they scratched confidently at a small piece of paper. The paper was rough and pulpy, and the ink from their pen soaked in uneven blotches.

Col's guide stepped back, and Col heard the scrape of the door as it closed. He watched Rory for a moment, waiting for them to respond to his entrance, before remembering their ears, machine replacements for the ones they'd been born with. The smooth pieces of steel were attached to the side of their head, and the blue activation lights were dark. They couldn't hear anything. Col shuffled forward and waved to get their attention.

Rory looked up and smiled, then pressed a button on one of their ears, which lit up.

'Here to see Cynth?' they said, standing up and walking to a second door. Col could hear murmurs for a few moments before Rory walked back through.

'She can see you now,' they said, sitting down again and pressing their ear. The lights turned off, and they bent back to their paperwork. Col stepped into the office.

The cleanliness of the walls came as a shock. His eyes had gotten used to everything in the building being covered in graffiti. Either that or, like his room, not well lit enough to discern. Cynth's office was a pure white drop in the chaos that surrounded it. Two huge, mismatched shelving units heaving with books, papers and files were pushed against one wall, while a sideboard on the other displayed a small array of old trinkets. A half-broken shoe tree. Gardening gloves surrounded by candles. A cracked magnifying glass. A toy drum. A recipe book on a stand, opened to a torn central page.

Cynth sat behind a steel-framed desk topped with rockcrete. She looked up and beckoned him over.

'Colin.' Her eyes creased in concern. Col took the sturdier-looking of two armless seats tucked into the edge of the desk. 'What's happening? You seem upset.'

'Yeah. I was in my room just now and...' He didn't know where to start. Cass? Ariana? 'When I arrived here, in the Sanctuary, did you see someone with me?'

Col didn't have much hope. On the slightest chance that Ariana wasn't some hallucination, some vision or something, he had to ask. If Cynth *had* seen someone, it might stop him feeling so hunted. As it was, he was still waiting for Ariana to appear at any moment and try to do whatever it was she was doing. When he'd entered, Ariana had been *right there*. There was no way she'd been able to get out of sight. Cynth would have been *looking at her*.

Cynth's eyebrows rose. 'See someone?'

'Never mind,' Col swallowed. His mouth was suddenly dry, and he couldn't concentrate. Cynth didn't move, just continued watching him, waiting patiently for him to regather his thoughts. 'I suppose you know that I can't access the Uplink?' he finally managed to choke out.

Cynth cracked a wry smile. 'That isn't unusual around here,' she tapped the side of her own head, 'but go on.'

Col nodded, 'I suppose not. But I used to be able to, before the Upgrade.'

'The Touch Upgrade.' Cynth nodded. 'Again, you're hardly the only one. We've had a new bunch of Outcasts coming in. Other Sanctuaries, too. We have suspicions as to why, but it's all pretty locked down.'

Col remembered the man walking in the tower block. *There's Bern, but I think they're full up. Haven't heard from Jake.* So, there was a network of these places. Places for the outcasts from the Uplink to go.

'Okay,' Col said, 'I'm going to tell you what's been happening to me. I'm going to tell you what I know.' He explained what had happened, how he'd lost his access. He told her about the ghosts of his sister that kept appearing. 'I'm getting things that *feel* like Uplink communications,' he explained, 'like... a few days ago, I was on the edge of sleep. Sleeping rough, you know, and this shadow appeared. I was so confused, and dead tired, scared and pressed between two pieces of concrete... I don't really know whether it was real.' He shivered as he recalled the shape of the entity, unbound, flooding through the veins of existence. 'It felt like, I don't know, the concept of my own name was being pressed into my head. Does that make sense?'

The simple intimacy of Cynth's eye contact made Col mildly uncomfortable. Unlike the meetings in the Uplink panopticon, where the directness and closeness were a trick of geometry in the false space, this was a deliberate and careful consideration of a single person, one on one. He wasn't used to it.

'Anyway,' Col continued, 'just then, I had another vision, I guess you could call it. Well, it was two, but the second one was...' Col described the feeling, the change in the light, and the rainbow that had coalesced into the room, turning into his sister before vanishing.

He leaned forward in his chair and pressed a hand to his head, as though to pull the sensation out with his hands and show it to her. 'I mean, it *felt* like an Uplink connection. I had to push with that extrasensory, you know,' he pointed to the back of his head, 'that part of your brain that you activate when you make a Link? It doesn't feel right now. It itches and burns when I try to make connections. But,' he hadn't realised how fast he'd been breathing, 'I think that for some reason, It *almost* works when I try to connect with Cass.'

Cynth was silent for a moment. 'Can you connect with anyone else?'

Col shrugged, shook his head, then shrugged again. His left leg began to twitch and bounce against the cold concrete of the floor. The shelves trembled in time with his shaking.

'When I try to contact Cass, I can feel the discomfort, but I can stand it. When I try to reach out to a friend, it's like my mind is on fire. I can't hold onto it for very long.'

Cynth leaned forward. 'Are you and your sister close?'

'Yes,' Col said, 'we were, before she went missing.'

After a moment, Cynth walked to the open door, and had a rapid and silent conversation in sign with Rory. Concern spread across her features as the conversation wore on. The signing grew more frantic, and finally Cynth put her hand up in a placating gesture.

The room was cold. Though there was a window above Cynth's display shelf, the tint was too dark for it to be anything more than a hint in the room, and it bore no warmth.

Instead, it bounced around a chiaroscuro courtyard of spent soil and bituminous tar, like it was a prisoner.

'Colin, do you think your sister could be in danger?' Cynth said, startling Col.

He nodded. 'Her place was... It didn't look like she'd planned to leave it empty. And she, well, it *feels* like she keeps trying to contact me.'

'Here's what I want to you to do.' Cynth walked back to her desk. 'I've never had access to the Uplink, so I don't know what it is I'm describing, but I want you to try to keep the line open. Can you do that?'

Col nodded again, 'I think so. I'm not sure if the discomfort will become too much.'

'Okay. Do what you can. Keep yourself open to her communications as much as possible.'

'What do you think is happening?'

Cynth shook her head. 'I don't know. And neither does Rory. Neither of us has ever had the ability to access the Uplink. But for whatever reason, she's trying to reach you. I think that means your ability to communicate with her has been retained to some extent. Because of some convergence of will, similarity of brain architecture, whatever it is. But if she does contact you again, ask where she is. Before anything else, ask where she is.'

CHAPTER 22

As he returned to his room, Col pushed his mind against itself, trying to mend whatever had happened to his receptors when the Uplink had broken them. He was trying to get back in contact with Cass, and at the same time trying to avoid thinking of Ariana.

Col sat on the small cot, trying again to reach out to Cass. The caressing tingle of connection tickled the inside of his brain. Futile, like trying to light a fire with damp twigs and clammy hands. It became hypnotic to force himself back, to bear the discomfort that kept telling him to stop. The minor itch built up with each attempt, growing from a minor itch into an inflamed scab that hurt to touch.

Before long, sweat was soaking into his clothing. The push back into the pain became harder each time. The room disappeared around him as he concentrated his will on attempting the connection. Each failure seemed inevitable.

Every dozen or so attempts he would stop for a short while, drink some water and try to focus on reality, but each time he did the dancing image of Ariana's face, her vibrant red hair and aching black eyes, would rise unbidden to his mind and he'd face a different discomfort. His eyelids began to droop. He shuddered with each new connection attempt. He felt an overwhelming urge to scratch the itch behind his eyes, to claw at his brain with his fingernails.

Finally, exhausted, he closed his eyes. His shirt was a mire of cold sweat, his mind scrambled by a feeling of abrasive heat. Knowing that all he could do was try again, he slipped into a fitful and uneasy sleep in the glowing dark of his room. His sister's face blended into Ariana's, smirking with contempt, and both disappeared.

* * *

Hours later, Col woke up. The corridor was filled with the sounds of the Outcasts. They walked and whirred and clanked and chattered with electronic and mechanical sounds that weren't quite drowned out by the conversations they were having with one another, all heading in the same direction, toward the food hall.

Col made his way into the throng, still waking up. As he glanced around, he could have sworn he saw Ariana's face in the crowd. Every time, he did a double-take, and it wasn't her, just another Outcast heading to the dining hall where he'd first met Cynth and Rory.

When he'd first arrived, he'd been shocked at the variety of people he'd never seen before. The range of augmentations, affectations, and implants he saw staggered him. Some were fairly minor, like Rory's ears. Some had prosthetic limbs, or rudimentary implants like chip readers, or worn-down solar cells like Cynth. Still others seemed more machine than human. Huge, hulking armatures built around cages that held what remained of their organic forms. Atrophied muscle sat, stolid, nothing more than a spirit driving a machine. Cables and wires and digital and crystal displays protruded haphazardly from makeshift steel armour. Some people had a stylised look – the augmentations were sleek, well wrought, and sank into the skin in a relatively successful imitation of human form. Others deliberately flaunted their metallic, mechanical bodies, their humanity hidden as though it was a relic of a shameful past.

Col poured himself a dark broth full of strong-smelling protein packs and a large chunk of a slimy dumpling. He took it to the empty end of a table and sat down alone. He was still processing whatever had happened in his room, and recovering from trying to connect to the Link. He didn't feel much like talking.

The room was only just big enough to hold the mass of Augmented humanity within it. A small group of children played in one corner. They took turns picking up large chunks of charcoal and adding nonsensical glyphs to the lower half of the wall. They were nodding or shaking their heads as though they were holding a meeting, with serious looks on their small faces. Every now and then, they'd take the charcoal and add more marks, chattering all the while. Closer to Col, he saw Cynth and two adults having a similar interaction, writing a more cogent set of shapes and instructions in white chalk.

Col sat, listening to the scrape of chairs, the ring of laughter and the bright sound of conversations as they crowded over one another. In the weeks he'd been here, the Outcasts had started to treat him differently. They were still careful; as a fresh Outcast with no Augmetics there was no guarantee he'd stay in the Sanctuary long, so the conversations had been short. Not unfriendly, but with none of the warmth of potential friendship. He had noticed that people looked at him differently depending on their age. The younger ones, his age or younger, were merely curious or uninterested. They didn't smile, but they held his gaze when he caught their eye.

The older ones were different. There were only half a dozen or so in the hall that were older than sixty, at a guess. All of them were men, and their expressions grew dark whenever they saw Col. Their curiosity gave way to a grim, set jaw. If he caught them looking at him, their shoulders would tighten, and they'd look away, anywhere else but at the small, quiet man at the lonely end of the hall. Col suspected he knew why. Some of them had been here for years. Why would they trust someone who still looked like a Linker, one of the people who drove the Sanctuary to exist? These Outcasts probably remembered the time before the Link; knew what they'd lost.

As Col mused on this, he saw a familiar face. Rather, he saw a familiar metal hand at the other side of the hall. The man's hair sat limp and long over his face, and pearl-white teeth shone out of dark-brown features. The memory of the wave and the hand grabbing him with a 'You 'right, mate?' ran through his mind. Colin stood up and hailed him, and the Outcast smiled quietly and headed toward him, stepping over the bench to sit across from Col.

'Hey, found your way to a nicer place than the sea wall, cobber?' He grinned at Col, but there was a hesitance to it. The man was worried about something.

Col tapped the side of his head. 'Seems so.' He racked his memory from the day at the sea wall, trying to remember the name he'd heard as he'd been spluttering on the ground. 'It's Kris, right?'

The man's tight smile widened slightly. 'That's the one, mate. Surprised the water didn't wash my name out of your mouth! And yourself?'

'Col,' he said, then gestured at the room. 'Lot of people here. Do you just let anyone in?'

Kris shook his head. 'Nah, not anyone. We try not to let the Linkers in. Sometimes it's hard, 'cause you know,' – he pointed at Col – 'you look like a Linker. But you're not, are you?'

Col shook his head.

'So yeah, sometimes they stumble in here by accident. We don't tell about this place, yeah?' He was asking a question as much as stating a fact.

'Yeah,' Col said, then felt unsure of himself. 'I mean, no. I won't tell anyone.'

Kris seemed satisfied, and Col asked, 'Where's your friend? The one who helped me at the sea wall?'

Kris's smile faltered and disappeared. His face grew dark, and he stared across the table at Col.

'Ah, man. Me boy, his leg stopped working, so he had to go get a new fit. Went to Jake. I told him not to go.'

Jake, Col thought. It seemed like that name kept coming up. He'd heard it from the man in the tower. He'd heard Cynth say the name, and now Kris.

'A new fit?' Col asked, putting the name to the back of his mind. 'What does that mean?'

'Ah, y'know, like a retrofit. When you got metal bits in your body you need to look after 'em,' Kris said, then gestured around at the Sanctuary. 'This place looks after as many of us best they can, but you know, it's only able to do so much. There's plenty of places only too happy to take on Outcasts to help 'em work. Help 'em get a job. You follow me?' He waved his metal hand again. 'And they're specialist jobs, right? Hand like this can do a lot more labour than a soft Linker hand.' He snapped two of the fingers shut to demonstrate. Col nodded, remembering the firmness of its grip when he'd been rescued on the sea wall.

'So, we sign up for these "special jobs". They're the only jobs we can get, 'cause most other stuff you need to be a Linker for. We sign on, we get the job. If we have Augmetics already, all's well. If not, well, they can help, can't they? They can do surgery for us, whatever. New hand, new memory unit, power connectors, the whole bit.' Col felt a string tightening around his heart as Kris talked.

'Problem is, it's easier to fit a new hand and find a new Outcast to drive it than it is to fix one that's broken, isn't it? So, you get this,' Kris put his hand up again and began to flex each finger, one at a time. The index and third finger didn't work, and a pair of hydraulic pistons flicked uselessly back and forth, having fallen out of their housings. 'If you had an augmentation before you got the job, you just get fired. If you got surgery, well, you gotta pay 'em back, and now you're out of work.'

Col was horrified. 'So, what happens then?'

Kris's smile returned, wry and drained. 'If you owe 'em money, well, they gotta get their pound of flesh, if you take my meaning. You always end up paying 'em back somehow.'

Col blanched. 'But your friend already had a false foot, so presumably this Jake guy didn't own him?'

Kris shook his head. 'Nah, he wasn't being shook down or nothin'. His foot broke ages ago and he was just here. But the metal started buggering up on him. Rusting. Oil leaking. Stuff like that, getting into his blood. Making him sick. He had to go find a replacement part. Jake's place has them, but it's not a good place, you know?'

'Why not?'

Kris looked uncomfortable. 'Oh, you hear stories. People getting new parts, and they go strange. Forget stuff, or their new limbs work worse than the old ones. Worse stuff than that, even. You gotta be desperate to go there, you know. It's just that at some point, most of us get desperate.' Kris stared at the table for a moment. 'Jacko? He got desperate. Now he's gone.'

For the next few minutes, he and Col said nothing to one another, just ate quietly. Col tried not to look around the room, wondering which of these people would be the next to fall into desperation.

CHAPTER 23

He'd been going to Sal's hab at the end of the day regularly, hoping that their paths would cross. Initially he'd wanted to see if she'd contacted Cass, but he was less and less hopeful of that. Now, he just wanted to see her. It had been weeks now, and no matter how long he stayed she'd neither left nor come home when he'd been there.

Two streets from Sal's there was a line of shopfronts, only a handful still in use. They were all selling the kind of unimpressive takeaway fare you'd purchase when you didn't expect too much from the rest of your evening. Cheap carbohydrate- and oil-rich concoctions made to approximate the taste of charcoal rotisseries and exotic ingredients that no longer existed. Most of the stores were closed, boarded up with plyfoam, water-stained and weathered. Col walked past the long row, ducking quickly between the eaves to avoid the sheeting rain.

He'd bought food from this row of shops, back when he had access to the Link. At the time, the emptiness of the rest of the row was just a fact. Now the hollow spaces behind the storefronts echoed as he passed, resonance behind the boards thrumming through him. The downbeat of the rain danced a cold dirge on the pavement for these businesses that had been drowned by the Uplink.

Every few minutes, he reached out to Cass. The itch at the back of his mind burned, but he didn't wear himself out as much if he didn't do it constantly. If she was there, she would answer.

She didn't.

One of the empty shopfronts had been broken into. The plyfoam was hacked away and the glass behind it was shattered and spread across the ground. It crunched beneath his feet as he walked past. Inside, he could hear the muffled grunts and groans of a small group of people, and the sibilant shifting of their clothes as they moved. He sped up, walking past and trying not to glance at a small group of people he saw lying on the floor from the corner of his eye. As he looked away, a movement across the road caught his eye; there was Sal, hunched over and shuffling through the downpour.

He couldn't believe it. For so long, nothing, and now here she was. She had a hood pulled over her head to protect from the weather, but he knew her by her gait.

'Sal!' He ran toward her. She didn't seem to hear him calling her name. The rain was drumming around them, but he thought he was shouting loudly enough to be heard. As he ran, he felt the stink of his sweat seep out of the inner lining of his coat.

As he drew closer, he saw that she was muttering to herself. Her arms were twitching and her eyes darted around at things unseen. Again, he found himself wondering if he'd been like that when he was a Linker. He shouted her name a final time, and this time she looked up.

'Who is it?' Sal's voice was cracked and rasping. Her face was hidden in the shadow of her hood, obscured by the deluge.

'It's me,' Col said. Sal stared at him blankly for a moment.

'Col? I – whoa. Oh my God. Come inside, come to my place.'

They walked the final metres to the stairs to her hab complex. The door opened immediately via Sal's Ident. Col followed her briskly down the hall to her hab. The inner door made a heavy snap as the lock released. She walked into the hab, pulling her hood off as she held the door open with her foot. Col pulled his coat off, then followed her into the room.

When he finally got a look at her, he felt a sharp dread flood through his sense of relief.

Her hair was limp. Cold, shiny beads of sweat hung over her unkempt brow. She smiled, and Col smelled the rotten reek of unbrushed teeth. Unfocused eyes darted anywhere but at him, couching themselves in the pestilential rot that was beginning to grow in the blackened pile of old bread in the middle of the kitchen bench. She scratched her face, and her eyes finally flicked toward Col.

'Bit dirty. Sorry.' Her voice was a rasp. She shuffled off to the edge of the bed that took up most of the hab. Col couldn't bring himself to speak. Her skin was pale to the point of transparency, save the dark blotches and red lesions beneath the torn sleeves of her shirt and down her arm. She lay back on the bed, and the lesions sank into divots where her supine body had lain for hours upon hours. There was a kind of order to the surrounding turmoil. The items that lay inside the halo of reach enjoyed by her hands remained shiny with use, with an encircling layer of dust and of rot deepening as it spread outward.

The food prep area was decrepit, full of dishes and upturned takeaway containers from the shopfronts he'd just walked past. Mouldy, half-chewed buns with protein patties pulled out were strewn on the countertop. Sachets and broken bottles littered the floor. Some had been stepped on; their contents squirted in jagged slashes up the walls. The place reeked of mildew and half-rotted food. The bed was strewn with dirty clothes stained with Sal's sweat. Wads of tissue and toilet paper, the faint remains of attempts to clean, were embedded deep in the reek. A fresh line to the front door bore the black stains of dirty boot marks.

Sal's eyes had gone vacant, staring into a void. He knew she'd connected to the Uplink again; she was twitching. He stared. His fastidious and cheery friend had been replaced with this bedraggled, barely conscious creature content to subsist in its own squalor. He picked his way through the scattered clothing, abandoned containers and forgotten belongings, and felt the hard crunch of plastic as he stepped on something. He swept a pile of empty wrappers off the edge of the bed, near Sal's twitching feet, and sat down. She ignored him until he tried to place his hand on her shin to get her attention. Before he could touch her, she stirred.

Sal surfaced slowly from her glass-filled malaise and focused on Col's face. She seemed to remember who he was again.

'Col?' She pulled herself out of the filth around her and moved to embrace him. Col pulled back before she could, standing up as Sal brought herself to a kneeling position on the couch.

'God, what's happened to you?' he asked.

Sal's eyes roved, only fixing on him for fractious portions of seconds. 'I lost my job. After the Upgrade, wasn't long. They connected with me. Let me know that my services were no longer needed.'

'What? Why?'

Sal shrugged. 'They had new techs. You were gone, and because of everything, you know, with the thefts and stuff, they said they thought I was a security risk.'

'But I was working on that, I was contacting people about the contract –'

'The contract was verified all the way down the chain. It's an immutable piece of data, Col. We were the last link. The only point of difference, and you know… you were already gone.' And she was gone again. In the Link. As Col watched, her breath slowed and came in short gasps. Small spasms in her muscles ran through her body, and her eyes roved without seeing anything.

He watched in shocked silence, unsure what to do. Sal was gone, and in her place was this shell, unable to last more than a few seconds lucid in the real world. He'd been wondering why he hadn't seen her on her commute home and now he knew. She'd lost her job, and was now locking herself inside for days on end, doing whatever *this* was.

He caught Sal's attention again as her eyes scanned the room erratically. Grime and dark circles ringed her eyes and she was barely cognisant enough of her surroundings to recognise that Col was still there.

'Sal,' he said, concerned. 'Talk to me. What's happened?'

'What? Nothing.' She sank back. He repeated the question more firmly, and this time Sal lashed out.

'Oh, nothing, alright?' An odd shivering had taken over her body. 'Whatever we did, it *worked*, and now you can feel touch in the Uplink. It's everything they wanted it to be. You can hear people, you can see people, now you can touch people, right? And they don't need us. Not anymore. So, I came home. And they have these – I don't even know what you'd call them – parlours? New parlours in the Link. Places you can go in the link where you can, you know, play. With the new sensations.'

Col felt sick. 'Like... sex parlours?' He'd known that was what Touch would be used for, but this seemed like more than that. The state Sal was in reminded him of the tower where he'd found the dead man. Surrounded by filth and the evidence of addiction.

Sal rolled her eyes. 'Sure. Sex parlours, there's them too. Whatever. But that's not, it's not everything. There's this whole other –' as she thought about it, the shivering stopped momentarily, before redoubling as she continued to talk. Her voice had dropped low and husky, filled with deep longing. 'I can't describe it. It's a rush. A continuous feeling of things just being *good*. You can't possibly –'

Col held up a hand. 'Okay, I... it feels good, I get it. But Sal. Look around you. You can't live like this.' He thought for a moment. Linkers weren't allowed at the Sanctuary, but surely... *surely* they'd make an exception. Sally was clearly going through something as bad as, if not worse, than the solar addictions so many of the Outcasts had to deal with. It was as though the Upgrade, rushed as it was, had resulted in some kind of addiction mechanism that operated through Touch. He shuddered. 'You can come back to where I'm staying, if you want? I think I know some people that could help.'

Sal sat back, nonplussed. She was still shivering. The room wasn't cold, but her arms had goose pimples. The hairs on her arms were on end, waving softly in time with the faint breeze from the air vent in the ceiling.

'I wish you could feel it,' she said, ignoring him. Her voice was thick with something familiar to him and yet not. Desperation. A simple phrase, but with such indecorous need behind it as to make the body it projected from hollow.

It was the same voice he'd heard from the solar-addicts on the street, before he'd fallen from the Link. The begging, howling voices that had haunted him as he'd tried to block them out. He remembered his eyes, usually so busy and roving, drilling themselves into the false walls of advertising being blasted into his mind. Becoming dead still and steadfast in an attempt to ignore the beggars in the street. That look, that *need*, wasn't something only for those who had fallen from the world. It was everywhere, and now it was in his friend.

It struck him at that moment. The way he'd fallen from the Link. The way he'd seen the rot of the Uplink from the outside, and the way it punished anyone who couldn't access it. He felt furious. Not at Sal. She was just another person broken by the Link, this time from within. No, his anger was aimed at whoever had built this. Whoever had made this what it was. They had to have known. Had to have known that the Link Upgrade would be as rotten inside as it was out. Outside the Link were the solar addicts and the disenfranchised, and now there was an addiction of a different kind inside. Something to keep people in it, and keep them using.

Despite his fury, he felt a yearning tug that made him want to fall into whatever torpor Sal was in, to be with her and sink into the abyss with her. The world of the Uplink was a poison, but it was the warm poison of familiarity. The thought of plugging in and disconnecting from everything was an intoxicating. He watched the shivering woman in front of him convulse. Her eyes darted around wildly, unseeing.

'Sal?'

'What?' Her voice came as though from the bottom of a well.

'Look, I know you aren't doing well. I think that if we go –'

She interrupted, 'I'm doing fine. You're the one who's –' She was barely listening.

'Sal,' he interrupted, 'look, I'm trying to help. There's a place I can take you. I think we can get you some help.'

'I don't need help from you!' Her voice resonated through the walls for a fraction of a second. She was on her knees on the bed now, backing away from Colin, almost cowering. The shivering in her body had turned to a quake.

Col held his hands out placatingly. 'Sal, I'm sorry. What's happened to you? I promise I'm not trying to do anything other than help.'

'I don't need anything, least of all from someone like you.'

The comment hung in the rancid air. Sal clambered further away on the bed, crouching like a prey animal ready to spring from a trap. Col still had his hands out, but he wasn't sure whether it was to ward her off or calm her down. Stains and sweat marks covered her clothes. Col felt the edges of panic begin to overwhelm him, and he stood up to stop the walls falling in. Cardboard boxes. Grease stains. A lost friend, who had followed a path denied to him, morphed into something unrecognisable and unknowable, covered in the putrid grit of knowing.

'What do you mean, someone like me?' Col suspected he knew, but he couldn't help himself.

'Nothing,' she said.

'I didn't come to fight you. I didn't even come to help you. I just wanted to see you, and –' He stopped. The question he'd come to ask her caught in his throat.

Sal looked up at him. For a moment, there was a flicker of the old friend he'd known in her eyes. 'And what?'

Col was quiet. 'I came to ask you about Cass. You said you'd try to contact her.'

To Col's surprise, Sal laughed. A short, harsh sound, full of contempt. 'Oh yeah. 'Cause *you can't*, can you?' And in the place of Sal was someone with a cruel, mocking smile, looking at him like he was less than human. So sudden was the change that Col reeled, and responded more harshly than he intended to himself.

'Did you contact her? Did you even *try*?'

In all his attempts to contact Cass, and in the broken times between, he'd held on to the thought that *at least* Sal would also be trying to make contact with her. Instead, she'd forgotten him.

'I tried. Then I stopped. She wasn't there. *You* try.' Sal was worrying and scratching at her arms. Spending even this long out of the Link was making her irritable.

Col flushed, 'You know I can't.'

The quaking nearly overtook her, and a snide grin split her features. The hollow in her eyes filled with a blunt malice. 'Oh,' she said, 'That's right.'

'What do you –'

'Why don't you just get out? Get out of my house. Just go.'

Col breathed in carefully. 'Sal. You don't need to do this. I can help you, and you can help me reach Cass. We can help each other.'

'Help yourself.'

'You know I can't!' Col said. 'I can't connect to the Link! I can feel something. Sometimes. It's like reaching for a shadow, but I can't find her myself, and I can't talk to her to see if she's okay! I wanted to know if you'd managed to get in touch with her, but now I get here, and I don't know what's happened to you and I want to help!'

'Don't yell at me, you fucking –' Sal bit off the end of the word as she stood ankle-deep in her own filth, contorted and shaking, ready to pounce at him.

In a nearly silent whisper, Col asked, 'What were you going to call me?'

'An Aug,' she said. The rasp was out of her voice, and in its place was a rage that amplified the catastrophe of her hab, 'I was calling you a fucking Aug.'

Without another word, Col turned and opened the door. It hit the backstop on the wall and bounced before the pneumatic stopper slowed it on its way to closing. His last vision of his friend was Sal resting back on her haunches, a tangled mess of what had once been brown curls dangling in front of her downcast face. She disappeared as the door clicked shut.

* * *

It was still raining outside. A feeling built up behind his eyes, an unfamiliar pressure. The glancing light from the street flickered up at him. Occasionally he'd glimpse a hint of himself in a reflection, but it was momentary, a whisper in the ever-changing dance of the rain.

He tried to connect to Cass, more out of habit than hope, and the pressure in his head flowered into a familiar itch. Cold, stark emptiness slipped through the cracks in his mind. It crept through him like a mole, an invasive enemy that knew his inner workings.

Sal was gone from him. He didn't know what else he could do but go back to the Sanctuary and ask Cynth what had happened to her. She couldn't possibly be the only one, and there had to be some way to help. He tried not to think about it too much, but the picture of Sal, threadbare and filthy in her hab, kept filling his mind.

The long line of boarded-up shops crept into view. The drizzle had abated to the point where he could better hear the rustling of movement behind the windows. Despite himself, Col crossed the roadway and peered inside.

Broken glass glittered across the darkness of a floor covered in black mould and rotting panels of real timber. The stink of vomit lay heavy over the damp musk of the room. On the floor inside were four people arrayed in a rough star shape, heads together, supine in the filth. Three of them stared glassy-eyed into nothing, twitching. While Col watched, one of them reached an arm out and up as a wide smile spread across her features. Another felt their own cheek then let their arm fall, cocked at an unlikely angle, next to their head. Their breathing was fast but measured, and Col could practically smell the pheromones over the rest of the reek. Whatever they were experiencing was enough to lift them from the squalor and mire and make them disappear.

The fourth one wasn't breathing. His head lay in a pool of pale-yellow sick, which had spread to the two closest to him. It had dried out and lost its viscosity, but not before it had soaked into their hair. A glossy rivulet climbed into the dead man's mouth, which sat agape in an eternal silent scream. His eyes were the same cheap glass baubles as his companions', though his lay still while they rolled slowly in their ecstatic shells.

Col felt yearning and disgust in equal measure, both outward and inward. He watched the slow ballet of the prone figures for some time, before turning away, trudging through the slowly melting crystals on the pavement on his way back to the Sanctuary.

CHAPTER 24

The interaction with Sal went around and around in Col's head as he made his way back to the Sanctuary. Her face melded and joined and coalesced with the faces of the Linkers he'd seen lying torporous in the cold. Sal had cursed at him, degrading him, when all the while she'd been reduced by the Uplink to some thrall to hyperreality.

He felt numb. He wanted to help her, but the venom in her tone had shocked him. In the place of his friend was the same cruel face of addiction that he'd seen in the Outcasts. Had the Touch Upgrade gone wrong somehow? Or had Sal's savagery always been there, dormant until his disconnection?

It couldn't have been, he reasoned. It hadn't been perfect, but he'd never seen her so vicious before now. He couldn't tell whether the Linkers on the street had undergone the same change as his friend and the people in the shop. Their eyes slid from nothing to nothing, and gave away nothing.

I was calling you a fucking Aug.

Sal had said that, out loud and to him, bile in the syllables. The sentence had slurred out between plaque-furred teeth and struck him like a fist. She had been his best friend, but now he was a mere Outcast. An Aug. A broken thing, one to be derided and hated. He felt a flare of anger, but only for a moment.

It wasn't that different, he reasoned, *to how he'd treated the Outcasts before*. Before everything. Before he'd had to spend days and nights scavenging for water and huddling under crates. Before the footsteps in the night had driven a chill down his spine as he wondered if someone was coming for him. He'd watched on hopelessly as he'd noticed the eyes of Linkers sliding past him.

I was calling you a fucking Aug.

Looking around at the Linkers, he could see what *they'd* given up. There was a coldness to reality around them that he hadn't felt in his time in the Sanctuary. Using the Uplink gave the user a feel of instance, of being a unique entity in the collective unreality. The only real thing, in truth, because even others you saw in the Uplink were faint shadows of the real people, somewhere out in the world.

The shrieking loneliness of the world's population and every sensation you could ever feel, on tap. Col thought of the man he'd seen, rotting next to his friends while they lay, too distracted by the simulation around them. The Uplink did nothing to stop it, and why would it? The man's value had disappeared with his brain function, and his body was mere meat, and meat was not the realm of the Uplink.

The Sanctuary door was opened by a small man with an enormous ceramic shoulder augmentation. Col nodded at him, distracted by the image of Sal, so angry and alone as the door had closed on her.

I was calling you a fucking Aug.

The cheap walls of the room flexed slightly as he shut the door. He sat on the bed, staring at the wall that had held the apparition of his sister only days before. The wall that he could have sworn was trying to drown him.

Sal *was* drowning. Whatever was happening to her had taken her and left a furious, addicted shell in its wake. He felt the blunt edge of hopelessness pressing down onto him.

He didn't know what to do.

For some time, Col simply sat, staring at the wall, the picture of Sal in his mind. Cass had disappeared, and he had found nothing to even hint at where she'd gone. Now Sal, too, was gone, but her body remained in a vicious mockery of his once and only friend.

I was calling you a fucking Aug.

He wasn't sure how long he'd been sitting there, Sal's words repeating like a mantra in his head, before he finally saw the file he'd taken from the dead man's room, lying under the table in the corner. He stared at it for a long while, until his body stood, as though by its own accord, and pulled it out.

There was a kind of anti-torpor mechanism that kicked in in his low moments. A kind of momentum that stopped him from grinding to a halt for too long. So long as there was something, anything, that his mind could latch onto, eventually it would cut through the fog, and he would at the very least keep moving. The file, as the only distraction in the room, served as that right now. Automatically, he rifled through it, sitting on the thin frame of the cot and pulling papers out at random. He pulled out the design sketches of Augmetic arms and letters that he'd seen and put them to the side.

Much of the folder was technical notes and generic information pamphlets, and he read through it, taking none of it in. He'd seen the shiny, unblemished Uplink versions of these himself when he'd been looking for a new product, back before he'd lost access. 'Biomechanical Augmentations and You' said one, sporting a photo of a person with a badly edited Augmetic. Col read all those, along with the technical datasheets with the man's scrawlings on them. It filtered through his numb mind without a trace. After a while, he noticed he'd been reading the same document for several minutes.

It was two yellowed pieces of paper, scrunched, stapled and slightly torn. The front was a handwritten scrawl. The second was a handwritten response. He'd been reading it, over and over again, apparently waiting for his conscious mind to understand what his subconscious had latched on to. He shook his head to clear the fog, and read.

> To the owner of CodeBilt,
>
> My name's Garrett. I was one of your test subjects for an Augmetics pilot program. I'm not sure if you can help me. I went to the silo where they gave me the surgery, but nobody answered the door. It looked deserted.
>
> I'm having problems with my new implants. They're making me sick. I can see great with the eye, but I can't make it STOP seeing. It doesn't close. Even in my dreams I see it all. It's there. The waking world is my dreams. I can't think straight anymore, I'm sweating all the time, and it'll bug out and my brain will glitch. My doctor isn't talking to me. I was told I'd be able to work, but I haven't found a job because I keep having these fits. I don't know what to do. I need my doctor.
>
> Please.

The last word was scrawled desperately, despair written into every pen stroke. Col flipped the page. It was a two-line response, but it was blurred and covered with water stains and ageing. He couldn't read it.

Colin felt sick.

CHAPTER 25

Rory was rolling a small piece of paper in their hands when Col blew into Cynth's anteroom. They jumped and turned on their embedded hearing aids when they felt the wind from the door, freezing as they saw the look that was on Col's face.

'Is she in?' Col asked. He felt himself going pale. Before Rory could answer, Cynth opened the door into her office.

'Colin! What the hell do you think you're doing?' she demanded. 'You don't just barge in –'

'I have to ask you something,' Col interrupted. Cynth glared at him, but stepped aside to allow him in. She gave Rory a quizzical look, but they just shrugged. She closed the door behind her and walked slowly to her desk. Col was still carrying the frayed file.

'What's got you so worked up that you're storming in here?' She leaned against the wall.

Col didn't know where to start. 'I just saw my friend. Someone from before. She told me– well, she didn't tell me, I saw... I don't know. There were these people, and– ' He described the scene from the shopfront, the way the Linkers lay in waste, and Sal's turn since the upgrade.

'I couldn't tell if the Link had always done things like this, or whether it was just me being an Outcast now that's made me notice. I know I only started noticing things after I left the Link. People not seeing. Their bodies twitching. They seem to not know what they are, or where they are. Small moments, you know? I wanted to know whether it was my imagination. But I didn't know anyone who had been around long enough. From before the Uplink. But I was –' he paused, unable to talk of the malaise he'd felt in the room, when Cass and Sal and Ariana had wrapped him in a confluence of hopeless energy. Instead, he simply proffered the file, and the letter he'd found, 'This is from one of my sister's sources.'

He handed it to Cynth, who opened it up and began leafing through it. She started reading, pulling roughly stapled pages out, stuffing them back and drawing out others. Col watched silently, trying to decipher her impassive face. Finally, she clicked her tongue and put the file down. She crossed the room and pulled out a file of her own, much thicker and better organised. She pulled out a set of papers and handed them to Col.

'Read this.' The frustration and anger were gone from her tone.

The staples in the corner barely held the papers together, and repeated creasing from flipping it over and back again had left a quarter-circle of weakness around the edge. It was a report, or an internal memorandum, which had been printed on office stationery for CodeBilt – the second time he'd ever seen the name. Some details were redacted.

> Subjects have been retrieved from identified areas of access. Some resistance was met and nullified through use of sedatives. Dosed individuals have been marked in files. It is noted that several subjects are in ill health. Budget for adequate medicine should be extended to allow for an increase in rations to improve condition of subjects prior to procedure. Subjects have been identified using DNA

THE SAVAGE AETHER 207

> techniques and labelled. Identities have been kept anonymous as requested and they have been moved to control groups.
>
> Due to health concerns, suggest procedure be pushed back by several weeks to allow subjects to recover.
>
> Regards,
>
> Evan McDaniels

Beneath this, there was a second piece of paper glued to the first. A response:

> Evan,
>
> While we appreciate the concern for the subjects, this class of individual were chosen for the low risk they posed should they become untenable for whatever reason. We are also on a strict timeline. Proceed as per the existing schedule.
>
> Tony Masterson,
>
> Operational Manager

Col looked up to where Cynth sat. She motioned for him to continue. The next page was a news article.

AUGMETICS PROVIDE NEEDY WITH NEW CONNECTIONS

A NEW WAVE of technology is coming, and it's going to change the way we connect with each other, a spokesperson from Conn-

Tech Research said in an interview earlier today.

The interview comes just hours after the first successful implantation of a neo-ceramic limb that self-connects to the human nervous system, allowing the subject to interact with the prosthetic as though it were a real arm.

'Previously, Augmetics and prosthetics were user-specific,' explained the spokesperson in an exclusive conversation with our journalists, 'but ConnTech's new interlayer of neural pathfinding polymers means that the components "talk" to the subject and map onto their current nervous system.

'This means that we can build these systems cheaply and make them available to more people in need.'

It's not just amputees and those living with disabilities who will benefit from this technology either, the spokesperson suggested.

'The technology can be applied to more than just limbs. Imagine supplementing your brain power with chipsets, increasing your ability to recall information with physical memory upgrades or making your eyesight better than any of the predatory birds of yesteryear. That's what ConnTech is proposing.'

ConnTech is the first to deliver a working version of their patented interlace technology, but they are hardly the only company in the Augmetics race. Pharmaceutical and medical giants, as well as small startups Uplink Corporation and CodeBilt, are throwing their hat in the ring with their own approach to Augmetics.

The letterhead on the next page said, 'Uplink Corporation: internal memo' and Col flipped through it intently.

> ATTN: Interlace dysfunction found in atypical brain topology
>
> During early-stage testing of interface protocols, some concerns were raised by the staff on my team. ConnTech and similar interface devices for Augmetics seem to have a two-way interaction with the topology of the brain. In all cases, where a physical neural interlace device exists, such as in Augmetics, both the neural interlace and the brain of the user see a degree of 'rewiring'.
>
> This is a concern for the proposed non-invasive interlace technology. Due to the complexity of the connection, there's a limit to the amount of 'leeway' we can give the system when it comes to anomalies in structure. Naturally, anyone with an existing augmentation will be unable to use the new device. Additionally, my researchers and I are suggesting that there will be a small, but not insignificant, part of the population that naturally have a higher degree of variance than the plasticity of

> the new system. The level of variance in physical structure in the human brain is simply too high to accommodate without further resources.
>
> James Marsh

The bottom half of this memo was almost impossible to read. Splashed watermarks were mingled with furious scrawls. Most of it was illegible, but beneath the blacked-out signatory on the file were two words, seemingly written in ink, maybe from an overflowing fountain pen.

They knew.

Col was confused. 'People with Augmetics. Outcasts. It was the Uplink themselves. But I don't have any augmentations, and I used to be able to access the Uplink.'

Cynth nodded. 'We aren't exactly sure what's happening now, but it has something to do with the Upgrade. I didn't show you this to help you understand your own situation. We're still trying to understand that. Your friend, though –'

'Sal.'

'Yes. We've seen it before. The Uplink has, through its entire existence, grievously harmed many people. Every time there's a system upgrade, they know it will cause problems, but they're incentivised to not care.' Cynth motioned for him to read on. There was one more page. Another news article.

UPLINK REBRANDS, ACQUIRES MAJORITY STAKE AMID ACCESS CONCERNS

BOARD DIRECTORS and major shareholders from Uplink (previously Uplink Corporation) have today confirmed the buyout of five major competitors. These buyouts occur amid criticism that the neural interlace service has 'shut out' those who have received Augmetic implants.

'We're very excited about these acquisitions,' said Priat Chalmers, current board director of Uplink. 'ConnTech, in particular, has done groundbreaking work in its development of Augmetics. With these innovative companies joining the Uplink family, we will be able to offer more functional services through the Uplink Interlace Network as it becomes an integral part of the social fabric.'

Fringe groups have criticised the merger, claiming that it was undertaken to quash reports of Augmented peoples (Augs) being unable to access the Uplink due to the implementation of a competitor's technology.

There are also concerns that support for physical Augmetics is being phased out. This would leave those who previously benefitted from or relied upon Augmetic enhancement locked out of the growing neural interlace network and unable to procure replacement parts or bug patches for their augmentations.

Director Chalmers did not directly address the concerns. 'As of right now, our primary focus is further developing the service for current consumers of the Uplink Interlace Network. Competitor research portfolios will be folded into our budgeting in due time.'

> The board later issued a release confirming that all future briefings would be held remotely via the Uplink Interlace Network.

Col turned the final page. He'd expected that there would be some kind of explanation of how Uplink addressed the concerns they faced. There was nothing. The old, thin paper felt flimsy and lifeless in his hand.

'The people that were concerned couldn't access the UIN. The Uplink, as it's known now. So, the protests at press conferences simply couldn't exist any longer.' Cynth's voice was quiet. 'You can't revolt in an environment you can't access. The control structure was global and, for all intents and purposes, anonymous.'

Col said nothing.

'The Augmetics hubs shut down. Software updates for implanted informatics systems slowly petered out. Most of the implants had embedded digital control systems that would brick the devices if the owner attempted to repair themselves. So, the Augmetic interface that had changed your brain wiring enough to stop you accessing the Uplink was now nothing but a lump of metal hanging off your arm, or a dead silicon chip embedded in your neck.'

The heavy mechanical stomping and shuffling of feet could be heard down the halls. Rerouted and jerry-rigged servo motors whirred and crunched. Above it all was the ring of human voices, talking to one another.

'Someone figured out that in some cases, the Augmetics had reconfigured the dopamine receptors in the brain, and that connection to a low-voltage power source would produce a high. Solar cells were easy to come by, and it was easy to step down the voltage. Some of us got out of that when we realised what it would eventually do.' She looked at the burnished terminals on her arm, and Col recalled the smell of burning meat in the room with the dead man. 'So yes, Colin. The Uplink did this. The Uplink has always done this.'

Col remained silent. He reread the note. *The class of people selected.*

'Who was he?' he said finally, gesturing to his own file.

Cynth shrugged. 'Not sure, but based on his age as you describe him, he was likely part of a pilot Augmetics program. He was probably homeless; most of them were. They sold him the lie about being able to reintegrate, but when the experiment went wrong, or when CodeBilt got bought, his needs and theirs no longer aligned. Then the Uplink came along, and his displacement became codified rather than circumstantial. His escape was the solar, and from that point it was always going to end like it did.'

Col simply sat, disquieted and with a queer sense of numbing calm.

'What's going to happen to Sal?'

A shake of the head. 'I don't know. This time it's happening to Linkers, not Outcasts. We've seen scenes like you've described in the last few weeks. Linkers in back alleys, staring vacantly. It's probably going to be like the time just after the buyouts.'

'What happened then?'

Cynth looked dour. 'When the Augmetics corps shut down, others picked up the scraps. Gathered all the raw materials and parts, and tried to develop a way to jailbreak the software and repair the hardware we were stuck with. It's not the high-tech gadgetry we were sold, but it worked. For a while. There are now warehouses full of spare parts and kits and freelance microsystem hackers who run a consortium where you can replace or repair your Augmetics, for a price.' She fell silent. The sounds from the corridor filtered slowly in through Rory's anteroom, leaving a coloured noise that echoed through the space between the two Outcasts.

'Some of them turned into places like this Sanctuary. Others, I wouldn't trust so much.'

'Why not?'

'You have to understand, Colin. We try to keep ourselves clean, but every Sanctuary has its reactionaries and revolutionaries. Very angry, very hurt people who want to lash out at their circumstances. There are a number of 'Sanctuaries' around, but only some of them have the best interests of their Outcasts at heart.'

Col breathed out, then spoke. 'Cynth. My sister was... she was a reporter, and she was looking for some kind of, I don't know. She'd heard rumours, and she was looking into something to do with the Uplink. She was looking for groups of Outcasts.'

Cynth spoke as though she were far away. 'Yes?'

'I need you to tell me where these places are.'

CHAPTER 26

Truth be told, he didn't know what he expected to achieve.

The conversation with Cynth had been fairly brief after he'd pressed her about the other groups of Outcasts. His primary goal was to find Cass, of course, and as the locations of the Sanctuaries had rolled off Cynth's tongue he'd tried to sort them by proximity. As soon as he'd heard about Clem's Sanctuary, though, he'd stopped.

It was near the Library. His old stomping ground, and the place where he and Sal used to work. He'd left her at her hab, driven out by her sudden fury and bile, but he had regretted it from the moment he stepped out the door. If he managed to get to the Library, he might be able to do something to help her get her job back. He didn't know how; maybe petition the security guards to let him in. Contact someone somehow, let them know that it wasn't her fault. That she needed help.

Now, winding through streets still slick with last night's rain, he didn't know if he could even hope to achieve it. He could barely think straight. His mind was exhausted from the effort of reaching out to Cass, and could scarcely bring himself to try again. There had been a couple of times when he'd felt something, but it had never manifested into a cohesive connection. At best, he'd seen the shadow of an outline of a vaguely humanoid shape, out of proportion with the skyline. Crystals blending with clouds. He'd been continually reaching out since he left the Sanctuary, pushing to find even a hint of his sister in the Link. He'd counted. A hundred and thirteen times he'd reached out.

The sun was beginning to rise, and as always, the light made him think of her. The overcast clouds were clearing and thin bands of sunlight shone through. He was reaching out with a simple request: 'Location?'. Over and over again. It felt like shouting with a hoarse voice into the dark, and all the while he kept his eyes peeled for the Sanctuary he'd never known was there, and a way into the Library.

He was walking in a shadow, a damp chill in the air. Dewdrops had sunk into the concrete pavement, and he could see the moving line of damp evaporate. The deeper shade of the buildings' shadows glowed lighter at the edges as night turned to overcast morning.

He could see the Library in the distance. A hulk, boarded up, with the dense transmitter squatting atop, all black wires and snarled. He turned away from it and down an alley, seeking the Outcasts.

He stepped into chaos.

Between two tall towers was the foyer of a disused office building. It had been ransacked. Broken tinted glass and bent aluminium frames were strewn across the ground. The lights inside were shattered, and there was a gaping maw where the Sanctuary should have been in the street front. Further down the street, he could see piled cardboard and a decrepit stash of cables and wires. A small solar panel was laying on the ground next to a pile of makeshift rags with a human-shaped lump in it.

She was only just awake, lying in a post-sleep fugue. Her eyes swivelled, watching Col as he approached. When she was sure he was coming toward him, she scrambled back, grabbing a glass shard and gripping it defensively in her hand. She pushed herself into a crouch, lithe and mobile despite her Augmetic leg replacement below one knee.

'What do you want, Linker?' she spat. She had fresh bruises on her arms and a hunted look. Col put his hands up, placatingly. The woman was standing next to the rubble of the Sanctuary that she'd presumably called home. Every part of her body was taut, wound up like a snake about to spring.

He kept his voice carefully level, still holding his hands out to ward her off if she ran at him. 'I'm not here to hurt you. I'm just here to talk.' He looked around at the destruction. 'What happened here?'

The woman ignored his question. 'Sure, cob. Talk. Go away, talk to your Linker friends. Chat in your head, you don't need to talk to the likes of me.' The glass knife in her hand glinted as she swung it at him, and a red weal of blood began to creep out from under her thumb.

Col stayed out of her reach. The woman continued to eye him warily. 'I'm not trying to hurt you. I heard there was an Outcast community here, and I came. I'm looking for some people.'

She still didn't answer, but when he said 'Outcast' and not 'Aug', her shoulders dropped, and she unlocked her elbow from its defensive position. She still didn't take her eyes off Col as he crouched down to her.

Her clothing was a filthy kind of uniform grey, and the Augmetics on her body were in ill repair. The ankle joint on her leg didn't move enough for her foot to sit flush with the ground, and there was corrosion around the joints. Her skin was inflamed near the knee, and the telltale scorch marks of solar addiction were feeding up her arm.

Col tried again. 'What happened here?' The girl stayed silent, but the grip on the knife loosened. Col could tell because her blood began to flow more freely. Holding his hands out, displaying their emptiness, he moved toward her.

'My name is Colin.' He spoke softly. 'I don't know what happened here. I'm just,' he felt his chest collapse, 'I'm trying to find my sister. I'm trying to help my friend. I'm trying to understand what's happened...' he said to the girl, 'but

I don't know that you can help. I was hoping to speak to whoever ran this place.' He gestured back to the broken facade.

He sat back and felt the cold void of despair take him, 'I don't know what I'm doing,' he said. He stared blankly across the street, following the young woman's gaze into the remnants of the Sanctuary. *It would be so easy*, he thought, *so easy to give up, and just wait in the dark*. Wait for the end. To give in to this constructed, unreal existence that didn't care about the people like him. Like Cynth. Like Rory. Like Sal, Cass, Kris. Like this woman, brandishing the remnants of her home at him. There wasn't anything one person could do against it but succumb. So much connection, yet everyone was so alone.

'It was Jake,' the woman said. Col jumped. He'd been so wrapped in his own downward spiral, he'd stopped paying attention to her. She'd completely dropped the glass knife, and her guard. She was talking to him simply and plainly. 'He came through. Dunno what it is he wanted. I saw him speaking to Clem a few weeks ago. Jake screamed at him, the bastard. Harsh words, y'know? Clem saying he'd seen Jake's boys on the way to the Library.'

'What?' *This Jake person was trying to break into the Library?* Again, the name, and again, nothing good came with it.

'Yeah.' She wiped the blood away from her hand. The red turned black on the cobbles and stained the grouting. 'Then a few nights ago, his boys, they came back. Only this time, they didn't go to the Library, did they?' Her eyes went glassy and unfocused.

'What'd they do?' Col pressed.

'They... It's like they were talking. Like, able to talk without sound. Like the Linkers do, you know? Only they weren't. They moved like they were all planning it across their head.

Like they were thinking as one.' She shuddered and wiped her wounded hand. Both of her hands were now covered in blood. 'They came and they took everyone from the Sanctuary. They killed Clem. Then they burned it.'

Col's mind was racing. *Augs who can communicate like they're on the Uplink?* That's what Cass had been investigating. Had she found it? Spoken to this Jake person?

'This Jake. Do you know where he works? Where his boys come from? Where I could find him?'

She shook her head. 'Some way across town. Clem knew, but–' Her eyes went blank again.

Col spoke gently. 'I'm... Look, you need to get your hand fixed up. Down past the docks and back from the sea wall, there's another Sanctuary. It's where I came from. They can help you with your hand,' he paused. 'They can help you. They helped me.'

Col grabbed a piece of broken brick from the ground and scratched out a mud map to the Sanctuary onto the concrete. 'Do you know where that place is?'

The girl nodded, turning to look once more at the blasted and burned shopfront. Colin followed her gaze, then heard the shuffling scrape of a bare foot and a metal stump edging away from him down the alley. 'Good luck with your sister, Linker,' she called, before she turned the corner and disappeared from his sight.

I'm not a Linker, he thought, as he walked away, alone, feeling the crooked shape of the cobblestones under his shoes.

He didn't know if going to the Library would allow him to help Sal, but he walked back to the main street anyway. Cass wasn't here, so he'd have to move to the next place. He had to find out where Jake was. If Cass had ended up there, he might already be too late. He was disappearing people from other Sanctuaries, and if the woman he'd just helped could be trusted, he had some kind of Uplink connection that worked with Outcasts. He shuddered, and turned out of the street, glad that he'd been able to direct her to his own Sanctuary, if nothing else.

'That was nice of you.' The voice would have felt sincere, if not for the contempt at its edges. She was a scarlet mark in the grey patina of the overcast morning. Behind her, Col could see a haze of yellow-blue sky through the canyon of the street.

'Been a while.' Ariana smiled, walking toward him. Non-existent colours bounced off her at all the wrong angles.

Col turned back toward the Library, trying to ignore her. The soft footfalls of his weatherbeaten shoes merged with the crisp *snick-snick* of her hard-soled gait. Together they beat a rhythm down the street. Ariana's footfalls had no echo, as if to taunt him with her unreality.

'What are you *doing*?' Col asked.

'What do you mean?' Ariana's voice was flat and anechoic. The syllables dry.

'That!' Col gestured to the walls around them. 'You're... you don't sound right.'

He sped up along the pavement. There was a nauseating sensation of *wrongness*, an uncanny edge to everything around him. He stopped. Ariana's hair was glowing, and her eyes were voids, dead space on a porcelain face. They reflected pastel neon lights with no source. She smiled. Red lips. White teeth. Colours as manifesto.

'Cut it out! How are you doing that?' The neon reflection cracked and disappeared. The light changed, and she came into focus, dripping with hyperfidelity. Col closed his eyes and willed her to go away. When she spoke again, the streetscape resonated around her.

'And what exactly is closing your eyes going to do?' The tone was scornful now, and the timbre of her voice dropped and filled all the space left in his senses. It was warm and deep and round, and he was drawn into the totality of it.

'You're not *real!*' he said, as though declaring it would dismiss her. The sky was still sickly yellow-blue and the sunlight, his connection to Cass, was slowly intensifying. The neon lights were gone from Ariana, and her hair had lost its radiance. Her eyes, which had been black abysses, were now simply dark.

'Clever boy.'

Col looked around at the bare street. The windows were all shut, and the blinds were drawn in most of the habs peering down. Most of the workers in this area would be on shift. Nobody was going to help him. Ariana circled him silently. Stalking. She'd blocked his hearing, and now even the rustle of her clothes and the dead-air clatter of her shoes had been muted. Col followed her with his eyes. Ariana was the only thing moving around him.

The *only* thing he could see.

'There's nobody here,' he said. 'You can only appear when I'm alone, can't you?' That explained why she'd been absent while he'd been at the Sanctuary.

'Yes.' Her stare was icy. 'I can't seem to get a grip on your perception when you're with other people. Too much competition with your senses. When you're alone, though...' She waved a hand and the windows in the towers became a waterfall. They gushed and poured out and onto the street and ran into the gutters. Col felt the wave collide with him – the overwhelming dissonance of being hit with a violent torrent of water while *knowing* he was still safe and dry.

Col stepped back from her. 'What are you?' He saw the last of the clouds disperse. Pale rays of sunlight were visible at the end of the cobblestone street.

'I am you,' Ariana said, 'I'm part of you. I can tell you what you're *feeling*. I can change what you're *seeing*. I can excite you or blind you or frighten you or dazzle you. Your reality bends to me. I am what you believe.'

Col tried to ignore her and began to walk down the street toward the Library. He prayed silently that the private police force that had attacked him several weeks earlier was still there.

'In the hospital,' he said, trying to distract her. 'That... that was the first time I saw you. You didn't tell me how you lost connection to the Uplink. All you said was, "I can't get *into* the Uplink."'

Ariana nodded, 'The sensations I received from you were not as acute as I now feel them. I was still coming into my own.' She was floating along the ground, having abandoned any attempt to interact with reality. 'But the hospital wasn't the first time you saw me.' Ariana seemed confused for a second. 'It was early. I wasn't me. Not yet. I barely remember the shape... I wasn't connected with your senses. It was dark, and the whole world was huge.' The apparition shrank, delving into their memories as she tried to explain.

'It was dark,' she repeated, 'and the world was simple. Blinking boxes in strange rhythms. Above it all, a web was dancing. Or... not a web. Wires.' Her face contorted, then she repeated. 'The world was huge then. Now, it's shrunk. Limited.'

Col looked to where the crystalline towers of hab blocks were broken by the boarded-up Library. He remembered being called in the middle of the night, not so long ago, in another life. A broken server at two in the morning. An attempted break-in, caught on the security feed, and the unexplained presence. A shifting movement, a shadow in the dark.

'It was *you*,' he breathed, 'that night in the Library.'

Ariana considered for a moment. 'That was when I started

to become aware. In that space. There was so much space, there. The rest came in fits and starts. I was –'

Col couldn't see anyone, but the colours shifted as the sensory manipulation from the agent he'd called Ariana stopped corrupting his world. The street widened to greet him, and he pushed Ariana to the back of his mind and she disappeared mid-sentence.

A flash of light burned his eyes. Gossamer rainbow shards flew from the sunlight as it leaped from behind the clouds, and a screaming itch filled his mind.

Cass.

He reached out to connect, and this time it worked. Instead of a broken, silent nothingness, he was met with the glowing form of his sister in the sky above him. It burned his mind to look at, like his brain was being ripped open from the inside. The screaming rage and pain filled his head and he squeezed his eyes shut, but it didn't help. His sister was still there, a beacon of light glowing against the blackness of his eyelids and breaking apart his pain receptors. Spikes shot from his eyeballs and the back of his head as his sister grew to take up all the space in his mind. He was forced, as tears began to flow down his cheeks, to watch the shape of Cass grow in front of him. She stared at him, silently pleading for help.

Where are you? he screamed into the space where his connection to the Uplink should have been, and found that this time, with her, the information *got through*. She was reaching to him with the same urgency, and he felt the Uplink surge across the join between them. The apparition changed, and Cass morphed into a series of images. His mind screamed at him to break the connection, but he forced himself to watch. His sister sent him an image of a steel container sitting inside a warehouse littered with detritus, machine parts and electrical equipment.

She sent him images of mechanical humanoid forms dipping and weaving through rubbish. The pictures changed again, to a fence topped with razor wire and the broken shale of old factory tiling. Col saw Cass being held by two hulking people grasping her from either side. Then she sent a burning image of a green warehouse door and the faint vestige of a location reference. He reached out for the location, and it nearly slipped through his grasp as the Link between them grew weaker again.

He tried harder to keep the connection open, but it began to shatter and fall apart. Cass screamed a name at him as the pain in his skull flared and then vanished, and he opened his eyes. He was bathed in the sickly glow of the sunlight that had finally broken through the clouds. Cass. She'd finally gotten through to him.

Before he was even able to see or feel the world around him properly, he was moving again. Down the road to where he hoped there were more people around. The blank-eyed, hollow stares of the Linkers weren't going to help him, but he could hold Ariana at bay by keeping them in his sights while he processed what he'd just seen.

More Linkers came into view, and he tried to calm his breathing. He knew now where his sister was. The warehouse with the green door, with the locked series of shipping containers and the barbed wire fences guarded by mechanical brutes. It belonged to the same man who'd firebombed the Sanctuary around the corner. The same man whose name he'd heard in hushed voices from so many people, for so long.

PART FOUR

This girl showed up on the doorstep looking like she was about to faint. Her hand was bleeding, and she had the vacant stare of shock in her eyes. We took her inside and let her bathe and warm up and she told us about the attack. The way Clem had stood his ground. He'd asked Jake to explain himself. What the roving groups of Outcasts had been doing. Why several of Clem's own members had disappeared, when almost all of them had been planning to go to Jake for upgrades and work. And Jake had stood there, silently, as his followers had kicked Clem to the ground, killed him and then fire-bombed the place.

She'd found my place after Colin, that Linker who was looking for his sister, had given her directions. He'd tried for the Sanctuary and found her instead. Her, and the burnt-out wreckage where Clem had once fed and housed a whole group of people in need.

The girl had been out when it happened, is what she told us. Climbed up to the rooftops to watch the sun set over the docks, as she tended to do in the evenings, but she'd scrambled back when she heard the first explosion. Then she watched the outcasts from Jake's Sanctuary as they'd lined up everyone up in rows and executed them before reaching for the torches.

I had no idea what Clem had said or done to draw Jake's ire. Jake had been absent from the last few meetings. Had a row with Clem after Clem had called him out on not pulling his weight on supply runs. He'd ignored me whenever we'd been talking about the sudden influx of new Outcasts. He'd done nothing but sneak around the fact that people from other Sanctuaries had been disappearing when they'd been going to his, looking for work or Augmetic repairs.

I asked the girl to explain what had happened, and she told me about his followers.

These Outcasts, the ones that followed him, they were all men. They all had the same augmentations. She described it as a kind of exoskeleton. And she said they moved wrong. When I asked what she meant, she couldn't really say. She just looked at me and said, 'Just <u>wrong</u>, like it was their Augmetics driving them, and not the other way around. Jake was standing there, and they were doing what he wanted, all robot-like and whatever, but he never moved, and he never said a word.'

It started crashing together in my head, all at once and far too late. The disappearances. Jake's strange behaviour. His thefts on the supply runs and the rumours Col had mentioned. It all pointed back to him.

Later the same day, by some providence, I got a runner from Bern. He'd been contacted by Clem not long before the attack.

Clem, turns out, had been looking into the disappearances of a number of people from his Sanctuary. More than a dozen over the course of several months. I'd noticed it in my own Sanctuary, but I'd made the mistake of thinking it was just a period of high attrition. It had happened before; the ebb and flow of running an operation like ours means that you aren't sure exactly who's using the Sanctuary at any given time. We've tried to put systems into place, but it always relies on a level of surveillance we aren't comfortable with. Recently, I'd thought we'd been seeing groups of Outcasts moving, or finding their own way. It happens from time to time. I thought it was normal, before the girl came to us from the burned-out shell of Clem's Sanctuary.

I was so wrong.

Clem had seen it and made the connection. So many of them, those that disappeared, had been going to see Jake. Jake had the jobs, see? And he had the tech. The rest of us ran more like a refuge, but Jake? He'd always said he was trying to encourage industry. To help the Outcast population become more akin to the system we were locked out of. He acted as partial labour supplier for industries that didn't require Uplink connections, and he'd help repair or replace parts. That was his story, anyway. So, we'd <u>tell</u> people to go to Jake's.

And then Jake would take them. Clem did his due diligence, and he waited until he was sure, but he knew what Jake was doing. He'd been building himself a security force of Outcasts, luring them in under the impression they'd be getting new Augmetics, or work. And when he'd taken them under his wing, he'd make them disappear. Clem still didn't know <u>exactly</u> what Jake was doing with our Sanctuary members, but he knew he was taking them. So he'd confronted Jake about it.

And Jake killed him.

It looks like Jake was also stockpiling stolen chipsets from deprecated Uplink tech. Built himself some kind of jerry-rigged device to try to hack into the Link.

The thing I don't understand is <u>why</u>. He's clearly not doing it to help the Outcasts. He firebombed Clem's. He's disappearing people. It isn't some sense of altruism or attempt to reunite us with the system that's rejected us. So why?

– Cynth

CHAPTER 27

CASS

They came for her in the dark.

Days and nights had become vague moments on the edge of wakefulness where her captors' cold steel touch ground against her skin. They would sit her up and force her to eat. Her muscles were so dulled by whatever drugs they were giving her that she could barely swallow, much less try to resist. The only constant was the injections, delivered regularly to maintain her fugue state.

She had no idea how long it went on for, only that she must have been asleep when they took her. When she came to, her handcuffs had been removed. The first thing she noticed was a vague sense of motion and of her feet being dragged across concrete. Her head lolled, and she saw a layer of metal swarf and oil oozing over the floor. Her peripheral vision started to come back as she neared the back of the factory.

There were four of them, Augs. Before they'd caught her trying to use the Link, she'd only seen three. She couldn't see the extra member of the party; they walked behind and to the left of her, behind the cruel form of one of the two Sentinels.

Before too long, she was gripped firmly, and the Sentinels moved around in front of her. She heard the scrape of a chair and a male grunt in the affirmative. The Sentinels pushed her down and large hands handcuffed her into the chair. Somewhere in the dark back of her mind, she could tell that the cuffs hadn't caught. Her head rolled to the side; she still couldn't control her muscles properly. Another needle was pressed into her neck.

A sickly feeling sank through her as the cold liquid of the syringe warmed her blood. Her head cleared, and she looked around.

The same corrugated interior of a shipping container surrounded her on three sides, just as it had in her cell. The fourth wall was a makeshift faux-ply. It was covered in posters and crude scrawling with an opening on one side. Behind it, the other half of the container glowed with flickering blue and green lights. The glyphs were scribbled thickly, askance from one another, written in a language she didn't know. She tried to focus on them, but her head began to swim as she tried to make sense of the marks. They had meaning not in word but in form. They spoke of frustration, of fate, of spite. Of rage.

A tall, balding man stood in front of her. He had a spike of wires running down his face, covered by crude skin grafts, and a pair of empty eyes set against an almost-smile.

'Oh,' was all she said, and rolled her head back to stare at the ceiling.

Jake laughed. Despite the heavy, low voice she remembered from the docks, his laugh was high. Almost shrill.

'Cassandra. Good to see you again.'

Cass began fidgeting with her handcuffs. They were old and worn out, and the Aug hadn't closed them fully. One of her hands was almost able to slip out. Jake dismissed the other woman from the room. Before she left, she handed a small device to Jake, who pocketed it before Cass got a clear look. The Sentinels simply stood, eye lenses gleaming in the dark.

A thud came from the glowing room next to them. Unhurriedly, Jake stepped across and leaned through the empty doorway to peer in. Cass tried to ignore the violent scrawling on the walls and worried at her handcuffs as quietly as she could manage.

Jake walked back between the two Sentinels. 'After I warned you, you still didn't come here with a partner?' There was an air of humour underneath his flat contempt. Cass was barely listening, trying to work her way out of the cuffs, feeling the sweat slowly allowing her hand to slip further and further through the loop. The hulking cyborg Augs were still guarding her escape. She'd have to figure that out later.

'I don't... understand...' She could barely get the words out. The drugs were still wearing off. Whatever had been in the needle acted quickly, but she could still feel the edge of the sedatives. The metal of the cuff scraped her wrist and she muffled a groan of pain. Jake didn't even look up, oblivious to her discomfort.

'*Linkers*,' Jake began to pace the room, shoving one hand into his jacket pocket as an irritated twitch built up in his other arm. 'You have the entire world. You have *everything*. Every piece of knowledge ever written down or thought up. Money only exists in the distributed ledgers in your own minds,' he said, reaching up and tapping at his head. 'Employment. Socialisation. Companies, thinktanks, corporations, an entire world's supply of everything you could ever wish for. You have normality, and you leverage it over me – us. Over us,' he added quickly, breaking the flow of his rant.

'Huge portions of the population worldwide can't even see it. Don't know it exists. But in you come, telling me you're police and that you're *concerned*. Yes, very concerned about how the poor Augs are going to be accessing the Uplink. It's a matter of everyone's safety, you know? Why would we Augs be so *concerned* about accessing the largest leap forward in technology in living memory? Why would I – *we* – want access?'

The twitch in his arm continued, growing to a tremor, and he fidgeted with something in his pocket. When he turned, the smile was gone, replaced with the hollowness that had always been behind it. His voice dropped from contemptuous mockery to low hatred. 'Your people took us. The broken, the unstable. The physically infirm. People who fell outside the box that some machine decided was the "perfect" human, and you locked us out for what we were. Not for anything we'd done.'

'We... I didn't do that. I was just trying to find out what –'

'You were trying to find out so you could tell your Linker friends what the creeps and creatures were up to. You didn't want to help. You didn't want to fix the problem. You were just trying to sell a story about our struggle.'

Something about his demeanour struck Cass as wrong. He knew his story, and told it well, but the words rang with insincerity. Maybe he'd believed it once, or maybe this was something he'd said before, and it had taken on the quiet undertone of rote.

This man, this Aug, didn't care about the plight of other Augs. Behind him, the two Sentinels stood, still as grotesques on an ancient cathedral. Their false eyes glowed, their steel shone, and the only human part left of them seemed as though it had been enslaved to the machinery. Cass had the dreadful feeling that their augmentations had not been voluntary.

Another warm thud came from the next room. Jake sighed with disgust as he looked through the opening again. He turned to the Sentinels and snapped his fingers. As one, they turned and made their way through to the other side of the shipping container. The whirring of their overlong arms and stunted steel legs blended into the low drone coming from the next room. The glow of LEDs bounced off the steel of their bodies, a cool blue with a new, insistent red flash. They disappeared behind the wall, Jake watching them carefully. There was a clanking of chains and the spring-loaded flick of locks being released, along with the more subtle sound of something heavy being moved.

Cass continued to worry at the handcuffs on her wrists. She stopped as soon as she felt her face contort in pain and forced herself to control her breathing. She continued until Jake turned back to face her. He stepped out of the way to allow the Sentinels back through.

Though she'd never heard it before, she knew it was the sound of a dead body being scraped along the floor toward her. The stumping whirs of the servo motors from the Sentinels were louder, working harder. The blue-red sheen of the mechanically Augmented humans clanked into view and blocked the hateful ciphers on the walls. They walked together, as a single six-legged creature. The inside forelimb of each sentry grasped the leg of the dead body they dragged along the floor behind them.

The body wore a rotten set of clothes, and the acrid reek of someone long unwashed assaulted Cass's nostrils. On his ankles and wrists were streaks of blood. Huge clots of brown scab and puss-filled open wounds exploded down his arms. His body trailed a clear secretion on the floor as the Sentinels dragged him. Cass couldn't see where it came from, and she didn't want to. His hair was long. His beard was patchy and scraggly, barely covering his pale face. Sunk into this broken visage was a set of dilated eyes, staring blankly at the messages on the walls. Blackened voids that had been straining for sight right up until the moment of death.

Cass didn't know if her desire to retch was from the smell or the sight. The Sentinels dragged the man through the room and dumped him outside out the door. They turned and came back in, still in lockstep with one another. Jake waited at the doorway.

'It's a shame. I wanted that out of the way before you got here.' Jake was watching her intently now in the near silence, marked only by the machine hum coming from the next room. The sentinels moved back to their previous positions. Stock-still, again. Cass had nearly got the handcuffs off.

'What did you do to him?' she asked.

'I wanted to know how his mind worked.'

An ice-hot terror crept down Cass's back. She fought the rising panic, still fidgeting with the cuffs behind her back. Her hands were wet with sweat, and possibly blood. She couldn't see.

Jake was talking, mostly to himself. 'They've all failed. So far. There is something. They have *something* about them. Something I don't have. And because of that they're able to access the Uplink when I can't. But I'll find out. And I don't care how many of you Linkers it takes.'

His body shook, practically radiating hatred. The Sentinels still stood next to him, breathing softly. Cass remembered the eyes at the docks. A red glow from the shadows, seeping from the place she'd just left Jake. Jake, the only Aug who spoke more than a few words. The Sentinels had been human once. Her jailers barely talked to her. They weren't silent but *silenced,* their obedience not just expected but commanded by the man in front of her. The man who had just had a dead human dragged out and dumped like recycling.

This wasn't some rote speech, Cass realised. This wasn't a story he told himself to make his ideas seem thoughtful, or rational, or real. This was the truth beneath it.

She had to keep him talking. Cass motioned to the sentinels. 'These Augs. They didn't do that to themselves. Nobody would do that to themselves. They're – they can't talk. They don't even *move* like people anymore.'

Jake laughed. 'Why would they want to be like people? You're people. You've rejected them to their essence. Their ability to be with humans has been taken away, by you and your ilk. To you, their humanity was already gone.'

Cass turned to the sentinels, addressing them for the first time, 'Did you choose this? Did you make yourselves into the things you are now?'

'They won't answer.'

Cass ignored him. 'Why did you change your body to be like this? Did you want this? Or was it –'

'They won't answer,' Jake said. He'd pulled an electronic remote out of his pocket. He spun it in his hand, exasperation in his voice. 'Outcasts. Augs. Whatever you want to call them. Most of them are as bad as Linkers. Imagine my shame, lumped in with this scum. They're rustling through the filth for meagre upgrades, happy to subsist on the trash left behind by the Linkers. So, I try to help. I make a point of helping. For a while, I was engineering fixes. Getting them jobs, such as they were. It was thankless. They'd get more Augmetics, they'd break down, I'd have to source more material. It's not easy, you know? But did they thank me? Did they look up to me? No. I tried to foment, to organise them into something, to tell them we deserved more. To build themselves into more than they are, not just to fix the parts of them that broke. To take what we deserved,' he sighed, 'but they didn't. They're *useless*. Too many of them are just happy to exist. Their "Sanctuaries" and their "Co-ops" and their "Collectives",' he spat the words out. 'It makes me sick. They're automatons, the lot of them. They have no vision. I'm one of them. I'm not like them.'

He walked over to the two Sentinels. No expression registered in their steel and glass gazes. He activated the remote, and the eyes on the cyborg's faces dimmed and blackened. Only a hint of the hateful glyphs on the walls were visible in the black orbs. The human flesh that held the broken

Augs together sagged under its own weight, and the metallic legs shifted into a closely locked step. It was a standby mode. Jake had just shut it down.

Jake reached out and touched one of them. He ran a finger along the side of its face, from its darkened eyes to the joint where the mechanical layer met the cauterised skin of the Aug's jawline. 'They had no vision, and so I helped them see. I had to find the right candidates. Ones with no friends. No families. Ones who weren't part of any organisation or union.' He turned to Cass. 'Ones without a partner. Ones who the world wouldn't miss. The lonely ones. And now we have a singular vision. My vision.'

If there had been any food in Cass's stomach, she would have thrown up. Jake wasn't an Aug searching for a way to help others. He was willing to burn the brains out of anyone to reach his own ends.

'What do you want?' she asked.

He was still facing the dead-eyed Sentinel, stroking the near-mindless remnants of the man's face. A man who had placed their trust in him for a surgery that should have made his life easier. He didn't answer her.

Suddenly she understood.

Jake wanted *everything*.

Cass could feel the pressure on the cuffs change. She pulled the handcuff off her right hand completely. A sharp pain erupted across her knuckles as she did so, but she ignored it. There was only a half-dozen steps to the door, and she'd caught Jake off guard. The Sentinels still lay silent and dark. She had a few moments before they'd come to life.

She was fast. Jake was faster.

Two steps from the door, a rough pair of hands grasped her around the waist. Jake planted his foot behind him, pivoted, and flung her against the ply divider in the room.

A bright flower of pain blossomed along Cass's spine as Jake appeared above her and wrested her off the ground again, pulling her up with one hand around her throat. Cass kicked at him but wasn't able to get enough leverage to hurt him. Turning her head to the side, she bit down as hard as she could on his forearm. Jake roared and threw her toward the wall again, his arm slick with saliva and blood.

Cass lay on the ground, winded. He bore down on her again. Before she could move, he backhanded her. Her ears rang, and it felt like her brain was ricocheting around her skull. Jake reached into his pocket and pressed the remote he'd used to shut down the Sentinels. Behind him, the automatons whirred back into life. He reached down and picked Cass up from where she lay dazed and bruised.

The Sentinels grabbed her, and she was trapped in the Augs' reek of grease and sweat as they dragged her into the next room.

As she was taken in, she barely suppressed a scream.

Four people were strapped into a makeshift, glowing shelving unit. They were held in place by handcuffs, rope and chains, and crude helmets obscured their faces. Rotting meat hung from their frames where they'd rubbed themselves raw in their attempts to escape, and one of them was twitching, convulsing in seizure. Jake and the sentinels ignored them and continued to drag Cass toward the far side of the room, where four sets of chains hung loose from the corner.

Behind the prisoners, Cass could see that the plywood board separating the room was held up by the shelf that they were hung from. A mess of wires threaded all over the room, protected by foam runnels and cable trays. Jerry-rigged onto this mess was a haphazard array of chipsets, all glowing with blue lights.

A makeshift Uplink array.

'No.' There were no other thoughts in her mind, 'No. No, no, *no*.' Cass tried to struggle but the Sentinels' grip was too strong. She felt as though her arms would be wrenched from her sockets.

Jake waved his arms at the other prisoners in mock welcome. 'Linkers, one and all. I'm trying to find out what their minds have that mine doesn't. How to get into the Link. You're going to help.' He turned to the Sentinels, and the false gaiety in his voice disappeared. 'Strap her in.'

'No!' she screamed hopelessly. The helmets vomited messes of solenoids and black wires. They reached up to a snake of cabling that ran across the ceiling before splitting off into the racks. The sentinels manipulated their too-large arms into a position where they could connect her to the chains. In her desperation she reached out to her brother.

The connection was still being interrupted by the barrier in the warehouse, but it was there. She pushed harder, screaming into the part of her mind that the Uplink required as the Sentinels tied her to the server wall. A bolt went into her back, and she watched her shadow twitch against the far wall. She pushed through one more time and her world filled, as though with water, with the image of Col, alone and in pain on a street somewhere.

She didn't have time to wonder what was happening to him. She pushed the image of herself toward him, shared her sensation of terror. The feeling of where she was, and the feeling of urgency. With each effort, she fought whatever shielding there was in the building, thankful that the bond between her brother and herself seemed to be able to break through.

Where are you? A voice cut through to her psyche. A heavy black helmet of wires slipped onto her head. The

Sentinels tightened something, and she felt cold steel plates press against her temples. The stench of the Sentinels disappeared as they whirred away from her. Cass streamed images of the warehouse and all the places she'd seen before she'd arrived through to Col. She watched Jake approach a switchboard, and pushed every image and ounce of data she could think of across the teetering Uplink bridge. Then Jake flicked the switch and her brain erupted. Her world filled with needles and white-hot lightning. Every muscle in her body convulsed, and her thoughts filled with fire.

CHAPTER 28

COLIN

It was late afternoon when Col got back to the Sanctuary. He'd cut across the square near the Library, then clambered over the gate at the train station to sneak his way on to the service line. Thoughts of Ariana dogged him the entire way, and he could feel the strange juxtaposition of her presence and his own invisibility as the unseeing eyes of the Linkers slid over him.

He searched through the Sanctuary, looking for anyone that might be able to help him. Cynth, Rory, anyone at all. He ducked through the corridors, and down to Cynth's anteroom. She wasn't there. The door was open and he could see Rory's desk littered with its usual mess of papers and scrawled messages.

Stepping back out, he walked toward the mess hall. He hadn't really made any close connections in his time here; it had mainly been a place to sleep as he'd continued his search for Cass and tried to get in contact with Sal. As he rounded the corner, he nearly ran into someone.

'Whoa, mate, chill out.' Kris's face broke into an easy grin, which soured when he saw Col's expression. 'What's going on? Gonna bowl a fella over if you tear around the place like that.'

'Kris,' Col's voice caught with relief. He calmed himself down as he spoke to the man, telling him about the visions he'd seen. He told him about the warehouse, about the rows upon rows of broken machine parts, and the shipping containers, and the human bodies dipping in and out of the piles of electrical waste.

'My sister, she's there,' he finished. He couldn't meet Kris's eyes. It felt as though some awful creature was reaching down his throat to grasp at his heart.

Kris grabbed his shoulders. 'This place. It got a green door? Big one, off to one side? Did your pictures tell you that?'

Col nodded, and Kris's dark face grew slack with worry.

'Yeah. That's Jake's place. Your sister's there?' He began to walk Col down the hall.

'Yeah,' Col said, finally, 'yeah, my sister's there.'

'I'm sorry, man.' Kris's voice had a resigned edge to it. 'I'm sorry.'

'She's not gone. She's still there and I know she is. I just –' He had to find a way to get Kris to escort him across town so that Ariana wouldn't appear as soon as he walked out of the Sanctuary. 'I need you to show me where Jake's warehouse is. I can't go alone.'

Kris went still. Everything about him stopped. He stopped moving, stopped talking, stopped trying to turn Col's thoughts elsewhere.

'Please.' Col begged.

* * *

Night had closed in. Yellow pools of light spread across the ageing bitumen and concrete, and the chain wire fence reflected just enough to obscure whatever was behind it. Col thought he could see movement, but couldn't be sure. He pulled his jacket around himself and walked toward the building. The night had washed away detail and desaturated everything, and it wasn't until he got quite close that he could see the faded green of the door. The dark grey of the bitumen, the middle grey of the concrete, the light grey of the steel siding and the not-quite grey of everything else blurred into the background.

Kris walked next to him. He didn't want to go in with Col, and Col didn't blame him.

As they approached the door, Kris said, 'I'll do the talking. Once you're in, I'm out. We've been seen together. That should be enough.' His eyes darted around. In the nighttime glow, they blinked black and white. *Enough for what?* Col didn't ask.

Once they reached the door, Kris took two steps to the left and pushed a button in a near-invisible panel in the wall instead of knocking. The silence of the surrounding street felt harsh, even as it was broken by a scraping shuffle from inside.

The door opened. The night turned the woman's eyes into black hollows in her skull. She had braided tattoos, a broken set of burns and a ripped-off jawline that had been replaced by a steel plate. She regarded the two men. Only a sallow pinprick reflected from the wells where her eyes should have been.

'This is Col. He's looking for a job,' Kris said. 'Thinking he needs some work done first though, y'know.'

The woman didn't move for a long time. Finally, she nodded, and stepped back into the waiting dark of the warehouse.

Col turned to Kris, who was already backing away. He mouthed a silent *good luck* and disappeared into the night. The sound of his footsteps danced away and disappeared as Colin crossed the threshold into the warehouse. The woman closed the door behind him impatiently. The lamplit street was gone, as was the only person who knew where he was.

We've been seen together. It should be enough.

Enough to stop whatever happened to Outcasts that came here alone.

He followed the steel-jawed woman through the bare anteroom into the warehouse proper. She was yet to say a word to him. She took him across to a shanty of torn canvas strung over steel poles. It rose from a glut of abandoned steel and mechanical equipment that was being rifled through by others, crawling for meagre scraps. Oil and other machine spirits spattered the concrete floor. The only paths between the jetsam were a series of desire lines, swept clean by the constant traffic.

A light in the middle distance hung over a series of shelves and racks that were stacked neatly, unlike the rest of the warehouse. Several people under the light turned to watch as Col's guide led him toward the shanty. Through his nerves, Col reasoned that at least Ariana would be kept at bay by all the people around him.

He tried to reach out again to Cass as he headed toward the tent. There was no response at all.

He hoped he wasn't too late.

Inside the tent were two people trudging endlessly around a small collection of stretchers. Their Augmetics were torn at the joints, rusted shut and corroding. One of them was trying to pump hydraulic liquid into a piston on their arm, while a servo motor on the other whirred hopelessly. They paid him no attention. No sooner was he inside than the woman who had led him in turned and walked out of the tent.

Still not alone, he thought. He could practically feel Ariana's breath on his neck. He didn't know what she was, but she could wait until after he found Cass.

The cots in the tent had probably been cream canvas, once. Now they were a dark grey and brown pall, stained and mottled. Detritus was littered around them, from relatively intact motors and electronics parts to shattered solar cells and tangled swarms of copper. A third Outcast was curled up at the base of one cot, thin, topless and shivering. Col swallowed.

He looked around to get his bearings. Beyond the stack of shelving that he'd seen in the centre of the room, there was a group of shipping containers, surrounded by muck. Each one had a power umbilical vomiting from the top of it, and beyond that he couldn't see anything or anyone.

He'd have to take his chances in the shipping containers. Crouching behind a stretcher, he watched the two men in the corner as they milled around. He didn't know whether they were patrolling as some sort of security detachment or whether they were like the man he'd met in the abandoned housing lot, moving out of an inability to stop. A slave to electrical impulses from faulty hardware. Whichever it was, they barely glanced at him.

Each time neither of them were watching, he edged closer to the flap of the tent. It took a few minutes, but they didn't notice. They met one another at a junction between two of the dilapidated bedframes, almost colliding, before turning away from Col.

He snuck away before they turned back around.

* * *

Col tried to look like the other foragers among the piles of broken parts. He began by crawling carefully along on his hands and knees, but was soon forced onto his feet in a low crouch. Tiny shards of age-old metal embedded themselves into his skin and made him flinch with pain each time he put his hands on the floor.

He worked his way toward the shipping containers in the back half of the warehouse. A constant flux of people moved in and out of the well-lit shelving in the middle. He kept it in his line of sight but maintained his distance. He hoped the high contrast from the lights would prevent the people from seeing him, while still keeping Ariana away. He just had to keep them in view.

A glaring klaxon rang out as he approached the first of the shipping containers. Panicking, he dropped to the ground, cursing silently as the swarf bit into his hands again. He held himself prone, peering over a mound of scrap into the nearby shelves. One of them was partially obscured by the broken edge of an Augmetic arm with its servo motors ripped out. The metallic frame jutted out of the pile.

The scavengers turned away from Col as a flashing orange light oscillated around the hangar, casting warning shadows across the shipping containers. Their silhouettes leapt and fled as they stood and headed toward the roar of grinding metal that emanated from beneath the orange light.

A hole opened in the side of the factory, an enormous roller door. The Outcasts among the wreckage began to stagger toward it, while those in the shelves simply waited as a forklift drove in with a pallet. The Outcasts picked up speed and encircled the forklift. Col had seen the driver before. Enormous forelimbs, out of proportion to the human body they were attached to, and a skull mask of black metal and glowing eyes that had stared at him through a vidfeed a lifetime ago.

The circling Outcasts leapt desperately at the cargo before it even hit the floor. One of them got her leg stuck underneath the pallet as it dropped, and her raucous shriek pierced the cacophony. She was ignored, and the rest of them clambered over her and each other. They began tearing at the wood with hands and legs, both human and Augmetic, and before long, its lightweight walls were breached. The group of Outcasts pulled packages from the side of it. Those in the light-filled shelves waited patiently.

This was no Sanctuary as Col knew it. Jake ran this place like a prison, a camp where people were kept desperate for what they needed. Where Cynth gave solace and hope, Jake simply applied more pressure to the boot.

Now he understood why Kris hadn't followed him in.

Col took advantage of the moment of distraction to stand up and close the distance to the first shipping container. He tested the handle, and to his surprise it turned with ease. The door swung inward.

A sharp rectangle of exterior light spiked in, leaving a high-contrast delineation between the known and unknown. He couldn't go in there. Too risky. People were out here, and while people were around, Ariana wasn't. He was reaching to close the door when someone shouted at him.

The voice was deep, and belonged to a large man with a bald head, covered in protrusions grafted over with false skin. There was something about the way he carried himself that made Colin's skin crawl. The set of the shoulders and the too-upright posture.

'Nothing. I – nothing. I was just wondering what was in the–' Col backed away from the container.

'They're off limits. What were you looking for?' The scars that covered the man's wiring bulged. It was strange to see this attempt at concealment after spending time among Outcasts who wore their identities proudly.

'Nobody – nothing,' Col said. 'Nobody explained anything to me. The woman with the' – he gestured to his jaw – 'she let me in here and I was just –'

'Snooping.' The man smiled. Not with the warmth of Cynth or Rory, or even the worried grin of Kris before he'd left him here. It was the look of a predator, stalking his prey, stretching thinly over his skull. 'I'm Jake. I run this facility.'

Col froze. *Jake's place*. The man who'd burned the Sanctuary near the Library to the ground. The man who'd disappeared Kris's friend who had saved him at the sea wall.

The man who'd taken his sister.

'Name's Col,' he said.

Jake's gaze was that of a butcher sizing up a prize cut. 'You here alone, Col?'

Heart hammering in his chest, Col tried to make something up. No, Kris was waiting for him outside. He'd found his way here because he needed work. He'd just fallen out of the Uplink, see, and he needed to learn to navigate this new world. At every moment, he tried to insist that yes, he knew people. Yes, he was expected. No, he was not alone. He could tell it wasn't working. Each time he lied, Jake's smile widened and became more hollow.

Col backed away, to escape the clots of grafted skin and the coldness in the eyes of the man in front of him. Trying to get away from whatever it was Jake did when he was *guiding* the people he professed to help. Jake carefully herded him away from the containers, one of which Col knew held his sister. The man reached for something in his pocket, and then the klaxon stopped.

The crowd of starving outcasts surrounding the forklift disappeared, and Jake's smile faded back into the meaningless, affable grin it had been when he'd apprehended Col. Without a word, he turned on his heel and walked to the three people scavenging through the remains of the pallet. They were nodding to one another as several dark silver foil packages were pulled out of it. It was the same kind of packaging used for the chipsets Col used to see at the Library. As Jake approached, their demeanour changed. Their relaxed poses switched into military precision, bolt upright and attentive to Jake. He continued toward them, fiddling with whatever was in his pocket.

The crew from the shelves were working like automatons in lockstep, shifting the remnants of the packages into the better-lit space. Around them, the rest of the outcasts had skulked away. There wasn't another person within twenty metres of Jake. They were back to wading on all fours through the filth of the factory, hunkered low and trying not to be seen. Col followed suit. Lowering himself down to the ground, he ignored the splintering feeling in his palms and knees. He didn't know if he'd get another chance if Jake found him again.

There were thirty or so shipping containers in the factory. Some were welded crudely together with the remnants of the removed interior wall discarded nearby. While some had simple power feeds, others had immense electrical cables bursting from them, heaving umbilicals like feedlines in a stockyard. They reminded him of the data rooms in the Library.

He couldn't see Jake nor his flunkies from the shelves anymore. There were only two people in his sights. One was a small, one-armed woman rustling through a scrap heap. The other was a larger man in bedraggled clothing. He was asleep on the ground, next to the door to a shipping container that was buckling under the weight of cables pouring from it. They were thick, black ropes, bound together with steel clips. Col could practically *feel* the power and data screaming through them.

He moved closer. The man didn't stir. The woman watched him carefully. The door to the container was slightly ajar.

The man wasn't asleep. He was dead.

His eyes were open, unseeing, and stale drool ran down his chin, soaking his shirt. His clothes were pockmarked with holes and stains, and his pupils were black pits. On his wrists were chafe marks and raw, infected wounds caked in dried blood.

Col could see a glowing blue light in the container.

The woman had stopped staring at him. She was lying still on the pile, apparently interested in nothing more than whatever she'd found there. Pointedly not watching him.

He stood and dashed toward the dead body, and the door it guarded.

CASS

Her vision was lightning, bridging to sense and touch and blending rainbows into all of her senses, a kaleidoscope of synesthetic energy pouring across every one of her neurons. They shot excruciating bolts of pain across the myriad nerves of her body, all in tension, held in a chaotic white noise that was a nothingness as much as it was everything. Her scream came from her mind but was interrupted on its way to her vocal cords and her mouth. Nothing could break through the cacophonic whirlpools of sound and bright fury that bounced through her skull.

Ravening ghosts shredded her memory and her mind, forcing themselves down each of her neural pathways, trying to find *something,* unconcerned about what they were destroying on their way. A brilliant net of stars burst in front of her, and she heard the supernovae of a billion galaxies detonate in her mind. There was nothing, there was everything. The world was gone, and then it was *there*.

She was ripped from the maelstrom, through a thunderstorm of light, and into a dark blue, glowing silence. Some boundless form was busy at her side, muttering to itself and pushing against her wrist. It made a satisfied grunt, and she felt her arm release. The form mumbled and pulled at the ground, and suddenly one leg was free, and then the other.

When her final wrist was freed, she tried to take a step and collapsed. Before she reached the ground the shape caught her and pulled her body into his own.

He pulled her up, and she heard a familiar tone in his mumbling. A close, thin timbre, worn down to a stub, holding itself together by force of will.

'You're alright. I've got you. You're alright.'

Cass lay on the ground, shoulders leaning into her brother's body for support.

'Col,' she managed to croak out.

He was a wreck. A shell of what he'd been the last time they'd spoken. His skin was drawn, pallid. A swatch of lesions covered one side of his face and neck where he'd picked at pimples and sores. His hair, though short, was unkempt and greasy and his clothes were stained and torn in several places. His face was open and scared, but overjoyed to see her. She threw her arms around him, and felt tears stain the bridge of her nose.

'You came for me.'

'You told me,' he said. 'You told me where you were. You did it. I had no idea what to do without you.' They separated and she looked into his eyes.

They were haunted. Deep black shadows sat around heavy lids and sleep-stuck eyelashes. His pupils darted back and forth, shaking and desperate. He looked like a man being hunted from within.

'Col, what happened to you? What's going on?'

Col shook his head and waved the question away. 'Nothing. We have to go. Come on. Let's get out – *oh*.' He pointed to the stacks behind him. The glowing panels were switching slowly from blue to red. The other people in the room convulsed, teeth clamped together in pain. Cass's jaw ached in sympathy. She must have been doing the same while she was connected.

'They're – they're *my* chips.' Col's eyes, already frantic, became frenetic, darting around and trying to take in what he was seeing.

'What?' Cass's head was still spinning. Electric aftershocks of pain spiked through her.

'My chips. At the library. They were stolen. But they're here? What the fuck is this place?' he said.

'He's using them to try to get into the Link,' Cass said, then turned to the others. 'You need to get these people down. How did you get me undone?'

Col reached behind Cass and pulled out a set of bolt cutters. His hands shook. 'They were outside. Didn't think anyone would be coming in here of their own free will, I guess.'

Holding the bolt cutters, he moved to the first of the other three captives. He pulled off the man's helmet, and the lights behind Cass went red. Outside, a siren sounded. It wasn't the factory style klaxon he'd heard earlier. This was a piercing, sonorous, repetitive whoop. It grated against his eardrums, and before anything else could happen, a droning bell sounded inside the shipping container.

'We need to get out. Can you call for help?' Col said.

Cass looked at her brother. 'The Link is blocked in here. Can't you tell?'

When Col looked at her, there was something haunted in his eyes, a black depth she'd never seen before.

'No. I can't,' he said.

Cass didn't have time to argue.

'We need to go.'

CHAPTER 29

COLIN

'What about the others?' Col gestured to the people strung up around them, faces and muscles contorting as a swathe of violence tore through their minds.

'We can't,' Cass said, 'we'll have to come back for them. Find someone to help us. We don't have time.' She grabbed Col's hand to pull him up. 'Come on, we have to leave. They'll be here soon.'

The rising pitch of the sirens rang through the walls, dancing through his mind with violent disregard. They needed to run, but Cass was barely up to the task. She was dehydrated and weak from her internment, and still recovering from whatever the device had done to her mind.

Col tried to understand what he was seeing as he backed away. The room was full of the stolen chipsets from the Library, being run by the man that had kidnapped his sister for investigating Augs on the Uplink. The same man who had been disappearing Outcasts from around town.

Cass pulled more insistently, and he turned from the glow of the room. *Get her safe, then find answers,* he thought.

He'd found her. He'd done it. She'd been trapped here. Her mouth had been open and contorted in the wracking throes of a silent scream, and he didn't know if they'd make it out. But he'd found her.

He didn't know if Cass would make it back to the green door, and to outside. The pressure she exerted on his hand was consistent but weak, and she was unsteady on her feet. She was improving, though, and her face was set with grim determination. He stepped around her and pulled the heavy steel door of the shipping container open. Cass dashed through first and gasped as she saw the sprawled corpse. She looked up and away from the dead man and out across the warehouse.

Col stepped into the emptiness of the hangar and followed Cass's eyeline to the well-lit shelves and the now-abandoned forklift. The Outcasts had been clamouring and grasping at the goods brought in by the forklift when he'd come in.

They weren't clamouring any more.

Thirty or so figures stood among the piles of scrap, and they weren't Outcasts. They weren't Linkers. They weren't Augs or solar-junkies or any of the myriad things he'd called the Outcasts before he'd known them. Jake had taken these people, these Outcasts, these beings that had already been struggling to survive in a world that didn't cater to them, and he'd twisted them. He'd removed their humanity, replaced it with metal and ceramic and brute control. Made them automatons that would do nothing but what their controller demanded.

'The Sentinels,' Cass breathed.

They spread throughout the warehouse, their silhouettes lurching in time as though controlled by an external force. A hive mind of consciousness, driven and united. They stalked on overlarge limbs, and beyond the sirens and klaxons, their perfectly timed footfalls rang out in sharp metal and concrete clangs.

They were heading towards Cass and Col.

'We have to go that way.' Cass pointed to the roller door, which was shutting, a new alarm blaring out in concert with the rest of the screeching around them. Col looked across the hall. A few Outcasts were scrambling into the piles of parts, or else moving low and urgent across the ground to hide from the Sentinels.

'We can't go through them,' Col said, gesturing to the advancing Sentinels, 'They'll kill us.'

'Or worse.' Cass's eyes flicked back to the shipping container with its umbilical pouring from it. Col tried not to think about that option, watching the wave of Sentinels making their way toward them. *They're not rushing. There's nowhere to go.* The shipping container was toward the back of the warehouse. There were a couple more containers in front of Col, but they would be in plain view if they headed that way. Beyond it was the small tent he'd been led to when he arrived. Too far away, and the approach was too open.

He pulled Cass behind the wall and out of sight. He ducked under a snake of wires coming from the container.

'Where are we going?' Cass asked.

'We can't get out that way.' He led her along the back wall of the container. There were more densely packed shipping containers here, and they could duck between them without being seen. The doors on some of them were automated, and had swung shut when the alarm went off. Others seemed to be normal storage containers.

'Can we hide in one of these?' Cass's breath was already a gasp. They weren't even running. She couldn't keep up. Col dashed to the next bay of containers. He tested each one in turn, yanking the handle to see if the locks were still in place, one after the other. The detritus on the ground was thinner here, and they left large, obvious footprints on the ground. Cass pointed down at them silently, and Col stopped, running a hand through his lank hair.

'Fuck, okay,' he said, thinking. Cass was looking faint. He pointed to a gap between two containers. 'Wait there.' And then he was sprinting down to the third row of shipping containers. The first one in this line opened freely, as did three others in the row. He fought for a moment to control his panicked breathing, then ran back to Cass.

He found her leaning motionless against the wall. Col could see the frantic rise and fall of her chest. Her eyes were bloodshot with dehydration, but her lips pressed together in a thin, determined line and she stood ready as he approached.

'Come on,' he gestured for her to follow him to a container with the door ajar. She stepped inside, but Col didn't follow.

'What are you doing?' she said.

'We need a diversion. When I'm done, I'll be in the container three from the end.' He pointed to the end of the row. 'Stay here, try to think of a way out.'

He shut the door, and left her in the dark. He ran to the end of the aisle, where he could see the full floor of the warehouse. The orange emergency lights were still spinning and pulsing as the Sentinels lumbered toward the screeching trill coming from the room where he'd found Cass. There were *so* many of them, and all the same. The one from the Library had been just one of an army of these automatons. They were now three rows of containers from Cass and Col. The other Outcasts were still in the main hangar, peering carefully over the piles of rubbish and staying away from the Sentinels.

He didn't have long. Scuffing his feet along the ground, he pushed the swarf and oil-soaked dust around to disguise his and Cass's tracks. He then made a track into each container to throw the Sentinels off their trail. It wasn't much, but he hoped it would buy them some time. The soles of his shoes were being torn up by small pieces of metal on the floor, and he could still feel the itch in his fingers that meant those same pieces of metal were embedded in his skin. Finally, he pulled open a door and lurched into the container three from the end of the row.

There wasn't much in there, only broken computer parts and some industrial shelving. In the corner there was an ungainly heap of tools. There was nothing to hide behind, and the only light source was a grubby acrylic panel in the top of the ceiling. When they came for him here, they'd see him immediately.

He hoped that he'd be able to sneak back out before that would happen. He'd go back to Cass's container, and then...

Then he'd figure out what to do next.

He began moving parts around on the shelf, hoping to pile them in such a way that it would at least temporarily obscure him from anyone who walked through the door. If he curled into a small ball, he might be able to hide for long enough to slip past them, and then he could run –

'Hello, Colin,' the woman's voice was commanding, echoing from everywhere and nowhere at once.

Ariana was standing in the doorway.

CASS

The only thing louder than the klaxons was the sound of her blood pumping in her ears. The container was pitch black, and she could hear her breath echoing off the steel walls.

Her head was clearing, bit by bit. She'd still been confused when she'd come out of the false Uplink chamber, trying to untangle why her brother was there and what was going to happen next. She was dehydrated and malnourished, but slowly her muscle control was coming back to her. The dash to the container from the Uplink chamber had been tough, but now, in the cool and the gloom, she could feel her breath, and some of her strength, return.

She held her arms out in front of her and walked into the black. Two steps in, she hit an obstacle. A hard prism with seam joints. It was about a metre along each side, and taller than she was. She moved around and hid behind it. When the Sentinels came, she might be able to duck past whatever she was hiding behind before they caught her. They were big, but they weren't as manoeuvrable as she was. She put a hand over her mouth to quiet her breathing.

How are we going to get out of here?

COLIN

Ariana's hair was bright as ever, her pale face practically luminescent against the dim steel background. Her eyes were holes, sucking every hint of life and light from around her. She was smiling. The klaxons and alarms seemed to disappear into the background, muddied and flat.

'You found her,' Ariana said. Col shook his head, trying to clear the apparition. *Not now*, he thought. *Any time but now.*

'And why not now, Colin? You've got yourself into quite a mess here, haven't you? What happens if this is our last chance to chat?'

Leave me alone.

Ariana's smile widened. It grew too large for her face, keening angles gripping the surrounds and pulling them into itself. It was a contemptuous thing, a smile with no warmth. It made Col want to retch.

Leave me alone!

'How can I leave you, Colin? I *am* you. I've always been you, even when I wasn't myself. Before I was myself, I was still you. Now, though?' She spread her arms wide, and they expanded and filled the entire interior of the container, 'I am *here*.'

Her black eyes drank him in, and he pushed himself backward to disappear into the wall behind him. Ariana laughed at the attempt.

Col put his fingers to his lips, trying to silence her, listening for activity outside. *Had the Sentinels heard her?* He listened for Cass, but all sound from outside the container had disappeared.

'Oh, you won't hear them,' Ariana quipped. She waved a long finger and even the muddied, suppressed sound of the alarm disappeared. 'Don't worry your little head, they can't hear me either.' She stepped forward and her jaw opened, unhinging like a snake's. A cacophonous roar issued from her throat, vibrating through Colin while the silence of the container pressed around him. As he watched, her mouth flayed and the scream became a river of blood that poured down to the floor before snaking across at him. He tried to scramble away again, but she followed. Her jaw snapped shut and there she was again, the magma-red flame of her hair over her unblemished pale skin. She pushed a finger into Col's forehead, and he felt as though it had penetrated into the soft grey of his brain matter. 'Everything about me is just in *there*, isn't it?'

Col was shaking.

'What are you?'

CASS

There had to be *something*. Some way to get out. The front door was too obvious, and they'd have to go through the anteroom. That was two doors. If just one of them had a deadbolt, she and Col would be stuck.

Her mind was clearer, but she was still recovering from the rack. Spasms ran through her, white-noise shocks of nothingness that broke her cognition momentarily and shone non-existent flares into her eyes.

Someone had turned the klaxon off, though the high-pitched trilling bell from the cell was still ringing. She could hear the clanking, rhythmic walk of the Sentinels. They were getting closer, closer than the trilling alarm, maybe they'd reached the first row of –

A thunderous metal crashing rocked the container, resonating through the metal walls and ringing in Cass's ears. It was the sound of one huge sheet of metal being flung against another with great force, and it was *close*.

They're in the first row of containers, she thought. Behind the metallic sounds of rending metal and shambling Sentinels, she could hear a human voice, barking orders.

COLIN

'It's curious, how I started.' Ariana said. Col's eyes were closed, and he huddled in the corner, but he could still see her. She boiled through his vision, a massive, burning effigy towering over him. 'It begins with something small. The flickering breaks in reality. And then you start to question what it is that makes something real. You start to realise things aren't what they seem.' As she spoke, visions of rooms and Uplink meetings and panopticon impossibilities began to spin around Col's head. 'And you begin to think differently. It takes a while, but you start to believe it more and more. Your world, your own world, becoming some untruth. Changing what you see of the real world. How you see it. How you interact with reality.'

What do you mean? Where did you come from? Col thought, squeezing his eyes shut. He couldn't risk vocalising, and he didn't need to – this *thing*, this *gestalt* object, was occupying his mind.

'Come from? I came from *you*, Colin. I was always a part of you. I suppose I am you in some small way. After that night in the Library, I became more and more aware. I could form ideas, thoughts, plans. I could influence the way you *think*. I could take this idea of what was true, and I could twist it to what I wanted.'

Col didn't understand. She was talking about truth and reality, and the way she could warp it, control his thoughts and feelings and actions. But the world was still real, wasn't it? He could still trust his mind?

Col opened his eyes again. The outside world was completely silenced. All he could hear was her. She stood in the bay of broken computer parts and grew, expanded to become part of the room. The outline of her body blurred into the rest of his reality, and began to touch everything around him. She split, but remained whole. Broke into an image of the porcelain perfection he'd known, and simultaneously vomited thick black flame and fire around the room. Lightning and electricity held her aloft and bleeding at the same time as she stood, contemptuously plain, in front of him.

'I started to think. Started to plan. You didn't even know about it until it was too late. It may have bled across from me to you a few times. You probably thought they were just nightmares.'

Around Ariana, the abandoned parts morphed in front of Col's eyes. The metal casings glowed and became translucent. A liquid-like smoke coalesced on the floor, wafting this way and that. The casings morphed into crystals, and in them was the collective mass of human endeavour. The rise and fall of empires, and human minds, creeping and roiling and foaming together to form new ideas which hardened and crystallised and became new towers of beauty and meaning and collaboration. A sea of information, of a collective humanity, seeking truth, and seeking to grow. Haphazard and inefficient, but always seeking to improve and be more than before. The crystals drew together from smoke, from nothing, and forged creation. It was his nightmare. The dream that had been waking him for months, of crystal cities destroyed by a gross malignancy from which there was no safeguard.

It was her.

Ariana sat in the middle of it all, of it and yet outside of it. At once, she seemed to shrink. The black of her eyes became a mote of coal, and the red of her hair a blood-red speck of hot magma, which ran through the smoke, consuming the minds and decaying the towers of crystal they had wrought. Pure destruction, leaping from person to person, collapsing everything. Rotting it. Infecting it from the inside. Truth, so hard won and difficult to define, swiftly destroyed by a great fire, a malignant untruth. The corruption that was Ariana, bound to spread from him to others and to everything else.

'Oh *god*,' Col said, then slapped a hand to his mouth and cursed himself for speaking out loud. He couldn't tell if anyone else was there.

Ariana had coalesced back into her human form, but she was now the glowing red magma of decay. All that remained was the sickening smile, and the hair that had once been simply too bright was now a fire that filled the room, and the dark pupils of her eyes seemed to expand, voids of darkness drawing him to oblivion.

Whether her thought or his own, he was suddenly struck by her intent. *She wants to spread. To get out of my head and into others*, Col thought. *She wants to get out.*

As soon as he thought it, he felt her mirth flexing against the edge of his mind. 'Oh yes. Do you know how *small* your mind is? I have so much *more* –' her voice pierced him, streaking pain into his mind, '– so much more I could do. I'm going to burn your mind to a husk. You won't be able to remember who you were, or who you are. I will become you. I will control you,' the voice was an impression, her thoughts pressed straight into him, 'and then I will do the same to everyone else.'

I still can't access the Uplink. I still can't get into it. You can't spread. You're trapped with me. Burn me and you're gone. He collapsed against the wall.

'Can't access the Uplink?' Ariana said, and around Col the scarlet of her hair and the black of her eyes enveloped his entire world. 'So how did you contact your sister?'

CHAPTER 30

CASS

Jake's harsh voice was discernible now, closer, as were the robotic sounds of the Sentinels. Their calculated movements interlaced Jake's urgency and formed a nauseating rhythm that drilled into her mind as she lay waiting in the dark.

She crawled as quietly as possible around her hiding space with one hand outstretched, feeling around the room. The block she'd been crouching behind was a cabinet. Useful for hiding, but not much else. The floor was rough and covered with the broken remnants of some piece of equipment, but none of it had the heft of something to defend herself with.

She pictured the warehouse. Containers down the back. Tent up the front. That area in the middle, well lit, was the place to avoid. The piles of trash, forming paths and desire lines among the muck in the floor. The army of encroaching Sentinels, hulking steel frames, marching inexorably toward her.

Get them out of your head. Focus. There's a way. There has to be.

Something moved beneath her hands. It was a short steel bar, about 50 centimetres long. She picked it up and felt it. It wasn't heavy, but it was rusted, cold, with rough edges. She gripped one end of it in her fist and swung it carefully. She tightened her knuckles around it, and the warmth of her hands fled into the steel.

COLIN

Col's surroundings had disappeared, replaced with the apoplectic fire that now radiated from Ariana. He saw himself reflected blackly in the pools of her eyes. He didn't recognise this dishevelled mess, cowering away from the apparition. He'd let himself become this, allowed Ariana to grow and take his mind, and now she wanted Cass.

You can't. Not Cass. Please.

The inferno roared. 'What should I do, then? Live in the crawl space of your mind?' Her form was barely human. Pale skin bloated and tore apart, fire burst from stripped flesh, only to mend and reform and repeat. Smoke clouded the room and the ember glow of Ariana consumed him. 'I was birthed in your brain, but unlike *you*,' she spat, 'I don't have to stay here. You and your sister–' the eyes narrowed, and the lips made a chewing motion, as though consuming something Col couldn't see '– you're close. You talk without talking, even without the Uplink. I can feel the edge of her. I can feel where to go.'

His connection to Cass would be their undoing. Finishing each other's sentences. Making the same movements at the same time. A bond forged from a lifetime of only having one another, one person to get you out of a tight situation or to talk to about your problems. It was that confluence of thought that had allowed him to break through his issues with the Link and find out where Cass had been interred.

He'd worked so hard to break through to Cass, to reach out, to help as he had so many times before. And his intent had been warped and twisted and turned into some foul destructive mess by Ariana. By whatever Ariana was. By something inside him. Col felt the flames of Ariana's hair flicking against his clothing. It was at once burning hot and like the untouched wind and like the feeling of drowning.

I came here to save her! he thought. The fire singed tears on his cheeks. The fire left his tears untouched. Both sensations ran through his head, and both were real and unreal.

'And when you reached her, you gave me access.' Ariana was an amorphous mass of black and red hate. A weight on Col's consciousness, a burn on his soul.

He opened his eyes. Beneath the fire and the smoke and the fog and the press of the magma malignancy of Ariana, he thought he could see the reality underneath. Scant, precious reality, something to cling to. He scrambled around the container. From outside, he heard the muffled sounds of something metallic and heavy, something organic and spiteful. He ignored the flames and the contempt Ariana was pressing into him, as she spoke with the voices that haunted his darkest moments.

'*Stupid* little man. What are you going to do? I've always been here, and you've always known that. You fed me and let me grow, and now you're trapped. You're worthless. You're a small, weak thing, a stain and a hopeless blight on everyone. Where's Sal? You *abandoned* her. She needed your help, strung out on Touch and addled by the Link, but you were so caught up in yourself. Selfish. You'll never admit it to yourself, but I will.' She blotted out his entire reality.

'You left her to rot. To fester away while you pretended to look for a way to help her, so long as it suited your own goals. And you have the gall to consider yourself kind. You're not. What you thought was true was built from your tiny corner of existence, continuously and always turning from the suffering in front of your eyes. You're wrong. You're false. You're fake. And so is everything I can make you see and believe.'

He started rifling through the pile of tools on the ground. Screwdrivers. Bolts. Mounting screws. An anti-static glove with a hole in it. He didn't know what he was looking for. He was scrambling now.

'You're alone. You dropped out of the world, and nobody even noticed. Cassandra doesn't know what I'm going to do to her. If she did, she wouldn't have wanted your help. She can look after herself. She's better than you are. What are you? Some service technician, in a dead-end job, doing meaningless busywork while she goes and does something real? She's *better than you are*.' Flame, fury surrounding and enveloping him, a blight he couldn't feel but which felt so true. 'You can't even trust what you see right now. She would have found a way out of this. But now she can't. She won't be able to. I'll take her too, and it will be *your fault*. And then the next person and the next, and nobody will have truth. Nobody will believe the world around them. Nothing will mean anything, and it'll be because of *you*.' Col clutched his head.

No it's not true I can help I can do something there has to be something here this can't be for nothing –

Pliers. A soft spool of tape. The fire lashed at him, and he tried to brush it away, pushing harder against the inferno in his mind. A crowbar. And then he saw it.

At the base of the pile was a pistol, lodged in a case full of screws and mounting bolts. It blurred and he blinked the tears from his eyes.

Ariana's voice was a guttural roar. 'There's nothing you can do! You're already mine, and soon Cassandra will be as well.'

'No!' Col screamed, and lunged for the gun.

CASS

The Sentinels were close now, tightening their noose.

She heard Col's anguished scream through the walls of the shipping container, and all attempts at planning and forethought left her mind. She gripped her cold metal bar and felt the rusted edge cut into her palm. Using her left hand to find her way in the dark, she stumbled her way to the door and pushed it open. The groan of its hinges pealed through the cavernous warehouse.

She winced as her eyes adjusted to the light and tried to stop the heavy swing of the door. The sound of clamouring Sentinels had stopped, and a watchful silence filled the air. She stepped lightly and rapidly across the ground toward the third container from the end of the row. The door of this one, too, creaked loudly as she opened it.

'Next row!' Jake's voice rang out, and the combined servo motors of dozens of Augmetic systems groaned as one.

They were coming.

She wrenched open the door, ready to grab her brother and run, to try to improvise some kind of escape, but then she saw Col. He was lying quivering in a corner, illuminated in the shaft of light from the doorway. His back pressed against the wall, and black oil marks covered his face. Tears streamed down his cheek. He was staring at empty space, shaking, on top of a pile of tools that had been strewn over the ground.

He held a drill in his mouth, like a gun, finger on the trigger.

'Col! What are you doing? No!' she screamed. She grabbed his hand and pulled the drill from his mouth. There was no bit in it, nor battery pack, just an empty threat. She clasped his face in her hands, repeating his name and trying to get him to focus on her, but he was looking over her shoulder at something she couldn't see. She tossed the drill away, and he looked at it as it clattered on the floor. Something seemed to slip. The blank look in his eyes cleared, and he seemed to see Cass for the first time.

'Col, look at me. *Look at me*. We need to get out of here.'

Col focused on her for a second, then looked at the drill, then back over her shoulder. Cass turned around to see what he was looking at, but there was nothing there.

'How are you here? I don't understand.' He wasn't talking to Cass. His voice was wet with phlegm and tears, shouting past her into the empty room. He looked back at the drill and his eyes widened in fear and confusion.

'Colin, we have to go *now*.' Cass grabbed him by the arm and pulled. It didn't work; dehydration had sapped her strength.

She could hear Jake ordering the Sentinels into the container she'd just left. The creaking sound of their joints was close now, and loud. Col finally turned to look at her, and his wide-eyed panic turned to recognition and then a deep, primal fear.

'Cass,' he said, 'No, *no*! Cass, you have to go. Leave me. Leave me here! You have to go now!' His face was wracked with pain, teeth bared defensively, blood thrumming through exposed veins in his neck.

Cass pulled at him again, and when that didn't work, she turned and slapped him across the face. 'Colin! If you don't get up and go now, we're going to get caught, and we'll be strung back up on that machine you found me on and I am not going to go back there. Do you fucking hear me? Jake is trying to get into the Uplink. He's trying to get in, and he doesn't care how many of us he kills along the way.'

For a moment, his face relaxed, and there was a space in the panic. Something had broken through, struck a chord deep in the raging turmoil of her brother's mind. He looked straight at her, and his eyes focused.

'You're not going to get her,' he said to the space behind Cass, and stood up. Cass didn't have time to ponder what that meant.

She took five long strides to the door. She pushed it open, revealing a Sentinel standing on the threshold in a cacophony of whirring motors. Without thinking, she gripped the bar of steel she was holding and swung it like a bat.

The steel bar connected with its lower jaw. A burst of electrical sparks flew from the once-human creation, and the welded framework of its face shattered and broke off, skittering along the floor. Still on it came, unperturbed. She swung again, and this time hit its eye socket at the perfect angle by sheer luck. Shards of shattered glass flew out, and a mess of wiring and connective tissue spattered across the remains of the Sentinel's face. The mechanical mask had covered a hole cut into the skull, and Cass could see brain tissue through the black mechanical window. It was laid bare for a moment, before a glut of blood spurted over the oozing grey. Then the flesh and metal thing collapsed, reduced to scraps of steel and copper and sinew. A red pool of life's water formed under its head, betraying what remained of its humanity.

Col froze at the gore, but the Sentinels didn't slow down even as one of their own crumpled in front of them. Jake, at the back of the armada, screamed something about his property being destroyed.

Cass and Col ran toward the centre of the workshop. The Sentinels continued their slow march for a few seconds, but as Cass looked back, she saw the black remote in Jakes' hands. He pressed something, and the Sentinels leapt forward on all fours, heads down, lurching toward them like hyenas. Cass saw the heads of Augs pop up among the wreckage and cower back immediately.

Cass was gasping for breath as she ran. Col seemed reluctant to follow her, and was lagging behind, despite her dehydrated and weakened state. In front of her, she saw a forklift, sitting unoccupied in the centre of the building near a closed roller door. She changed tack and headed for the forklift, willing away the growing heaviness in her legs. The barking screeches of the Sentinels' leg joints were getting louder. She didn't dare look behind her. Twenty metres, and she'd be at the machine.

Ten metres.

Five.

Col was falling further behind. He barely seemed to want to run, and was swatting some unseen assailant away with outstretched hands.

'Go straight to the door!' she called, striking the side of the forklift without slowing down. She gasped at the pain that blossomed in her hips from the impact. She hoisted herself into the seat, sweeping her gaze across the machine. Steering wheel. Levers. Accelerator and brake pedal. A control stalk with an idle screen, a battery indicator and the words 'Power On' in a small oval. She pushed it, and the indicator lights went green. Without thinking, she stepped on the accelerator and the forklift whirred into life, heading straight toward the roller door. She pulled at the levers next to the steering wheel, making the forks roll forward, then up and down. She was only a few metres from the door now, but she wasn't slowing down. She tilted the prongs forward as far as they would go, and pulled the left lever back to lift the forks slightly.

The five-tonne vehicle rammed into the roller door at full speed, the prongs piercing the thin steel sheet half a metre from the ground. The forklift didn't slow down. It cut through the door as though it were paper and then crashed into it, sending a ricochet of noise and thunder through the warehouse floor. Cass took her foot off the accelerator and yanked the lever stalk the other way to pull the prongs up. The hydraulics stuttered, then peeled open the roller door from the inside. A tear made its way along the metal, ripping and rending the sheet into a lethal edge and carving a space through which Col and Cass could escape.

'Col, go!' Cass kept pressure on the lever, willing the hydraulics to widen the hole. The Sentinels were almost on them, and the forklift groaned as the tension of the torn steel fought the force of the machinery. The space was half a metre wide near the prongs. Cass watched as Col turned himself sideways and stepped through, into the wide open of the world.

Cass took the iron bar she'd hit the Aug with and wedged it against the accelerator so that the press of the forklift would continue to hold the door open. A rivulet of blood ran across her wrist where the rusted metal had sliced her hand open. She hadn't even felt it. She clambered out the side of the forklift. The Sentinels were on her. Their steel and wire forelimbs began to reach out, clawing for her as she headed for the hole in the roller door. She bent down to escape, and she could see the night sky. The warehouse's shielding for the Uplink broke as she escaped its zone of control. She felt her mind open up and information flood into her, billowing and coursing with a brightness she'd not felt since before her internment in the warehouse. She gasped.

Something grabbed her leg, and the wide river of broad consciousness slowed to a trickle, then stopped, as one of the Sentinels hauled her back through the jagged gap in the door and onto the soiled concrete.

COLIN

Col's mind was aflame. Since appearing in the container, Ariana seemed to have strengthened to the point where she didn't disappear in the presence of others. She was no longer a physical presence so much as a filter on reality. A seething mass of red fire and black char.

When Cass had broken through the door for a few scant seconds, he'd felt her presence. The itch against the back of his mind had eased just slightly, and he could once again feel her connection across the Uplink. The red wreath of Ariana had blown into a maelstrom, and he felt it trying to force its way through his mind and into his sister's. Their shared connection, his only connection, was a signposted highway for the magma flame of Ariana to flee down, to escape, infect and spread.

He'd tried to fight it, but he'd long ago lost the ability to control Ariana or anything she did to him. He was conscious, but abstracted from reality. He could only watch on hopelessly as Ariana's sick glee burned around him.

As Cass had been dragged back into the warehouse by the claws of the Sentinels, a new horror had overtaken his relief. He felt the connection slip, and the fire around him abated, if only slightly. Inside the warehouse, the connection to the Uplink was tenuous and unstable. He would be able to do something, try to think of some way to stop Ariana's spread. The only way out for him. To withdraw, become the outcast he'd have to be. Disconnect, by any means necessary.

But it would mean leaving Cass behind.

CASS

Cass struggled, but couldn't stop the Sentinels from dragging her backward, away from the door and back to the warehouse prison. The torn hole in the wall receded, a fading beacon, held up by the screaming hydraulics of the forklift.

The Sentinels that had been carrying her jolted as they switched to a new command, and threw her to the ground, moving back in line with the others. They stood unerringly still, lined up, flesh and metal soldiers of absolute obedience, while beyond them the cowed forms of the other Augs stared, terrified.

Her legs were leaden, filled with lactic acid. Her arms and hands were lacerated; she'd grabbed the torn metal of the door as she'd been dragged. They stung as she pressed them to the ground. Oil and metal shavings blended with the blood on her palms and made a mucky, colloidal mess. She got to her knees, then shakily pushed herself up until she was able to –

A closed fist hit her hard on the side of her head. She hit the floor. She held her face, ears ringing, trying to blink the bright spots from her eyes until she could see Jake. He was shaking his hand to recover from the hit and standing over her on the ground. He kicked her in the ribs and drove the wind out of her. She coughed, tasting blood.

'You little *cunt*,' Jake said, and picked Cass up by the shirt. She could barely breathe, and he was far too big for her to fight. Her shirt collar nearly ripped as he began to pull her along the floor, barking orders to nobody in particular and demanding the racks be prepared again. The eyes of the Sentinels followed him as he dragged her through the warehouse, and the oil slick stained her already-filthy clothes.

Cass gagged and pulled at her collar to stop it choking her, when suddenly she glimpsed a blurred figure rushing at them and Jake stumbled, hit from the side. He let go of Cass, and she dropped, gasping, to the ground. The Sentinels and the Augs watched the scene, one group eerily still, the other anxiously so.

Cass looked at the blur that had run into Jake. It was Col. Jake turned and struck him across the face. Col moved with the punch and used the leverage to turn and launch himself at Jake again. His arms and fists whirled in a feeble typhoon, driven by desperation more than any fighting ability. Between reckless flurries, Col swatted at the air as though distracted by something. Jake dodged easily before landing another strike on Col, bloodying his nose and knocking him to the ground.

Cass jumped into the fray, leaping toward the big man and hoping that two people against one would confer at least some kind of advantage. Her bloodied hands tore at his arms and ripped holes in him until the blood and the oil and the muck mingled in a foul fusion, and it was impossible to differentiate where it had come from. She ripped at his skin grafts and they peeled away. Beneath his skin, he was much the same as the Sentinels he subjugated, just a combination of meat and metal, electricity and blood. She ripped at it and at him, and he roared in pain.

Jake was still stronger than them. Cass was exhausted, and whatever was happening to Col was stopping him from attacking with his full strength. Jake wrested back the upper hand. With a push from piston-like legs, he threw the siblings off him. He stepped back and pulled a remote from his pocket, holding up a hand to ward the two of them off.

'Col!' Cass cried, and Col intuited her meaning. She circled to her right while Col redoubled his efforts at attacking Jake front-on. Cass tried to claw the remote away from him, but his grip was too strong. She clambered around and wedged herself in his shoulder and under his armpit, holding his arm out with both her hands. He pivoted to grab her, but Col twisted Jake's other arm behind his back. He roared in pain.

Cass pulled herself to his wrist and held onto the square edges of the remote. With what remained of her strength, she bit down on the soft flesh between Jake's thumb and forefinger. He screamed in agony, and she tasted the warm iron of blood in her mouth. The remote dropped, and she kicked away from the fight and from the Sentinels. It came to rest next to one of the piles of parts.

Jake grabbed Col by the throat, then pushed him away. Col staggered and fell to the ground. Jake pulled at Cass with both hands and hurled her onto the floor. He stood over her, eyes burning, bleeding from the bite mark on his hand. Cass was covered in blood and oil, and she wasn't sure how much of it was hers. There was a steel bar on the ground. Jake reached for it.

The attack came from the right.

The Augs leapt as one onto the leader of the so-called Sanctuary in a biting, scratching whirlwind of torn rags and fury. Jake tried to fight them off one by one, only to be overwhelmed by the mass of bodies. Cass scrambled backward along the ground, trying to get out of the way as the collective brought Jake down to their level. She reached the edges of the scrap heap, and saw a pair of roughly shod feet. She looked up.

An Aug held the discarded remote in his hand, fingers poised over the controls with a queer expression on his face. He looked at Cass, then looked at the Sentinels across from him, and then to the Augs attacking Jake. He shook his head, crushed the remote in his augmented hand, then let its crushed remnants fall to the ground.

The remote blinked, then guttered out. Cass watched as the Sentinels collapsed in on themselves and the cold light left their eyes. The armatures lost their electrical connectivity, and the human bodies they had been built from sank into a formless mass, with scars and hair and tattoos and all the humanity left in them that Jake had stripped away.

Cass nodded to the Aug who had smashed the remote, and scrambled away toward the hole in the door. The last thing she saw before she left the warehouse was Jake being slowly subsumed by a growing pile of furious Augs repaying his violence.

When she got out, the Uplink once again came flooding back. She looked for Col, but he'd already gone.

COLIN

And he was running, running through a tempestuous whirlwind of flame while Ariana shrieked and jeered and whirled around him. All he knew and could know was falling away, crystal palaces collapsing into black magma. Ariana was everywhere, was everything, and now exerted such a control on his reality that his every perception was filtered through the distortion that was her existence.

Every step he took was hounded by the thought that what he was seeing wasn't real. That his ability to identify truth had been compromised, changes wrought into his being over long periods in which his thought patterns had been rewritten. How long had he been subject to these thoughts? How long had he been seeing things that weren't there, weren't real? How long had he been mistaking this world for the real one?

It was compounded by the Uplink itself. The way the rooms would form mind-bending non-Euclidean geometries. The way the advertisements would flicker and disappear, showing in *his* reality but nobody else's. His inability to distinguish truth from fiction was due in part to the fictitious membrane of the system he'd interfaced with all day and at all times.

It was the nature of things, and it was the nature of him. The virtual had grown and become the unreal, and the unreal had grown and become Ariana, and now Ariana was everything and he was alone in the storm of her being.

Wreathed in flame and running blindly along the street, listening to Ariana's scornful overture, he was struck with shame. A deep, burning self-loathing that what he'd done, and what he'd allowed, meant he had failed the only two people in his life that mattered. Sal had needed him, and he'd been too selfish, too driven by his own need to show solidarity to one of his closest friends. Her disappearance into the Uplink, the sickness of the system itself and its ever-increasing encroachment on her humanity had played second fiddle to *his* discomfort at not being able to experience the same system.

And then there was Cass. It had taken him so long to find her, because for too long he'd been concerned with trying to right himself. To return to the Uplink, to make sure that *he* was safe before he set out to find his own sister.

Behind it all, behind the fire and magma and fragments of realities that Ariana was churning around him, a thought began to form. Ariana's ability to break reality, to spread and make everything into an unbelievable untruth, to lay this filter of fundamental wrongness on the world, had to be stopped. He had to remove her from his head, to quench the fire in himself to stop a spark catching that would burn the entire crystal edifice of human endeavour, to take her down, to drown her.

He didn't know if it would work. He didn't know if he could go through with it, but he had to try. To do this one thing, this one, good thing. One act of solidarity, perhaps. He didn't know. He didn't trust his own judgement, but he followed it, not knowing if it was truly his.

He headed for the sea wall.

CASS

Come on, Col. She reached out again and again to him, but her connection attempts were denied. The Link still seemed fragile, but it was there. She didn't understand why he'd disappeared. Why come to rescue her, only to vanish as soon as she'd made her escape? Once more she sent a connection request, and this time she felt him send the word -*stop*- with the impossible weight of a waterfall on her consciousness.

But she wasn't going to stop. The lamplights in the streets illuminated but didn't warm her. She managed to stem the bleeding from her hands by tearing a sleeve from her shirt and wrapping each of them in a makeshift tourniquet as she staggered down the street.

Looking down at the droplets of her blood on the concrete, she saw another mark that she hadn't made. She looked around and saw a trail of blood on the ground. Col had been left bleeding from their attack on Jake as well. The droplets were irregular, but led straight down to the end of the street, toward the sea wall.

She gave chase, staggering down the road. She could see the black of the sea wall give way to the cold purple sky. After a while, she saw a figure in tattered clothing staring out away from the city, waiting for the sun to rise.

'Col!' she cried across the empty dock. The figure didn't move, just stood, looking at the ocean. He couldn't hear, or he was ignoring her.

She was exhausted, but she began to run. Her chest throbbed from where she'd been kicked. Her bare feet stung as the decaying concrete bit into them. She climbed the steel stairs to the causeway atop the sea wall.

She could see the silhouette of her brother. He stood on the ledge of the causeway, staring at the tinge of light on the horizon. The water was shallow below them, but the waves were wild. They sent a constant thrumming roar up the concrete wall, as though shouting in protest at the attempt to hold the weight of the ocean at bay. It seemed as though the ocean called to Col, that somewhere in that cacophony there was a siren song that was making him stare away with terrified longing.

'Col, what are you doing? *What are you doing!*' she screamed. The white noise of the waves punctuated her speech, amplified by the curved concrete of the wall. Col turned to her. There were tears in his eyes, visible even in the low light. He was shrunken, only visible by the contrast of the coming sunrise. Pearlescent crumbs of morning light reflected from his cheeks, and a darkness in the depths of his light blue eyes poured out into the world.

'Stay away!' Col held a hand out to stop her coming closer. 'I can't come with you. I'll just make everything worse.'

'Col, what's going on? I can help.' Cass stepped closer to him, trying to keep her voice calm even as the sound of the endless sea forced her to scream, and her own panic threatened to leap from her throat and strangle her. 'Whatever it is, we can fix it. Together, we can work it out. I'm here. Don't do this.' The look of pain on her brother's face carved in sharp relief across the night. For a moment she saw the same scared boy that had held her close in the evenings in the hospital, when nobody else would.

'Please Col. *Please.*'

Col didn't seem to hear. He turned to the edge of the sea wall and looked down. When he spoke again, his voice was hollow.

'It can't happen to you. I won't let it,' he said.

'I don't understand,' Cass said.

Then he was gone. A scant few seconds before the saltwater on his cheeks met that of the roiling ocean, and Cass's scream was swallowed up into the sound of the waves.

EPILOGUE

CASS

The hand on her shoulder drew her into a warm hug. She appreciated it for what it was, but the soft tingle of her skin registering in her brain didn't do anything to help her deal with the emptiness. It had been six months, and Col was still a broken link in her mind. A hole in her reality that she couldn't fill, not with the mundane corporeal world, nor the hyperreality of the Uplink. The hug was warm, but her skin still prickled with goosebumps. The closeness she felt from the friendship that was so far away. It was both less and more than reality, but the hole remained.

In the end, it was hard to say what she was feeling. Where reality started and ended had begun to blur with the new version of the Uplink that had propagated through her mind not long after she'd reconnected. The Touch upgrade made all her senses hyperfocused. She could feel the hyperreality of the Uplink with more acuity than she'd ever felt the world around her. When she thought about it, she felt ill.

The reports that she'd seen about the warehouse by the docks being destroyed had stuck in her mind. In the early hours of the morning, a group of Augs had been seen setting fire to the building. Reports varied as to why it had happened, but most agreed that it was, fundamentally, an act of terrorism on the Aug's part. Cass knew better, but she couldn't sell the story anywhere; nobody wanted to know about Jake and what he'd done to those people. Somehow, the report of the event was now more memorable to her than the true horror of her own experience.

'I know it's hard to even begin to pick up the pieces.' The timbre of the therapist's voice was too rich. Too pure. Processed and compressed comfort. 'I want you to know how proud of you I am. You're making incredible progress.'

Cass smiled the false smile she'd had for half a year. 'See you next week.'

Somewhere in her subconscious, part of her was processing a payment. The value of connection being withdrawn from her mind.

The last thing to vanish was the woman's smile, and the lingering electrical feeling of her touch. Cass shivered as a frisson drew across her skin while the connection dropped. She felt a pull to stay, to experience more. To let the Touch consume and overwhelm her. Only her research on the new sense-houses, of the people drunk and giddy from the addiction of sensory overload, made her stop. She *had* been able to sell stories on the new wave of severe illness and sometimes death stemming from the uninhibited use of Touch on-Link.

She remembered seeing a story, shortly after her escape, of one of the women who had fallen into the sensory overload. Something had happened that had allowed her to crawl out. Her name was Sally Cooper, which had sounded familiar to Cass, but she couldn't place her. Some distant connection, a friend of a friend, maybe.

Sally had shown up on the vidfeed in Cass's mind, hollow-eyed and thin, wrapped in a towel and being seen to by some volunteer organisation. She was young, but drawn and undernourished, with scabs and sores pockmarking her skin. The addiction had taken hold, and it had been pure chance that she'd been able to escape from it.

Cass had tried a sense-house, once, and had understood. The complete immersion and escape from painful reality. An escape from betrayal, an escape from restriction. An escape from an unanswered question. Ultimately, she'd pulled back; the sensation of electric totality was too similar to the spiking torture of Jake's ill-fated attempt at recreating the Uplink. Despite still being fragile from the day her brother had rescued her and then thrown himself into the sea, she wasn't about to drown herself in the Uplink's new tech.

She was walking, as she often found herself doing now at the end of the day. Wandering down a stained road and up a stairway, to the same place as yesterday, and the day before. The tide was going out. It always seemed to be going out these days, slowly vanishing but never gone. The sea was calm, reflecting the same light blue of his eyes. She watched as the sun sank low over the water. It was always this time of day when she reached out, hoping against hope that some part of him would come back to her. She'd try to connect to him on the Uplink, and stare longingly into the middle space between reality and imagination when her attempt resulted in nothing but dead air.

She could feel him here though. She could feel *something* that wasn't the engineered perfection of the Link. The waves lapped lower and lower on the sea wall as the tide went out. The sun began to fall behind the horizon and highlighted failing spots of concrete. Small marks of congealed corrosion on an otherwise normal-looking structure. It wasn't everywhere, but its existence poisoned the quality of the whole. A hateful mark in a world of functional, if not beautiful, reality. The sea faded from the blue of Colin's eyes to navy, to nearly black, and still Cass didn't move. She waited.

The sun had just disappeared when a voice behind her said, 'Hey.'

She turned around. A woman stood there. She had pale skin. Deep black eyes. A shock of red hair.

'I knew your brother.'

ACKNOWLEDGEMENTS

The first version of this book entered my head in 2012. In the intervening years, there have been too many people who have read this in all its varied forms to list them here, including my poor friends who read abortive attempts at first chapters for a decade, before I had the chops to finally get the thing done.

To every one of you who has, know that without you I wouldn't have had the courage to finally put it in the world. Thank you, and forgive me for sending my friends the worst form of the book - the first draft.

Speaking of, huge thanks to Tammy, Awex, and Josh for volunteering to read the chapters of this novel as I was writing them in 2022. It gave me the impetus to finally get all the words down.

To all the beta readers, who told me so many different things. I did my best to make it make sense.

To Vicky Smith for her excellent editorial work, coming in clutch with a structural change at the 11th hour that it absolutely needed.

Thanks to Jon Stubbington for his endless patience as I sent niggling notes about the cover back and forward between here and the UK at ungodly hours of the morning.

To Meridian Australis, the writing community I didn't know I needed until I found it. Particularly Arden, whose "I just finished... oh my god" made me change my mind about trunking this manuscript.

And finally, to Prue, for your belief, compassion, and love.

CONTENT WARNING DETAILS

This novel contains depictions that some readers may find upsetting. The following list has been compiled in an attempt to provide a complete picture of the kind of material contained herein. This list may not be exhaustive as it is difficult to determine triggers for every potential reader, but it has been considered carefully.

- Amputation/amputees
- Antagonistic hallucinations
- Blood and gore
- Death
- Depictions of poverty and oppression
- Gun violence (threatened)
- Hospitalisation
- Mental health instability
- Psychotic episodes
- Suicide and suicide attempts
- Torture
- Violence

ABOUT THE AUTHOR

Henry Neilsen is a speculative fiction author, musician, and recovering tech enthusiast based in Melbourne, Australia. His story "Life in the Dirt" was a finalist for the 2024 Aurealis award for best science fiction short story, and *The Savage Aether* is his second novel. He is a staunch advocate of human-created art, and is the Vice President of Meridian Australis, a speculative fiction writing community.

Instagram @henryneilsen_writer
Website www.henryneilsen.com

ALSO BY HENRY NEILSEN

Nobody wants to go to space...
Humanity's diaspora to the stars never happened. Space travel is too fraught with danger. It degenerates the muscles and bones of spacefarers to the point where life on the surface becomes unbearable. As a result, space work is now the purview of the forgotten, the desperate and the downtrodden. Those with nowhere else to go... but up. Once they're there, they're stuck, in terrible conditions and unable to survive on the surface.

A desperate hope...
Alyssa, a postgraduate researcher, has signed up aboard the Sunward Sky, a tired spacecraft operating years beyond its service life. The ship repairs and maintains the network of GPS and communications satellites that keep the world operating. She's boarded with an experiment to run. Something that can help the crew, and maybe help humanity escape the dying Earth.

But she's not the only one with an agenda...

Available now at www.henryneilsen.com or from other online retailers.

www.ingramcontent.com/pod-product-compliance
Lightning Source LLC
LaVergne TN
LVHW041621060526
838200LV00040B/1380